SHREDDED

SHREDDED

Charles O'Donnell

Moon Lit. Publishing
Westerville, Ohio
www.moonlitpub.com

SHREDDED

12-29-2019

Author's website: www.charlesodonnellauthor.com

ISBN: 1-970041-05-6
ISBN-13: 978-1-970041-05-7

To my wife, Helen
Everyone needs a dream advocate. You are mine.

Contents

ALSO BY CHARLES O'DONNELL

The Girlfriend Experience (Matt Bugatti #1)
Moment of Conception (Matt Bugatti #2)
Shade (Shredded #2)

Prologue

"People say there's no hell, but I know better."

"Grace, you're not easily discouraged. You're a positive, upbeat person. You don't talk this way unless you've had a setback."

"Not a setback, Madeleine, a reboot. I was doing it, you know I was—making good choices, staying straight—and I still am, but it's not enough. After four years of sweating it, day to day, I'm back in the pit."

"Grace, I'm concerned. I haven't seen you like this before."

"I've never been like this, not even in my worst days. I feel like I need oxygen to finish a sentence. My arms and legs feel like sacks of rocks, hanging from my body as I walk, dragging myself along, like those poor, sad cases I see in an endless line to my station every day, confused wrecks counting the days to death."

"Talk to me. Help me to understand where this is coming from."

"I don't know if you *can* understand, or if anyone can who's never been where I've been. You know what I did to myself, how low I sank, and what I had to do to fight my way back, but knowing's not understanding, is it? I buried myself under a mountain of trash, suffocating under it for years, but I dug myself out, I cleared the mountain away, I got myself clean, and I stayed clean, one day at a time. For four years, I never let the trash pile back up. Then last week I woke up in a panic because I was back under the mountain. Someone found the trash and hauled it back and dumped it on top of me."

"Let's talk about what happened."

"They hacked my life."

"What does that mean?"

"They hacked it. It's online, in the Worldstream, every bit of it, to hear those stream riders tell it, the perverts."

"How do you know this?"

"They told me, the stream riders did. Their v-grams."

"V-grams? How many?"

"I've lost count. Hundreds, I'd guess."

"What did they say?"

"Oh, Jah, Madeleine, everything—details, you know, where the devil is? Except there are zombies in these details. I thought they were dead, the zombies, that I'd killed them and burned their bodies. Then the weavers—that's what they're called, weavers—dug them up and all the details with them. The stream riders tell it like they were there, in the room, inside my body, like they were inside my mind."

"Tell me what they said."

"Must I?"

"Grace, you've always been open with me. Our sessions not only help me to understand what you're going through; they're therapeutic. Talking through your situation is part of the process."

"You're a big believer in the process."

"It's worked for you. Do you remember what it was like when you first came to me, when you carried all these things inside you, all alone? Do you remember the self-recrimination, the compulsions, the despair?"

"What I remember was that I was out of control. I hated that. And now I've lost control again. Why do you think I'm so worried?"

"Grace, you know you can trust me."

"You're always doing this, pushing me. I hate when you do that, like my mother, always pushing."

"Grace."

"All right, all right. After I lost custody of Dylan, there were a few weeks, a month or two maybe, every night with a different partner—man or woman, it didn't matter, sometimes two or three at once—anyone I could find VR and hook IRL, after a tab of Mandy X and a pint of apple vodka. I could get them to do anything I wanted, dom or sub, anything. I barely remembered those nights; I didn't remember them, not until Gogo read the v-grams to me, like a play-by-play with creepy commentary by low-life stream riders. Their voices, Madeleine, that's the worst part, like animal grunts, the men *and* the women. The first v-gram was bad, and it went downhill from there. Half of them are rubbing it out while they're dictating their v-grams, I swear."

"Grace, I'm so sorry. After all you've been through, especially after working so hard to recover, to put your past behind you, you don't deserve this."

"Doesn't *deserve* mean I have something coming to me? If there's one thing the last four years have taught me, and the twenty-five years before that, it's that I have nothing coming to me that I don't take for myself."

"And what will you take?"

"My life—not my old life, the life I killed and cremated, the one that the weavers resurrected and dumped on top of me. I want my new life, the life they took from me, that I dug out from under the mountain of trash."

"Don't you still have your life, Grace? I know this is very upsetting to you, but do you think this intrusion of your old life threatens the new life you've worked so hard to build? You've come so far. Your foundation is solid. Think of this new development as a storm that will pass, that your foundation can stand up to. I've seen how strong you are— you're a fighter. It's when you're in your darkest place that you're most determined. You can get through this. I can help you."

"Oh, Madeleine, if my past were only rumors, or what I choose to tell, just words, then the people in my life could make what they wanted of it. I could tell Andrew that he's not the first, or even the hundredth. I could describe the scene for him—the anonymous hook, the mindless coupling, the hollow feeling afterwards, the lingering, unsatisfied urge —and he'd work it into his romantic idea of me, because it *is* just words. He could pretend my past isn't real, that it's not me, not the me he knows, not the me he wants me to be. And I could tell Dylan that his mother made mistakes, and that he can learn from my example, and make better choices than I did. But I can't do that now. My past isn't mine anymore, to tell in *my* words, when *I* choose. It's out of my control. My life is now a lifestream, a full-fidelity, all-sensory, Virtual Reality venue, more real than Real Life, that any creep can rent for fifty cred. Andrew and Dylan can't even pretend I'm not that person. My lifestream is out there, and it's viral."

"Are you giving Andrew and Dylan enough credit? They love you, enough to know that the person you are is not the person you were."

"But I am."

"You are what?"

"The person I was. I listen to them, Madeleine, the v-grams—not all of them, not the raunchy, disgusting ones— who could stomach that? —but the others."

"What others?"

"Some of them, a few, they tell me what they're feeling, not how their bodies feel, or what we're doing together, the way most of the v-grams do, just mechanical sex acts, but what's going on in their minds, what they're thinking, about themselves, and about me. They tell me how *I* make them feel, and what they would do for me if I only asked. I delete them; I put them away, out of my thoughts. I focus on the wonderful life I've built, on the loving, caring people in my life, and remind myself I'm not that person anymore, the person in the v-grams. I start every day with a pledge; I end every day with a ritual, clean and sober. I brush my teeth and wash my face, like my mother taught me. I go to bed and lie awake until the urge gets to me, and I call out, 'read them, Gogo.' He knows what I mean. He even knows my favorites. And I listen, and I touch myself, until I fall asleep on my damp pillow, and Gogo senses that I've drifted off and the voices trail away."

"Grace, don't punish yourself. The path back from sexual addiction is not straight, and you don't walk it alone. You have me, and Edward, and Andrew, and Dylan. We love you. Your past is past."

"And it will stay that way. I've seen to that."

"What do you mean?"

"I know a shredder. He's agreed. It's a lot of money, more than I have, but I don't care. I'll spend that and more to be certain that my life is destroyed."

1
JUST FOR TODAY

"GOOD MORNING, GRACE. Today is your one thousand, three hundred and eighty-fifth day of sobriety. Well done, Grace. I'm proud of you."

Grace lay unmoving as the man's voice continued, like a tenor's speaking voice, its comforting tone precisely designed to wake Grace gently.

"It's now seven a.m. The sun rose at 6:56 this morning, just four minutes ago and it's already bright outside. The weather is clear, but clouds will move in before noon. No rain, though. You can leave your umbrella at home."

"Thank you, Gogo."

"You're very welcome. Would you like to hear your schedule for the day?"

Grace rolled to the edge of the bed, dropping her feet to the floor as she sat up.

"It's the same as yesterday, isn't it?"

The disembodied voice laughed, indistinguishably from an authentic human laugh, unless one had heard the exact same laugh a million times, as Grace had.

Grace splashed water on her face as she bent over the bathroom sink. She looked in the mirror. Her short, red hair was a spiky riot, tufts jutting in all directions. Her brown eyes were narrowed from morning puffiness; a path of wrinkles meandered from her forehead, past her right eye, across her cheek to her chin. Sighing, she pressed her fingertips to her face to smooth her creased skin.

Grace returned to the main room and slipped on her Virtual Reality gear.

"Gogo, Blue Ridge."

"Yes, Grace."

Grace was transported to a rock outcropping on the face of a wooded mountain. Birds chirped among the trees in the otherwise noiseless venue. The valley spread out below her, carpeted in a hardwood forest, still shrouded in purple darkness before the sunrise. The first rays of the sun peeked between the mountains on the far side of the valley.

"Hands to heart," said Gogo, his voice coming through Grace's headphones.

Grace focused on her breathing, standing straight, eyes closed, her palms pressed together in front of her.

"Forward fold," said Gogo.

Grace assumed each pose as Gogo named them—*plank, locust, down dog, crescent moon, warrior*—and others, ending as she started, hands to heart.

"Gogo, meditations," Grace said, eyes closed, still in her final pose.

"Yes, Grace. I'm ready when you are."

"Just for today…" Grace said.

"…I will reflect on the positive influences in my life, on my sponsor and the many other people who love me and care about me," Gogo responded.

"Just for today…"

"…I will be patient and considerate with my clients, who are less fortunate than I, and who depend on me for help."

"Just for today…"

"…I will treat my body and mind with respect, to stay mentally sharp and physically fit."

Grace paused before whispering, "*And just for today, I will make my life an act of courage.*" She took a final deep breath as she opened her eyes. The sun shone brilliantly in a deep blue sky, the dawn colors having faded. The valley floor below was an unbroken expanse of green.

"Gogo, suspend the venue."

The mountain vista dissolved as Grace was transported back to her apartment. She returned to her bathroom mirror. The wrinkles had disappeared, and her eyes were clear.

"Thank you, Gogo."

"You're very welcome, Grace. You have fifteen v-grams."

"Later, Gogo," Grace said as she stepped into the shower.

A pot of red rooibos tea steeped as Grace prepared her breakfast, whole-wheat toast with honey and banana, the best hangover cure she knew of, at one time her standard morning-after therapy. It was still her regular morning meal, a habit she'd retained through four clean years. She poured the tea and sat at the only table in her two-room apartment, in view of the wall screen, flashing pictures of architecture, people and nature.

"Gogo, v-grams, please."

The display showed the text of the first v-gram, scrolling past a photo of a middle-aged man with a friendly face. Gogo narrated the text, its voice more robust, a baritone with a harder edge.

"From David, Branch Manager, Northern Fiduciary Trust, yesterday, 9:00 p.m. Grace, a deposit in the amount of nine thousand, seven hundred International Exchange Credits has been made to your account, drawn from the account of State Live Services. Your balance is nine-hundred-forty-seven thousand…"

"Delete," Grace said. David's image and the scrolling text vanished.

"From Madeleine, dated yesterday, 10:05 p.m." Grace recognized the accurately synthesized voice of her therapist, a steady, silken, calming alto, as Madeleine's picture appeared on the display. "Grace, just a reminder, you have an appointment next Friday. I'll send you another reminder a day before. See you then, and stay strong. You know you can call me any time."

"Delete."

"From Andrew, dated yesterday, 10:10 p.m." A round, fleshy face appeared, fat-cheeked, like the face of a boy, but with an old man's eyes, surrounded by dark circles and wrinkled at the corners. The rough voice had a catch to it, as if the speaker were uncertain of every word. "Hi, Grace. I'm just thinking about what you said in the venue, about what I want for myself long term. I guess I'm so focused on the day-to-day, I forget about big picture things. Thanks for helping me keep my head up. After we closed the venue I kicked myself because we spent the whole time talking about my day and I never asked you what yours was like, and if you had anything to share. Sorry. We'll start with you tomorrow and I'll shut up. Bye, Grace. Love you."

"Reply. Andrew, don't worry about it. I can tell you've been struggling lately, so we should spend as much time as we need to make sure you're staying with the program. You were really feeling it yesterday, but I'm proud of you for keeping the pledge. You should have IM'd me. I can take a break from my clients for you. And if you're in real trouble, call. That's what sponsors are for. Take care. Love you. End of reply. Delete original."

"From Edward, dated yesterday, 10:30 p.m." The man in the photo was strikingly handsome, with classic features on a narrow face, silver hair and deep-set blue eyes. His thin voice seemed too weak for his face. "Hello, girl. I was thinking about you today. I was in a venue in China, at a meeting of our regional heads. My supervisor wanted me there as her technical backup—she gets lost sometimes when things get technical. Anyway, it got pretty contentious between the Asian and African heads—they're both pretty strong personalities. My super tried to get between them and they rolled right over her. That's when I thought of you. My Grace would've stood up to Africa and Asia and Europe, too.

"When is our next visit? You picked the last venue, so it's

my turn, and I choose the Boundary Waters. Surprised? There's a big ol' muskie waiting up there for me and I feel lucky. Just let me know when. Bye for now!"

"Reply. Hi, Edward. Let's do it on Saturday, after my visit with Dylan. Boundary Waters is fine. It's peaceful, the scenery is fantastic, and I never get tired of seeing you reel in the big ones. Dylan told me about the time you took him fishing up there and he had a ball. 'Hi-res,' he called it. We should all three of us go some time. Does the venue have a bigger canoe?

"It sounds like you're hanging with the big boys and girls at the firm. Good for you. I'm glad to see they're finally giving you credit for all you do for them. Go get 'em, Daddy. I love you. End of reply. Save, folder name Edward."

"From Dylan, dated yesterday, 10:40 p.m." Beside the text of the v-gram there appeared the face of a boy, barely a teenager, his hair the same ruddy color as Grace's and not much shorter, still young enough to sport dense and obvious freckles, the teeth in his wide grin a little too big for his face.

Grace set down her teacup, putting her fingertips to her lips. Dylan's image could have been her own face at Dylan's age, young and fresh, just as her reflection in the mirror that morning could have been Dylan, older and jaded.

"Hi Mom." Gogo recreated Dylan's voice nearly perfectly, high and thin, cracking but not yet broken, synthesized from tens of thousands of voice clips gleaned from the Worldstream, nearly everything Dylan had ever said from his first spoken word. "Guess what we learned today? I told you we were studying AI, right? So, today prof started on layered neural structures. Have you ever heard of that, Mom? It's hyper-res—computers that think like people. Prof told us they're pretty good at thinking but not perfect, so sometimes when you have to solve a really hard problem you need people and computers working together. I guess there are still some things people can do that computers can't. That makes me feel good, but I wonder if people will always have the edge. I hope so. What do you think?"

Grace lifted the teacup to her lips, pausing, staring at the display, as Dylan's exuberant voice narrated.

"Do you remember Wayne from school? He's got a girlfriend! Just a VR girlfriend—they haven't met IRL, but you'd have thought they were hooked to hear him tell. He keeps pushing me to get a girl in VR, but I don't want to make any commitments. Wayne says I can always block her out if I get tired of her, but I heard those blocks don't work; you can always find ways around them, and anyway that seems like an ugly thing to do. I don't think I would block someone if it would hurt her feelings.

"Aunt Donna is telling me it's too late to be on the screen and I need to go to bed. I'll see you on Saturday. Love you, Mom."

Grace finally took a sip from her cup. She set it down as she wiped a tear from the corner of her eye.

"Reply. Dylan, you amaze me. I wouldn't know a layered neural structure from a layer cake, but they sound fascinating. How do they work? Is it like trying to simulate a human brain? I want to hear all about them, especially if you think they'll get smarter than we are. I want to be ready for that, but I'm in no hurry for computers to take over. We people still have the edge for now.

"Girls, huh? You're fourteen, Dylan, plenty of time for girls. I'm sure your Aunt Donna reminds you that you have a lot to concentrate on without the distraction of girls, so I won't repeat it—ha, ha! And thank you for saying that you wouldn't hurt someone's feelings like that. You couldn't hurt anyone's feelings. I don't think you have it in you.

"I'll see you on Saturday, dear. Think about what venue you want to try. I love you. End of reply. Save, folder name Dylan."

"From Stream Ranger, dated today, 12:05 a.m. Grace, you are crazy hot. I just got off your lifestream after an hour and I still have a chub. Jah, what a wild ride. I ran it forwards and backwards, standing up and on my knees, underneath and on top. You are one insatiable lady."

"Gogo, pause!"

Grace stood up, bumping the table as she pushed her chair

back, causing the teacup to overturn. She approached the display, the coarse, phlegmy voice now silent, and began reading where the narration left off.

What you did to that guy with the bulldozer tattoo rewired my head. I never saw a white guy that big but you took him all in every which way. I rode that part third person and rubbed one out. I should have saved it. When I flipped to second person and let the Belt take over, my head got totally rewired, a complete reboot. Jah, you played that sumbitch like a steel guitar. What a kicker! I put it on an endless loop until I almost locked up. Jahbulon, Grace, that bulldozer guy was one lucky bastard.

The picture next to the v-gram text was that of a gaunt man, sixties or older, his thinning hair unkempt, the age spots on his jaws showing through heavy growth. Grace continued reading, her eyes wide, her breath coming in short spasms, stopping when she reached Stream Ranger's graphic description of sex acts, point by point, peppered with bulldozer metaphors.

"Gogo, *delete!*" Grace shouted, dropping into her chair.

"I'm sorry, Grace. I could have warned you."

"Why didn't you, damn it?"

"You have my filter at its minimum setting. If you like, I can increase the filter level. Would you like me to automatically delete similar v-grams?"

"Yes, please!" Grace turned her teacup upright. She mopped the spilled tea with her napkin. "How many more v-grams, Gogo?"

"You have no v-grams remaining."

"You said I had fifteen. How many did you read?"

"I've read six v-grams, Grace. The remaining nine I've deleted automatically, according to my updated filter level, as well as five more that arrived since seven a.m."

2

EARTH MOVER

GRACE'S FIRST CLIENT was already waiting when she arrived at her station at State Live Services, State Benefits Department, at five minutes before nine. The client was an elderly woman complaining that her credit voucher for September never came. The woman wore clothes that were stylish in the twenty-twenties, but not since, looking as if she were losing a battle to keep her personal dignity. The old woman's frustration grew as Grace fumbled, trying unsuccessfully to locate the missing voucher in the State Benefits system, having mis-entered the woman's personal data three times.

"Where m'vouch' li'l miss?" the woman cackled. "F'get that, where y'head, li'l miss? Wha' ya do las' night so's y'head so mess up? Been out wi' t' boys, huh? Some wine, maybe? D'ya hook late, tha' why y'so foggy?"

"Please, citizen, I'm trying. If you could just give me your state social services number again."

"Like I say fo' times, 9733-hyphen-560-hyphen-61440. Why'd t' voice thing not hear me? Why d'ya got t' punch 'tin for?"

"It hears you, citizen, but it's having a little trouble

understanding you. I have to verify the number."

"You sayin' I can't talk right, li'l miss? Sayin' that thing, Jahbulon, wh'ever, don' hear me right?"

"I've got it, citizen. According to our system, your voucher was delivered to your address on September fourth, by drone."

"There y'damn pro'lem. Them buzzin' things don' care f'm nothin', prob'ly drop it on the street or chew 'tup in 'em buzzin' blades 'n' nev' know."

Grace handed the woman a slip with a coded symbol. "If you'll take this to the desk right over there, they'll issue a duplicate voucher."

The woman snatched the slip from Grace's hand, drawing herself up as she stood. "Fine thing, y'dummies here't t' state service place, got t'waste m' damn time."

Once alone, Grace closed her eyes and drew a cleansing breath.

"What was *that* all about?"

Grace looked up to see her supervisor peering over the partition.

"Heidi," Grace said, forcing a smile, "the voice response couldn't pick up everything and I fat-fingered the entry. I've got it under control."

Heidi looked over at the service desk. The old woman appeared calm as she picked up her voucher.

"Sharpen up, Grace, or you're in for a long day," Heidi said, disappearing behind the partition.

"Yes, Heidi," Grace said under her breath.

Grace paused before calling the next person in line. She looked up, gasping as she laid eyes on a man in his sixties, his thinning hair unkempt, the age spots on his jaws showing through heavy growth. By the end of the day she would serve six similarly appearing men, some of whom spoke with coarse, phlegmy voices.

❖ ❖ ❖

On the community transit ride to her apartment, Grace

dredged up a memory from more than four years ago, of a well-muscled man, naked and hairless, standing in front of her as she knelt. On his groin he had a tattoo of a bulldozer, its driver gripping the levers, grinning maniacally. Painted on the bulldozer's square blade in block letters were the words EARTH MOVER.

"Good evening, Grace," Gogo said as Grace entered her apartment.

"Hi, Gogo." Grace hung her sweater in the closet, holding the closet door open for a moment.

"Gogo."

"Yes, Grace?"

"Any v-grams?"

"You have no v-grams."

Grace closed the door.

"Did you delete any v-grams?"

"Yes."

"How many?"

"I have deleted forty-two v-grams."

Grace was in bed by nine. At ten-thirty, she was still awake.

"Gogo."

"Yes, Grace?"

"How many v-grams have you deleted today?"

"I have deleted sixty-five v-grams."

"Gogo."

"Yes, Grace?"

"Recover them. Read them."

At two a.m., Grace pulled on jeans and a sweatshirt. She walked down the stairs of her apartment building, out into the street, in a direction she rarely went, toward a place she hadn't been to in more than four years. The sounds of early morning street life in the chill air stirred uneasy memories: a couple, laughing as they left a convenience store, strangers just minutes before, having gone there with a common purpose, now pawing each other amorously, drunkenly, heading off to one or the other's apartment for a hook; the buzzing of police drones, flying their surveillance routes in formation, scanning every movement, instantly signaling the civil authorities of any suspicious activity; the soft rush of the community transit auto-buses, empty of passengers or nearly so, stopping at intervals, opening their doors to the deserted sidewalks. Grace walked until she came to a storefront shop, with a sign in the window flashing its name: CITY BEVERAGE.

The layout had not changed in four years, as far as Grace could tell. She walked directly to a well-known shelf, lined with bottles of vodka, straight and flavored.

"One-half liter of apple vodka," the voice responder said as Grace scanned the bottle. "Sixty-five credits. Do you wish to make any other purchases?"

"No."

"Thank you. Please scan for payment. Look into the screen and tap."

Grace looked into the screen. Her own face looked back, over an icon labeled *Tap Here For Payment*. One tap and her image would enter the Worldstream; facial recognition algorithms would register her presence at City Beverage at 2:30 a.m., completing the purchase of a half-liter of apple vodka and transferring sixty-five credits from her account to the liquor store's, the entire transaction—location, merchandise, payment, image, identity—entering the Worldstream, never to be purged.

One thousand, three hundred, and eighty-five days of sobriety.

Grace stared at the bottle on the scanner, cheerfully labeled with a brilliant green apple.

Just for today.

Grace turned away from the screen and left the store,

almost running, nearly colliding with the convenience store couple as they entered the shop, as the voice responder repeated, "Please scan for payment."

3

Privacy Is Overrated

"Where's Grace, the dedicated public servant that I know?"

Grace sat silently as Heidi, her supervisor, dressed her down, after four clients of the State Benefits Department complained about the lackadaisical attitude and error-riddled service they were subjected to by the woman at station four —Grace's station.

"We perform an essential function at State Live Services," Heidi continued. "It requires empathy and patience. You have those qualities, Grace. I know you're able to handle it."

"Yes, I'm able," Grace said. "I know my job. I'm *doing* my job." She looked aside. "I just…I didn't sleep well."

"You know that's not an excuse, and it certainly is *not* the concern of our clients. They may not be the top layer of society, but they're entitled to their benefits and they deserve our respect."

"Heidi, I didn't disrespect anybody."

Heidi showed Grace her personal screen, displaying the pictures of the clients and the texts of their grievances. "I have complaints from four citizens who say you did. They're the final judge of whether they've been disrespected."

Grace looked up, eyelids drooping, her eyes red and puffy. "I've got it under control."

Heidi put a finger to her lip. "Grace, you're a good associate. You're better than this. What's going on?"

"It's personal, Heidi, but I'm managing it."

"Grace." Heidi softened her voice. "I said, *what's going on?*"

Grace looked into Heidi's face. Heidi was four years older than Grace but she looked five years younger, as if she were unaffected by life's vicissitudes. A career State Services associate, Heidi had risen through the ranks, known for her proficient practice of State Live Services people management methodology, especially important in the difficult field of dealing with the disadvantaged, deficient, lonely or merely stubborn and shrinking minority of citizens who insisted on transacting business face-to-face, eschewing the convenience and efficiency of Virtual Reality commerce. Grace admired Heidi's composure in even the most stressful scenarios, seemingly a daily occurrence at Live Services. Heidi, the defuser of crises, the arbiter of disputes, the smoother of ruffled feathers, her skills perfected through years of reasoning with the unreasonable, now applied that experience to her supervision of twenty-two associates of the State Benefits Department.

"I will not allow my personal situation to compromise my professionalism to the detriment of my clients," Grace said, repeating the mantra of State Live Services.

Heidi gave a single nod. "All right. Get back to work."

"Heidi," Grace asked, "what do you know about the Cloak?"

Just the mention of the Cloak was enough to startle Heidi. Everyone knew about the Cloak, but almost nobody discussed them, at least not in polite conversation. They were a secretive group who never appeared in public unless fully hidden from the view of surveillance cameras, police drones, personal screens, kiosks, or any of the other innumerable video and audio sensors connected to the Worldstream.

"Those guys with the weird robot voices that walk around in burqas?" Heidi asked.

Grace nodded.

"Stay away from them. They're criminals."

"Aren't they just people who want to keep their lives private?"

"What have they got to hide?"

"Nothing, maybe, or something, but does it matter? What if they'd just rather not have their purchases tallied up and analyzed and advertised? Maybe they want to enjoy a heavy meal without getting v-grams before they're even finished eating, from some drone delivery restaurant, or from State Health Services with a calorie count. Or be in a VR venue without a content provider monitoring their streaming habits. I think they just want their lives to have boundaries that *they* control, so that *they* choose what they want other people to know about them."

Heidi sat facing Grace, leaning forward, speaking softly.

"Grace, the Worldstream connects us, it ties us together, it makes us stronger—it makes us *happier*. The Worldstream knows your needs and how to fulfill them; it knows your desires and how to satisfy them. The choice it leaves to you. The Worldstream protects you. You can walk the streets at any time, day or night, and not be afraid: if you run into trouble, you only have to call on Jahbulon for help—and not just when you're in danger. When you're troubled, or discouraged, or needy, the Worldstream knows, and the resources of a whole community are there for you. But *only if you're connected.* Why would anyone cut themselves off from their community unless they're saying or doing things that are truly shameful?"

"Not shameful. Just private."

Heidi touched Grace's knee. "Grace, the Worldstream is the foundation of our modern state of security and prosperity. It works because everyone is a part of it. That's why the Cloak are so suspicious. They hide their faces and disguise their voices. They meet in secret, with no connections, and no accountability. You have to wonder why."

"For control of their own lives? For privacy?"

Heidi stood, as she often did to signal the end of the conversation. "Privacy is overrated, Grace. And the Cloak are dangerous. Steer clear."

❖ ❖ ❖

Grace stood at a corner, on a stained and fractured sidewalk, by a narrow, one-way street, dotted with repairs. Tall buildings formed embankments on either side, residences for the most part, tenements that were old when the twenty-first century was new. They limited the view of the sky to narrow strips, through which the fading twilight filtered to ground level. It was peak shipping time, after people had ended their days, finished their evening meals, and opened retail portals on their screens. Their purchases were delivered in minutes by commercial drones, hundreds of them, high enough overhead that the buzzing of their propellers softened as it echoed off brick walls, blending into an ever-present hum. The police drones were less numerous but closer to the ground, where their high-def cameras could conduct surveillance more effectively. Their formations passed at regular intervals, announcing their approach with a sharp sound, dropping in pitch as they passed. The only ground-based vehicles were the community transit auto-buses and the rare private transports, moving slowly, stopping when they encountered the occasional pedestrian.

Grace was in a part of town where people gathered in the evening—people who had grown restless inside the walls, who sometimes preferred Real Life to Virtual Reality, who felt that an authentic experience, however mundane, had an appeal that a synthetic experience, however remarkable, did not. They found it comforting to walk to an actual, physical shop, to take a breather between a want and its satisfaction, and fill it with human contact.

Some were people who lacked the means or the aptitude to live in the rich and varied Virtual Reality world. Real Life, where they spent the majority of their hours, was a trial; VR was their escape. They were patrons of the ubiquitous lifestream bistros, *streamboats* they called them, where they could rent the VR gear that the affluent took for granted—headgear, gloves, and the latest innovation, the Belt, strapped to the waist, coupled to the nervous system, delivering sensations directly to the spinal cord. They could select from a menu of VR experiences, exciting breaks from their gray RL existence. For a lousy fifty cred, the cost of a cheap meal, a person could be anyone he wanted to be for thirty minutes.

Some were Cloak. They walked among the uncloaked citizens, concealed from head to foot in one continuous, black garment, like the burqas worn by women in the less enlightened parts of the world, where people still worshipped gods and men still followed the words of the Prophet, shielding their women from all eyes but theirs. The street people knew enough to step aside when the Cloak approached, and they never spoke to them. The Cloak were not so much people as they were mobile features of the surroundings, indistinguishable and anonymous.

Grace watched from her corner for nearly an hour, studying the movements of the Cloak. They walked quickly, leaning forward, some in a near run, as if they wanted to spend as little time in public as possible. Several passed her where she stood, coming and going too quickly for her to confront them, until one approached from her left, coming directly at her.

"Excuse me," Grace said as the cloaked figure passed, never breaking stride. She repeated this near encounter four more times over the next hour, each time speaking more loudly, each time stepping aside as the Cloak passed without slowing down. She spied a Cloak on the opposite side of the street. Frustrated, she ran toward it, planting herself in its path.

"Excuse *me*, can I speak with you?" The Cloak stepped to one side to pass. Grace grabbed it by the arm.

"Hands *off!*" the Cloak said, its voice a synthesized monotone, a mechanical, emotionless sound, intelligible, but empty of any character. "I don't want to talk to you or to anyone else." Grace shivered at the sound of the android voice. She let go of the Cloak's arm, watching as it hurried away, its cloak billowing behind it, until it disappeared in the shadows.

Discouraged, Grace started to walk back to her apartment building. She slowed her pace as she came upon a line of people stretching out the door of a streamboat. The stream riders ranged from teens to senior citizens, of both sexes, in all manner of dress, but they were mostly men, sixties or older, shabbily dressed, most gaunt and unkempt, like the men at Live Services, or Stream Ranger from the v-gram. They kept their eyes down, or looked furtively around, like guilty children in the presence of a disapproving parent. Grace stood at the window of the streamboat, watching as one man after another stepped to the counter, scanned his image, then went in the back as another man emerged, hangdog, yet satisfied.

The stream rider enters the room, Grace imagined, *alone, closing the door behind him. He straps on the Belt, dons the VR gear, and makes his selection. He's immersed in the scene: a young girl and a well-muscled man with a bulldozer tattoo, engaging in all manner of sex. He looks and listens, and reaches out to touch, the Belt transmitting directly to his brain whatever sensations the VR programmer has coded. He wonders: Who is that girl? What's her name? Where does she live? How picky is she about her men? until his time runs out and the scene goes dark.*

Another man appeared from the back. He looked up, directly at Grace. His eyes got wide and his jaw dropped, as if he recognized her.

Grace turned away from the window, hiding her face. She sprinted down the sidewalk, caroming off the brick wall of a building, swerving to avoid a collision with an elderly couple carrying a bag of fruit. She turned into a side passage, an old alley lined with dumpsters, and leaned against the wall, her hands over her head, her cheek pressed against the gritty surface, until she caught her breath.

"Jah!" she cursed. After a moment, she wiped her face on her sleeve, took a deep breath, and turned toward the alley entrance.

Blocking her path was a silhouetted figure, an inch or two taller than Grace, covered from head to foot in a single, seamless garment.

"Grace, don't be afraid," the mechanical monotone said. "I've been watching you. You look like you could use a friend."

4

In Vita Occulta

THE ENTRANCE TO the passage was invisible from the street if one didn't know exactly where to look. Grace followed the cloaked stranger down the dimly lit corridor, bound by windowless walls, just wide enough for one person to pass. After twenty meters, the path widened, ending in an anteroom, softly lit by luminescent panels covered with a fine copper-colored mesh. Ten or so people filled the space, a mix of Cloak and others, like Grace, wearing ordinary clothing. The far wall had three doors, one marked with a stylized male figure, another with a female figure, and one in the middle, guarded by a large Cloak, with a sign that read:

CLOAKROOM
IN VITA OCCULTA LIBERTAS EST

"Go ahead of me, Grace," the stranger said, gesturing toward the doorkeeper. "You must be scanned."

Grace inched forward, halting when the doorkeeper raised a hand, holding a rectangular object the size of a pocket screen. The doorkeeper passed the device over Grace in two motions, one vertically, from her head to her knees, and a second horizontally, from shoulder to shoulder, then glanced at the device's screen before holding it out for Grace to see.

Grace squinted at the display. It was a list: *phone, pen, cosmetic case, handbag, government ID, state employee badge*. Every item in her handbag was on the list, and the list continued: *wrist screen, shirt, jeans, briefs, brassiere, shoes, stockings*. It listed every article of clothing she wore.

"What is this?" Grace asked.

"These are all the articles on your person that are connected to the Worldstream," the stranger said. "You can't enter the Cloakroom as long as you have with you any connected article."

"But this is everything! I'd have to leave my handbag behind and get completely naked."

The doorkeeper pointed to the door with the female figure. "You can get undressed in there. Leave your belongings in the changing room. They'll be safe and shielded from the Worldstream."

Grace's eyes darted from one Cloak to the other. If not for their difference in height, they would have been indistinguishable. She stared at the shorter of the two, the mysterious stranger, crossing her arms in front of her as if she were trying to cover herself.

"I'll wait here, Grace," the stranger said. "No need to worry. The changing rooms are completely private."

Grace entered a long, brightly lit corridor. She walked slowly past the doors lining the walls, each door with a glowing panel the size of her hand. Most of the panels glowed red, labeled *Occupied*. She stopped at the first door with a green panel and pulled it open.

Behind the door was a room the size of a closet. There was a bench against one wall with a steel basket on it and slippers underneath. The opposite wall had a series of hooks; on one of them hung a white robe, like a choir robe.

Grace removed every article of clothing, folding each one carefully and placing it in the basket. She put on the slippers and pulled the robe over her head. She spread her arms and looked down at herself. She remembered a picture from a book, one that her father read to her when she was a child, when people still owned real books, a fantasy about angels, and what heaven was like.

Grace closed the door behind her as she left the changing room. The panel flashed a message: *place hand here*. Grace pressed her palm against the glass. She heard the sound of a lock closing as the panel turned red.

Outside, the doorkeeper once again crossed Grace with the scanner. It flashed green with the message *Disconnected*.

"Welcome to the Cloakroom," the doorkeeper said.

The Cloakroom was as big as any room that Grace had ever seen, the size of ten or more large apartments, with tables arranged throughout. There were thirty or so people in the room, some seated, some wandering around, most of them in the black uniform of the Cloak, and a few in white robes like Grace's. The sounds of conversation filled the air, but unlike any conversation Grace had heard before, not a mixture of individual voices, male and female, rising and falling, but instead a mechanistic monotone, an undulating sameness, punctuated occasionally by an authentic human voice from one of the white-robed guests.

"This is where the Cloak gather," the stranger explained. "Here, we're free to speak our minds, to associate with whomever we choose, to pursue our passions, knowing that our lives are still our own, to keep to ourselves or to share with whomever *we* choose. The Worldstream cannot penetrate these walls, Grace."

"How do you know my name?"

"Out there, in the connected world, there's nothing about you that isn't known or that can't be discovered, unless you've intentionally concealed it." The stranger sat at a vacant table and invited Grace to sit. "It was easy to learn your name—anyone could do it—a query to a screen at a public kiosk, correlating your location with an image from a random video clip by a passing pedestrian—a total stranger, who doesn't even know you're in his field of view. He steals your image and sends it into the Worldstream without his— or your—knowledge, certainly without your consent. Facial recognition algorithms identify you and put a name to the image: *Grace*. That's the terrible power of the Worldstream—you have only to appear in public undisguised, or in VR, for that matter, and the whole world knows who you are and what you're doing."

"Were you spying on me?"

"The Worldstream is spying on you, always and everywhere. I just happened to notice you as you tried to make contact with the Cloak. You probably felt like you were being snubbed."

"You all don't seem to be terribly polite."

"We Cloak aren't rude; we're paranoid. Even when disguised, with our voices altered, we try not to interact with the connected world. That's why we have this place."

"The Cloakroom. I've never heard of it."

"We don't advertise it, for obvious reasons. This Cloakroom, and others like it, were founded by Vita Occulta, a society of freedom-loving citizens. The VO are fighting the ever-greater intrusion of the Worldstream into our private lives. By the time the VO created the Cloakrooms, the Cloak had already existed for years, mostly citizens like me, who rebelled against this insidious, invasive Worldstream. We hid ourselves from all forms of visual surveillance, whether by the civil authorities, commercial kiosks, or the random citizen's video feed. We synthesized our speech to foil voice recognition algorithms. We felt secure, but isolated. Then the VO created the Cloakrooms. They foot the bill, so that we Cloak can have a place to interact freely, knowing that our privacy is protected."

"Vita Occulta. I saw an inscription on the door with those words."

"*In vita occulta libertas est.* 'In the hidden life, there freedom lies.'"

Grace looked around the room. Some Cloak were seated with their guests in white; others gathered in groups of two or three. She saw one Cloak approach another, apparently at random, speak a few words; then the two of them left the room through a side door.

"Where are they going?" Grace asked, nodding in the direction of the door.

"It could be anything. It's not important. Let's just say they have a matter to discuss that requires a heightened level of security. The Cloakroom provides private rooms for such purposes."

Grace touched her arm, feeling the fabric of her robe between her fingers. She imagined what it would be like to walk the streets freely, cut off from prying eyes, knowing that no images or utterances of hers could enter the Worldstream, to be hacked for others' perverted pleasures.

"How can I join the Cloak?"

"That's why I approached you. Every one of us was introduced to this life by one of the Cloak. Too many of us have forgotten that we owe it to others to repay that kindness. You struck me as one in need."

"I am."

The stranger appeared to nod. "There is no formal organization. To join the Cloak, you simply become one. You'll still participate in the connected world, keeping your identity, earning your credits, buying goods—and guarding your words and actions. You must be mindful at all times that when you are uncloaked, you are under the relentless scrutiny of the Worldstream. Only when you conceal your face, cover your body, and distort your speech, will you be free." The stranger reached into a fold of its robe, pulling out a slip of paper. "Take this. You'll find everything you need here."

The slip had an address and a name: *Gavin.*

The stranger stood. "I have to leave now, Grace. You're welcome to stay as long as you like. You may find some of the Cloak here a little more talkative than those in the streets."

"Wait," Grace said, "who are you? I mean, do you have a name?"

"We Cloak choose the names we're called by each other. I'm called the Eye of Providence."

"Eye of Providence, how can I reach you?"

"You can't. But we'll talk again. As long as you're in the

Worldstream, uncloaked, I'll know where you are, and when you need me."

5

ARTIFACTS

The door opened quickly. Grace stood face-to-face with her sister Donna.

"Why couldn't you visit Dylan in VR like always?" Donna grumbled.

"Donna, please," Grace sighed. "It's been more than a year since I saw Dylan IRL, and that was on his birthday."

Donna silently stood her ground. A red-headed boy appeared behind her, grinning widely, eyes shining, in a close-fitting top and roomy pants, the style preferred by young teens. Donna looked grim-faced at the boy, then at Grace. She stepped aside. Grace held out her arms.

"Hello, Dylan."

"Mom!"

Dylan ran to Grace, throwing his arms around her, pressing his head against her shoulder. Grace hugged him back, her fingertips lightly stroking his coarse red hair. She closed her eyes, listening to the sound of her son's breathing, enjoying the smell of him, feeling his hair against her face.

Grace held Dylan at arm's length. He was three inches taller than the last time she'd seen him in Real Life, as tall as Grace and taller than she expected—VR encounters didn't always render relative sizes accurately, especially if one party had her own ideas about how tall the other party was, or should be. She looked him over. He wasn't as thin as she remembered—his shoulders were broader, his arms more muscled, his chin stronger—all well represented by Dylan's VR avatar, but striking in Real Life, in a way that surprised and pleased Grace.

"Oh, my," she whispered. "Who is this handsome young man?"

"Mom, you see me every week," he said, blushing charmingly.

Grace shook her head. "I see your avatar. It's not the same."

"You have four hours," Donna said. "I'll be in my workspace, Dylan." She looked at Grace with narrow eyes. "I have some *important* things that I need to get done."

"She's been grumpy all day," Dylan said as Donna left the hallway, "ever since I told her you were coming here IRL."

"Your Aunt Donna has a lot of responsibilities," Grace said. "She has her work, and she has you, and she has to take care of things all by herself. Are you good for her? Do you do what she tells you to do?"

"She's too strict, Mom. I'm fourteen. I'm old enough to figure things out for myself."

Grace placed her hand on Dylan's cheek. She saw her own face in his, fourteen years younger, when she was about Dylan's age. She smiled.

"But do you know how much there is to figure out?"

Dylan and Grace sat in the main room of Donna's apartment, each in VR headgear and gloves. They walked side-by-side in a virtual desert, the sun so intense that it tricked the mind, triggering an autonomic response, causing Dylan and Grace to perspire in the cool, climate-controlled apartment.

They approached a cactus, at least twelve meters high, one

of a hundred like it scattered among the brush, a cactus forest vanishing into the distance.

"What is this?" Grace asked.

"It's a saguaro, Mom. They were all over the desert in Arizona and Mexico but not as many today. Prof says they can live to be a hundred. And look!"

Dylan pointed to an opening in the cactus, ten meters up. A tiny feathered face appeared from inside. With a wave of Dylan's hand, he and Grace were levitated to the height of the hole. The bird in the cactus gave them a languid blink.

"It's a pygmy owl. They live in the cactus. They used to, anyway. They haven't seen any for ten years." Dylan held out his hand. The tiny owl hopped onto it.

"It's cute," Grace said. "What does it eat? It must be hard to find something to eat in the desert."

"Mom, life in the desert is fantastic! You can't always see it, and a lot of it only comes out at night, but it's there. Life is everywhere." He touched the bird tentatively with a finger. "Everywhere."

Grace looked on Dylan's avatar face, rendered in virtual space—lifelike, detailed, down to the fine hairs on his face—glowing in the simulated sun. He was smiling, eyes wide with excitement.

"Do you think you might want to be a biologist?" Grace asked.

"Oh, no. I mean, biology is interesting and all. I like learning about it. But I want to be a programmer, like Aunt Donna."

"That would make your aunt very proud." Grace's avatar looked pained, her state of mind inferred from her voice by the VR algorithm and represented in her rendered expression, not too subtly for Dylan to notice. "It would make me proud, too."

"Mom, you didn't go to university, did you?"

"No, Dylan. I made other choices." She reached out to pet the owl in the boy's hand. The tiny bird seemed unafraid. "I'm glad you're going, though."

"Well, yeah! Everyone goes to university." Dylan stroked

the bird, his fingers brushing Grace's, creating a tactile response in her VR gloves. "Hey, I want to show you something!"

With another gesture a menu appeared, suspended in mid-air, as the two of them floated above the ground. Dylan punched an entry: *Mars Rover.*

Grace and Dylan were instantly transported to a desolate landscape, dimly lit by the distant sun. The horizon glowed a dusky red, transitioning to a deep violet overhead. Boulders littered the field surrounding an ungainly, six-wheeled vehicle, the size of a personal transport, bristling with instruments.

"Where *are* we?" Grace whispered.

"Mom, it's *Mars!* This is a rover that landed more than thirty years ago, before the first people did. The rendering is so real. They wove together images from the rover to make it, then they synthesized the missing data to make the whole VR scene seamless. It's like you're really on another planet. That's what I want to learn—VR rendering. It's so hyper-res."

"Who did that, created this scene?"

"I don't know. Some of the old NASA scientists, maybe. And some really good VR programmers."

As they walked around the rover, Grace noticed flashes appearing on its surface, tiny flat polygons that transitioned from a dull, uniform shade, to brilliant white, then to black.

"Dylan, why is it doing that? Those little flashes of black and white?"

"Prof says those are *artifacts*. It's what happens when you try to render a scene with incomplete data. They probably tried to create this venue using mostly still photos, without much video. Hey! Do you want to see something really hi-res?"

Grace's avatar hand touched Dylan's. "Dylan, can we take these off?"

"But Mom, Wayne showed me something ultra-hyper-res. Wait until you experience it."

"Dylan, we can meet in VR any time. I want to spend some time with you IRL."

The avatar Dylan looked disappointed as he waved a hand. The surroundings went dark before the image of Donna's living room appeared in the visors. Grace and Dylan removed their gear.

"Dylan, come sit here with me," Grace said, placing her hand on the sofa next to her. She stroked his hair and rubbed his shoulder as he sat down. "Are you doing okay here with Aunt Donna?"

"Yeah, Mom, I'm okay, but she's so hard on me. Nothing's ever good enough for her. Like, I got a four on my calculus test, which is really good—I think only ten or eleven out of fifty got a four or a five. But Aunt Donna, she's all on me about why didn't I get a five? And I studied really hard." Dylan crossed his arms, falling back into the sofa. "It's integrals, Mom, they're really complicated, not like derivatives. And I did *good* on the test. Not good enough for Aunt Donna. 'You need to understand continuous math if you want to program VR,' she tells me. I know that. She doesn't have to keep hammering me."

Dylan's eyes were downcast, his lips pursed and his brow furrowed. Grace patted his knee.

"Is it worse than when you were living with Nana?"

Dylan groaned and rolled his eyes. "Oh, *Jah!* Not the Guantanamo Commandant!"

Grace locked eyes with Dylan, forcing a serious look. Dylan mocked her with an expression even more dour, until the two of them cracked smiles and exploded in guffaws.

"Did I miss something?" Donna stood in the doorway, fists on hips, as Grace and Dylan fell against each other in a fit of laughter.

"Nothing, Donna," Grace wheezed, catching her breath. "Dylan said something funny, that's all."

"Dylan? Funny? Now that would be unusual. Share it with me. What did you say, Dylan? I want to enjoy your sense of humor, too."

The laughter ceased. "It wasn't anything, Aunt Donna," Dylan mumbled. "Just a dumb joke."

"Judging from Grace's reaction, it can't have been too

dumb. Tell me. I never see you laugh. I'm not even sure I know what you think is funny. Tell me. I want to know."

"I said, it was just a dumb joke."

"He was telling me about his professor," Grace jumped in. "He's very demanding. Dylan called him the Guantanamo Commandant."

"The Grade Nazi," Dylan added.

"Der Flog Meister?" Grace continued.

"The Torture Chamberlain," Dylan said, grinning.

"How about Hannibal Lecturer?"

"Who?"

"You're right," Donna interrupted, "that is a dumb joke. I've talked with your professor and he's a very nice man. You're lucky to have him. You should be more respectful." Donna looked at Grace. "And you shouldn't be encouraging him." She looked up at the wall-mounted screen, displaying a news crawl, the current weather, and the time. "You have ten more minutes. Then Dylan has a VR cultural exchange session with a class in Brazil."

Grace and Dylan looked chastened as Donna left.

"She's hard on you because she loves you, just as your Nana loves you," Grace said. "And I love you."

"Aunt Donna says you gave me away."

Grace gasped. *"That's not true!"*

"But I grew up with Nana and Papa until I was ten, then I moved in with Aunt Donna. And you only came to see me once a week."

Grace closed her eyes, drawing a deep breath.

"It's very complicated," she whispered. "Do you remember when you asked me if I went to university, I told you I made different choices?"

"Yes."

"Well, they were bad choices, that left me in a terrible place. I couldn't keep you because I couldn't give you a home and all the things you needed to grow up right. Then, when Nana and Papa split up, and Aunt Donna asked you to live with her, I wanted you back. I wanted us to be together, but I still wasn't ready. I didn't know it at the time, but I know it now. You being with Aunt Donna instead of me isn't because she loves you and I don't. We both love you. She loves you enough to give you a home, and to take care of you, and to care that you do well in school. And I love you enough to be apart from you, to only see you once in a while, to know that you're getting everything you need, and to work very, very hard to be a better person, a person who won't make terrible choices again." She put her arm around Dylan's shoulders. "Dear, if I ever become the mother you deserve, I hope we'll be together."

Dylan turned to Grace and hugged her. "I love you, Mom."

"I know you do, Dylan. I love you too."

"I don't believe you were ever a bad person. I don't believe my mom *could* be a bad person."

Grace put her hand on Dylan's cheek. "Thank you for that." She glanced at the screen. "Our time is up. I should leave before your aunt tells me to go."

The two of them stood up.

"Oh, what was it that you wanted to show me? If it's in VR we can do it next week."

"Yes! It's so hi-res. Wayne showed me. You can actually live another person's life in VR. It's called a lifestream, Mom."

Grace kept her eyes down and her arms tightly crossed over her chest as she made the twenty-minute walk back to her apartment.

It's called a lifestream, Mom.

The streets were nearly deserted, as they always were in early afternoon, hours before people emerged in the evening. There were a few Cloak in their hurried pace, and the remnant population living outside of VR, some running errands, some walking their pets, and some just wandering. The number of people was a small fraction of the surging crowds like the ones Grace had seen in historical venues from barely a half-century ago, filling the city from before dawn until well past sunset, every day of the week.

Grace passed a few of the shops that still existed, making a living mostly from online sales, but keeping up a physical presence for the eccentric, or for the dwindling population who appreciated the charm of a face-to-face transaction. Most of the shops were deserted except for their proprietors and the occasional customer.

But not the streamboats. They were always well-patronized, day or night. Grace passed one, walking alongside the queue waiting to enter, the patrons' eyes down, none of them anxious to make eye contact.

She had just passed the end of the line when she stopped. She looked at the last man in line out of the corner of her eye. He was nonthreatening in appearance, dressed relatively neatly, somewhat well-groomed.

"Excuse me," she said to him.

"Uh-huh?"

"I'm just wondering, what goes on in there? In the lifestream bistro?"

"You know, right? It's a VR thing, like a VR game."

"But it's not just games, is it?"

"It's like living someone else's life. You can watch, or you can get involved, like seeing through their eyes." He chuckled. "And they have the Belt in there, so you can *really* get involved. Get it?"

"I'm not sure I do. What other persons' lives are available?"

"They have a whole menu. There are some famous people, and some guys that climb mountains, or skydive, you know, like that."

"Is that what you need the Belt for? To feel what it's like to skydive?"

The man's smile disappeared. He looked aside. "Look at me, lady. Look at these guys. You think we're here to jump out of an airplane?"

"You're here for VR sex."

"Yeah, so what? I'm not hurting anybody. Why are you

asking me all this?"

"I'm not judging you. I'm just curious. I've never been in there. What's popular?"

The man's smile returned. His eyebrows bounced. "I've heard there's a new one. I haven't tried it myself, but they say it's amazing. Someone named Grace."

Four more men had joined the line. One of them nudged the man behind him, tipping his head at Grace. The next man in line opened his eyes wide and mouthed the words, *no way!*

Grace hurried off as the two men followed her with their eyes. She broke into a run and didn't stop until she was back in her apartment. She closed the door behind her and leaned against it, panting, staring at the ceiling.

It's called a lifestream, Mom.

6

THE FARADAY CAGE

IN A PART of town she rarely visited, on a street she had never before walked, Grace found it. There was nothing about the shop that called attention to itself, just a curtained window, by a door with a tarnished brass plaque that read:

THE FARADAY CAGE

The shop sold all manner of goods—clothing, accessories, appliances—piled on shelves, on and under tables, like a haphazard storage shed. Despite its nondescript appearance and remote location, the shop was filled with customers, browsing the selection of wares from narrow aisles, pushing past one another, reminding Grace of videos she'd once seen of shoppers in crowded stores from the last century, but with a difference: besides herself and one other person, everyone in the store was Cloak.

The other civilian was an older man, tall and bald, with a thin face. He wore a tunic of coarse cloth, handmade-looking, resembling a costume from a Shakespearean play. He stayed close to a kiosk, identical to the payment station in any .other physical store. A Cloak customer approached,

40

handing him a basket with his selections. As the man called them out, the kiosk repeated the descriptions, listing the items on its screen. Once the total was tallied, the Cloak held up a small card to the kiosk's camera. The screen flashed, signifying a completed sale. The man in the tunic bagged the items, handing them to his customer with a word of thanks.

Grace approached the man, who addressed her with a smile.

"Hello, I'm Gavin. Welcome to the Faraday Cage."

"Hello, Gavin. My name is Grace. The Eye of Providence sent me."

"Providence," Gavin repeated, his smile disappearing. "He's slipping. Usually he tells me when he starts a new project."

"A project?"

"The Eye of Providence fancies himself as the chief recruiter for the Cloak. I'm guessing he found you out there, IRL, looking needy."

"Not needy. Curious, maybe."

"Oh. What are you curious about?"

"The Cloak, the Worldstream." Grace looked around the shop. "But for now, I'm curious about this place."

The man rubbed his lip, looking at Grace as if he were searching for meaning in an abstract painting. "Constance!" he shouted. A middle-aged woman with features resembling Gavin's emerged from a door behind the kiosk. "Take care of the customers. Providence has sent us another one of his protégés." Gavin walked toward the door. "Follow me."

The back room was at least as large as the shop, with more merchandise, boxed and unboxed, filling shelves and stacked on pallets on the floor. Gavin sat down behind a desk, not much bigger than he was, piled high with papers. "All right," he said, "go ahead. Ask me anything."

"The things you're selling here, they look like anything you can buy in VR. Why are the Cloak buying them from here?"

Gavin laughed. "*Nothing* that I sell here is available in VR! Not one thing." He leaned forward, resting his elbow on the desk, and his chin on his hand. "And you don't know why, do you?"

Grace slipped her fingers around the handles of her bag, recalling the list on the scanner at the Cloakroom. She touched the collar of her shirt. "They're not connected."

"Bravo! Providence sent me a smart one for a change. That's right, we're the only general merchandise store in the metro area selling one-hundred-percent, guaranteed, unconnected stuff and other Jahbulon-foiling technologies. If you want to poke a stick in the All-Seeing Eye, you've come to the right place."

"The All-Seeing Eye? Do you mean the Eye of Providence?"

"No, I mean the All-Seeing Eye, the Worldstream, Jahbulon, sees all, knows all, and eventually tells all, the dump for every tiny detail of your existence, from where you are, to who you're with, to what clothes you're wearing."

"My clothes—yes! Why is that? I mean, why are all my clothes connected to the Worldstream?"

"Big Data, sister. The transceivers cost next to nothing, so they go in everything. That shirt you're wearing, for instance. The company that made it knows it was you who bought it, when you bought it, where you bought it, how many times you've worn it, where you've worn it, how many times you've washed it, and they'll know when you throw it out. They know all that for your shirt, and for every shirt like it, bought by girls like you who give up their personal data without knowing or caring. That goes for your shirt, your pants, your shoes, your socks and everything else you're wearing. They're all connected, filling the mass data storage farms of multinational companies. You can be sure that there's not a single move you make, or word you utter, in VR or RL, that doesn't leave a trail in the Worldstream."

"That's crazy. Why would anyone, much less a big company, care about my shirt?"

"*Your* shirt? That's not how *they* see it. All the shirts, socks and shoes, that's *their* property, or at least the data from them is. It's not *you* they care about, it's the *data*. Before the All-Seeing Eye, they were blind. They had to go find scraps of data, at great expense, guessing about what they meant, like blind men feeling along the wall for the door. Now the data comes to *them*. They can run a thousand experiments at a time—use different fabric, change the color, alter the style—and know within days what the optimum product is for every market. It's all done in the name of customer satisfaction and low, low prices."

"That sounds like a good thing."

"If it's such a good thing, then why are you shopping with us at The Faraday Cage?"

Grace tightened her grip on her bag. "I think my life has been hacked."

"Oh boy. A weaver?"

"A what?"

"Weavers. They're VR programmers who crawl the Worldstream for a subject's life data, then they weave it into a lifestream and turn it into a VR venue. Is that what happened?"

Grace swallowed hard. "Yes, I think so, but I didn't know that's what it was called—weaving."

"Yeah. I'm sorry. I get it now. Well, I will say, you've got more reason to go under the Cloak than most of my customers. The vast majority of them are just paranoid, or black market, or horny for some RL action."

"*What?*"

"Oh, yeah, you didn't know? Think about it—everything ends up in the Worldstream—*everything*. If you want to get intimate, where do you go if you don't want your lovemaking piped into some corporate database? Or woven into a VR peepshow? Most of the Cloak won't even kiss unless they're totally isolated from the Worldstream. Did you think the Cloakroom was just a place to grab a cup of tea and discuss current affairs?"

"I don't know anything about it," Grace said, her stomach going queasy. "I just know that I've got a situation, and I intend to deal with it. I've lost my privacy, if I ever even had any privacy. My life's been woven, as you call it, and I'm going to take back my life however I can. That's why I came to your store. The Eye of Providence said I could buy a cloak here."

"Ready to take the plunge, eh? Fine. Stand up. You look like a medium." Gavin pulled a box from a shelf. He removed the lid, pulling out a cloak with one hand, and a head covering with the other. "Put the cloak on first, then fasten the closures for a comfortable fit. I recommend keeping it loose. Too tight and your contours will show. The Cloak don't like to advertise if they're men or women. Like I said—paranoid." He held up the head covering. "Put the hood on next. Make sure the microphone is close to your mouth. The synthesizer will disguise your voice. Speak softly or you'll over-modulate." He dropped the cloak and hood into the box, then pulled out a black mask, large enough to cover most of the face, leaving the mouth exposed. "And, of course, your mask."

"What's that for? I'll be wearing the hood. Why do I need a mask?"

Gavin blinked slowly. "It's for when you hook at the Cloakroom. You'll be taking off your cloak and hood. You don't want to give *everything* away."

"I don't...are you serious? I don't need *that*. That's not why I'm doing this."

Gavin dropped the mask into the box. "It's part of the set. Besides, everyone uses it, sooner or later." He pushed the box toward Grace. "Constance will help you pick out some disconnected clothes. No point in going Cloak if your underwear is broadcasting your location. You can pay me later, when you get out of the money stream. If you forget, Mr. Providence will hear about it."

"What you mean, 'when I get out of the money stream?'"

"The Cloak don't pay with face scans. That kiosk out there isn't connected to the Worldstream—it's on the stealth network. It tallies up the buys and sells and squares up the accounts, completely separate from the international exchange. And they don't pay with credits. They use cryptocurrency. You'll need to put some credits into a crypto account. Providence will explain how. It's not exactly legal, but crypto transactions are impossible to trace. It's kind of like the Shade."

Grace reached into the box, running her fingers over the fabric of the cloak. It felt like any other synthetic, smooth and light, but Grace found the texture strangely comforting. "What's 'Shade?'"

"Like Cloak, but taking it to the next several levels. Those are the guys that have completely disconnected from the Worldstream—eradicated every bit and byte of their personal data."

"How does that work? I thought that once data is in the Worldstream, it's there forever."

"It ain't easy, but it can be done. You need a crawler that hunts down your data and deletes it, more than deletes it, tears it up. Shreds it. Shredding, that's what they call it."

Grace replaced the lid on the box. Her mind returned to the previous day.

It's called a lifestream, Mom.

"I want that. I want my lifestream shredded."

Gavin's head snapped straight up. "Whoa. Don't go messing with any shredders. First, it's totally illegal. Second, shredders don't work cheap. They demand big credits for risky stuff like that. Third, and finally, once you shred out, you're out for good. There's no coming back. These Cloak, they all still have regular lives. They work, play, and shop, in VR or IRL, like regular folks. They only go out in their cloaks when they want to keep out of the Worldstream. The Shade? They're gone, out of the Worldstream, like they don't exist. You'd have to be damned desperate to take that step. Criminals and sickos, that's the Shade. Steer clear, Grace, that's all I can tell you. Go on, now. Constance is waiting."

Grace stood, picking up the box. "I have a question."

"Shoot."

"When you talk about the Eye of Providence, you say *he* and *him* and *his*. How do you know he's a man?"

Gavin raised his eyebrows. "I *don't* know, not really, but it doesn't matter. They don't care. Call a Cloak he, she, him, her or it and you won't get a reaction, not one you can see. I suppose if they know each other IRL, they might use the right pronoun, or they might not. Like I said, they don't advertise their gender. Anything else?"

"What's 'Faraday Cage?'"

Gavin smiled and nodded. "A Faraday cage is sealed off from all electromagnetic radiation, you know, radio waves." He pulled back the loose corner of the wallpaper to reveal a dull, copper-colored mesh. "See here? The entire room is lined with this copper screen. So is the store in front. Even the windows are coated with a conductive layer. No radio waves can penetrate, in or out. This space is completely isolated from the Worldstream. It's a service we offer our customers—no extra charge."

Back in her apartment, Grace removed her clothes and dressed in the undergarments that Constance had selected. She slipped the cloak over her head, fastening a closure at her neck and another at her waist. She looked at herself in the mirror, robed, as she had been at the Cloakroom, but in the black uniform of the Cloak, rather than the white robe of a civilian. She slipped the hood over her head. Through the fine mesh covering the opening over her eyes, she looked at her reflection, a Cloak apparition, indistinguishable from her fellow Cloak, invisible to the All-Seeing Eye. The tight throat, the queasy stomach, the muddy mind that had dogged her for the last four days, from the moment that Gogo had read the first v-gram, all vanished, as if a valve had opened and the building pressure had escaped. She was shrouded, cocoon-like, free to emerge at a time of her choosing—a butterfly in her chrysalis.

7

SEA OF DATA

MEET ME TONIGHT at nine. Follow the directions.

The IM was in Grace's IM stream, but it was unlike any IM that Andrew had ever gotten from her. Its terseness wasn't unusual—Grace always kept her IMs short—but it played not in Grace's voice, in an alto range, with a roughness that Andrew found attractive, but in an eerie, synthesized, mechanical-sounding voice.

The directions brought him to a narrow passage on a side street, leading to an open space lit by glowing panels. In one wall were three doors, one of them labeled CLOAKROOM.

Andrew checked his pocket screen: *9:03*. Besides him, there was one other person, a large figure in a dark gray cloak and hood, standing guard by the Cloakroom door. Neither of them spoke. Andrew considered whether to leave, when the door opened, and another cloaked person came out.

"Andrew," the Cloak hummed in a sterile monotone. "Thank you for coming here."

Andrew peered at the figure, its cloak and hood obscuring all identifying features—even the narrow slit over its eyes was covered with a fine mesh that appeared opaque from the outside.

"Grace?"

The figure appeared to nod. "Yes. But don't call me that. While we're here, please call me Chrysalis."

"Grace, I don't understand."

"Please. I'm called Chrysalis. I'll explain everything once we're inside." Chrysalis motioned toward the doorkeeper. "But first, we must scan you."

"Why 'Chrysalis?'"

Andrew sat at the table, wearing the white robe that marked him as a civilian among the Cloak, one who took no precautions to hide himself from the Worldstream.

"The Cloak try to separate themselves from the Worldstream in every way. When I'm in the connected world, I'm Grace. When I'm cloaked, when I'm outside of the Worldstream, I'm Chrysalis."

"But the Cloak, they're criminals. Why else would they cover themselves? What have they got to hide? What have *you* got to hide?"

Chrysalis stretched out her hand, clad in a glove the same color as her cloak, to touch Andrew's fingers. "I won't tell you that all Cloak have pure motives. Some hide from the Worldstream to break the law. Some are here for other reasons, not illegal, but not really socially acceptable, either."

"And you? What are your reasons?"

"Andrew, do you believe in sin?"

"Sin? Like a sin against god? Does *anyone* believe that anymore?"

"Maybe not a sin against god. But if I did something that hurt someone else, even if I didn't mean to, I think that's a sin. And what if I did something that made me a worse person instead of a better person? Isn't that a sin? There are a lot of things like that, sins, in my past that I've tried to put behind me, but I can't. I've heard that there was a time, before we were born, when sins could be forgiven, because sins could be forgotten. Not anymore. All of my sins are still there, in the Worldstream, and nothing, not prayer or penance can purge them. But I can stop adding to them. I can keep from inflicting my sins on people I care about, like you."

"Grace…"

"Please—Chrysalis."

"Excuse me, Grace, if I don't automatically buy into this Cloak thing."

"Andrew, *please*, at least keep your voice down. I don't want my name used in here. I don't want my Cloak name to be associated with my connected name unless *I* decide. Will you grant me that much?"

"All right." Andrew lowered his voice to just above a whisper. "*Chrysalis*. I know all about your past. Remember? We met in rehab, for Jah's sake. I know about the alcohol, and the Mandy X, and the other drugs. You told me your sins and I told you mine—we confessed, like everyone in VR rehab. When you and I partnered and met IRL, and I found out how strong you are, I knew that I wanted to spend time with you, and know you better, and maybe get some of that strength for myself. I know what you did, and I don't care. I don't judge you and you don't judge me. Can we get out of here so you can take off that silly cloak?"

"I love how you've accepted me, even with all the mistakes I've made," Chrysalis said in her synthetic voice. "Really, it makes you one of the most important people in my life." Chrysalis withdrew her hand from Andrew's. "But there are others who wouldn't be as understanding if they knew how I'd wasted my life. And if they *do* find out, I don't want you to be hurt. Your lifestream can't be linked with mine anymore, not VR, not IRL."

"Are you ending it between you and me? Seriously? Is that why you brought me here, to break it off?"

"No, Andrew. We can meet each other, but only here, only when I'm cloaked. And we can't meet in private, not ever, unless you're cloaked, too."

"No!" Andrew stood. He raised his voice. "Do you think I'm going to wear one of your disguises and hole up in a secret clubhouse?"

"*Andrew, please!*" Chrysalis rasped, the synthesizer masking the urgency of her plea. A few Cloak heads turned toward them. Chrysalis grabbed Andrew's arm and pulled it until he sat down. "You saw the scanner, didn't you? Did you see what you had on you that was connected to the Worldstream? It was *everything*, even what you were wearing. That's how pervasive it is, the Worldstream. We're walking through a sea, all around us, a sea of data, and wherever we go, we leave a trail; whatever we do, we leave an afterimage. I won't have it, knowing that everything I do or say is recorded and processed and consumed. And I won't compromise the people I care about by connecting their lifestreams to mine. Not with everything I've done."

"I told you, that doesn't matter to me."

"Andrew, it's not just you, but even if it were, my decision would be the same. From now on, there will be no more Worldstream records of the two of us together."

Andrew sat mute for a minute. He tugged at his robe. "I look like a Halloween ghost. And you look like a vampire."

"I can give you the name of a place where you can get a cloak. Once you're Cloak, we can meet here. There are private rooms if we want to be alone. Please, Andrew. I don't want to be away from you, and this is the only way we can be together."

"I don't accept that. We can be together like we always have."

"I've made my decision, and I won't go back. Please don't make me regret it."

"I'm getting out of this ridiculous robe. IM me when you want to talk again." He stood up to leave.

"Andrew?" the mechanized voice said flatly, with a slight rising inflection at the end.

"I don't know," he answered. "I need to think about it." He went for the door. Chrysalis watched through the opening in her hood as Andrew left the Cloakroom.

Chrysalis lowered her head, putting her hand to her mouth, pressing the synthesizer against her lips, partially muffling the sounds of her breathing.

"Chrysalis."

Chrysalis looked up at the Cloak standing behind Andrew's empty chair. "I'm called Chrysalis," she said.

"I'm called the Eye of Providence."

"Please, sit."

The Eye of Providence spread his cloak as he sat. "I overheard you. We all did."

"Have I violated protocol?"

"No. There are few protocols in the Cloakroom. But you'll want to be more discreet in the future." The Eye reached out and tapped Chrysalis's hand. "The separation from your loved ones in the connected world is the hardest part of cloaking. You can still be with them in the Worldstream of course, but knowing that everything you do together is visible to the All-Seeing Eye, you must be careful in your words and actions. Only here, in the Cloakroom, can you be completely free."

"It's more than that. I've done terrible things. It wouldn't be fair if that man—or anyone else—were to suffer because they were connected to me. They're blameless."

"I understand, Chrysalis, but look around. We all have our motives for joining the Cloak. Some of us want to believe we're protecting others, or protesting the All-Seeing Eye. Some of us are more honest about our motives. There's no one here who doesn't have history, buried in the Worldstream. Do you think you're different? All any of us can do is move on and keep that history from becoming richer. You'll have to decide whether you sort your relationships into Cloak and civilian, or bring your civilian relationships into the Cloak world, or cut yourself off completely. There's a balance point. The more honest you are with yourself, the more quickly you'll find it."

"I understand," Chrysalis said. "Thank you."

The Eye of Providence nodded and left the table without another word.

A balance point, Chrysalis thought. *What can balance a long and terrible past that refuses to stay buried?*

8

Circles of Hell

By ten a.m. Grace had settled into her routine, serving one applicant after another, bringing their petitions to State Live Services, State Benefits Department, hoping their requests would be granted.

"Citizen, your entitlement is fixed," Grace said to the man, unusually young compared to her usual clients, older than Grace, but not by much. His clothes were clean but well-worn, as if he'd scavenged the reuse receptacles at multiple corporate reclamation sites, finding the most serviceable articles, vaguely resembling what a job-seeker might wear for a final, decisive IRL interview. Grace wondered how many different data trails converged in this one man, each trail retained by a piece of used clothing, the braid of previously unrelated strands now a single path in the Worldstream.

"One thousand credits a week? That's not a living wage."

"I'm obligated to remind you, citizen, that your entitlement is not a wage. It's your guaranteed minimum income." Grace's desk screen flashed a detailed dossier of the man, retrieved within seconds of the man's first words, the voice response system having recognized his voice and recovered his identity. Grace perused the man's record. He'd received a weekly transfer since reaching the age of legal entitlement, almost twenty years before.

"This is the same distribution you've received since you were sixteen, with adjustments. You've never applied for an increase before. Has your situation changed?"

"No," the man said, barely whispering, "not exactly."

"I'm sorry. What was your answer?"

"Nothing has changed. I'm still a writer. I still create with language. I still don't have the skills to render a 360-degree VR venue, or to stimulate a response in the human brain through a neural interface. Those are highly technical skills that I don't possess. I have other skills. I write. I have no immersive sensory apparatus, no tactile feedback, no galvanic interface to the limbic system to work with. Just words, and my reader's mind. My words have to penetrate a lot of layers in the reader's psyche to make an impact. What VR programmers do is too hard for me." The man looked Grace in the eye. His voice gained a hard edge. "What I do, touching the reader's mind with words, is infinitely harder."

The man's eyes turned tired and moist. He suddenly seemed ten years older.

"Citizen," Grace said, "I'll ask you again, has your situation changed?"

"I create content for VR advertising. Nothing more than outlines, really, not even screenplays—just storyboards in words. There's no premium for creativity, and there's a penalty for subtlety. The VR programmers take it from there. They get the accolades—and the money." The man shifted in his chair and looked away. "I don't want to do it anymore. It's not writing. I want to write."

"Have you been discharged from your position? If you have, you could be eligible for an unemployment benefit."

"No, I'm still employed."

"Citizen, if your situation hasn't changed in any material way, we can't alter your stipend."

"I need to *create*. I need to *write*. I don't program, I've never even wanted to program." He leaned forward. "Do you use VR? Do you like it?"

"I have," Grace said. "There are some VR venues that I like."

"I hate it. Plugging my mind into a machine that controls my senses, putting pictures in my eyes, sound in my ears and feelings in my fingers. Making myself a receiver for whatever the VR machine jacks into me, a human peripheral, no more active than a wall screen. But with language." The man paused, smiling for the first time. "With language, the reader is a participant, my partner in creation. Do you read?"

"A little. Poetry, mostly."

"I've been reading since I was four. While my friends were strapped into their VR gear, I was reading. While they bungee jumped off of virtual bridges, I walked the streets of Victorian London. While they rode rafts down whitewater rivers, I hunted whales in the Pacific. While they drove race cars on oval tracks, I traversed the circles of hell. Their epinephrine surge lasted a minute; literature changed my life. Who's better off?" The man covered his mouth with his hand, speaking through his fingers. "I have to leave my job so that I can write. And I can't live on a thousand credits a week."

Grace turned back to her screen and studied the man's case file. "Your mother is still living, is that right?"

"Yes."

"She's on a pension. Do you provide any support for her?"

He shook his head.

"You're eligible for a supplemental support stipend on your mother's behalf. Three-hundred-eighty credits per week, payable to you." Grace lowered her voice and spoke with exaggerated slowness. "This is provided on the condition that these credits are applied to your mother's welfare. It's the best I can do."

The man nodded with resignation. "Thanks," he said as he left Grace's station. Grace watched him leave, wondering what he could have meant by *traversed the circles of hell*. The screen beeped a reminder.

"Supplemental support stipend, three-hundred-eighty,

authorized, Grace, associate 216412," Grace said, watching her screen as the voice response system transcribed her words, verified her voice, and finalized the change to the writer's entitlement. "Next client."

The man who entered Grace's station was older than her last client by two decades at least, and far less fastidious in his appearance. He was a large man with soiled clothes, emanating an acrid odor, recognizable as the smell of street people who hung around the community disposal plants, scavenging from the refuse bins lined up for the incinerator, the majority of them, the street people, being too impoverished even to afford the modest fee charged by the corporate reclamation facilities to browse their containers of castoffs. He sat down heavily, laying a fleshy hand on the desk, holding a plastic card with what was once a glossy finish, now scuffed and dog-eared.

"My voucher came up short," the man mumbled.

Grace took the card from his hand and held it up to the screen to be scanned. *Pogue, Freeman* the screen displayed, next to a photograph of the man. A list appeared, the tally of purchases recorded against his voucher; at the bottom of the list was the remaining balance of seven credits.

"Mr. Pogue, do you recognize these purchases?" she said, rotating her desk screen toward the man.

Pogue squinted at the screen. "I don't know 'em all. Don't matter. I got to buy food and my next voucher don't come for another week. I know I had a hundred cred on that card but they turned me down at the shop."

"You can see, citizen, that every transaction was validated by face scan. They're all legitimate buys. If you're short, I can grant you a small advance, but the total is correct."

"Listen, lady, I can keep track. I been buying on vouchers for twenty years. I can keep track. I don't give a damn what your screen says, I…"

Pogue stopped abruptly. He seemed to be staring at Grace's chest.

"Citizen?"

Pogue's mouth slowly dropped open. "You—you're

Grace!"

Grace looked down, then back at Pogue, who now stared at her face. She tapped her name badge:

Good Day Citizen
I'm Grace
216412
I'm here to help

"Yes, citizen, I'm Grace. I'm here to help."

"You're Grace!" Pogue repeated. He leaned forward, draping his ample arms across the desk. The smell of the community disposal plant assaulted her nose; his sour breath caused her to turn her head. *"I've had you fifty times!"* Pogue inched forward; Grace pushed back staying just out of reach.

"What, are you shy?" Pogue said. "I don't believe it. What you did to me, whoa! What I did to you, whoa-*oh*! Jah, what a head job. I'm getting a chub right now just thinking about it."

Pogue lunged forward, now off his seat, his stubby fingers waving inches from Grace. Grace pushed further away, until she hit the back wall of her station. Desperate, she looked for an escape path, her eyes settling briefly on the screen.

The list of transactions from Pogue's voucher included a string of identical entries, all in the amount of fifty credits, all to the same vendor: *Head Trip Lifestream Bistro.*

A thick, sweaty hand grasped Grace's wrist.

"Jahbulon, help me!" Grace shouted.

Within seconds, two security guards appeared, dressed in black, equipped with taser pistols. One put a choke hold on Pogue, while the other one expertly peeled Pogue's fingers from Grace's wrist. Pogue proved surprisingly strong, standing with two security guards clinging to him, staggering backwards, pinning the guard with the choke hold against the wall. The second guard unholstered his taser pistol, pressed it into Pogue's side, and fired point-blank.

The taser round buried itself into Pogue's flesh with a spray of blood, the impact triggering a burst of fifty-thousand volts, sending Pogue into convulsions. The guard released his hold, pushing Pogue away from him. He sat down hard on Grace's desk. "Yeow, baby, I felt that," he said, shaking his hands to restore feeling.

A crowd gathered around the scene as the guards applied restraints to the big man quivering on the floor. Grace stayed plastered to the back wall of her station, breathing hard.

"That's a messy one," one guard said to the other, moving his foot to avoid the stream of blood meandering along the floor.

"No option," the second guard replied. "Caught me off-guard. Strong bastard, huh? Quick, too."

Grace's supervisor Heidi pushed through the crowd. "Are you all right?" she asked as she broke through the ring of gawkers.

"He grabbed me. He had my hand. I had to call Jahbulon. I had to."

"It's okay, Grace. Jahbulon is our protector. That's what he's for." Heidi turned back to the crowd, a mixture of State Benefits associates and clients. "Citizens, Jahbulon has this under control. There's no danger to any of you. Please, take your seats and we'll be with you shortly. Associates, please return to your stations. We have clients to serve." She turned back to Grace. "Take a break. We'll need you back in ten minutes."

Grace rolled her chair back to her desk. She gripped its edge and stared at its blank surface until her racing heart slowed and her breathing returned to normal. She looked up at her screen, the list of transactions of *Pogue, Freeman*, still visible, including his purchases at the *Head Trip Lifestream Bistro*, twelve total, eight of them on a single day.

"Erase screen," she said. The list disappeared, along with Pogue's photo and identifying information.

Grace closed her eyes and covered her face with her hands.

If only it were that easy to erase my life.

9

CROOKS AND CREEPS

HE WAS CONSPICUOUSLY conventional in a room of indistinguishable rebels. Though seated, he was obviously a tall man, and thin, with a long face and sharp features. His skin was creased but not wrinkled, brown but not too dark, and clean-shaven; the overall effect was that of carved and burnished wood. His eyes were close-set, and small, with prominent brows; he looked as if he were scanning the horizon, like a lookout on a sailing ship, ready to shout a warning from the crow's nest. His hair was long, parted in the center, rippling down his shoulders in a silver cascade. He wore a loose red shirt with buttons, the kind that was popular in the twentieth century, and a black vest, another relic of the past. He was the only one wearing what could be called *ordinary clothing* in the Cloakroom, among black-robed Cloak and white-robed civilians.

As she approached his table, Chrysalis recognized him instantly from the description given to her by the Eye of Providence.

"I'm called Chrysalis."

The man cocked his head toward an empty chair. "And I'm Raúl, friend of the Eye. Have a seat." His voice was firm, though slightly rough, an old man's voice with the confidence of his years, a sharp contrast with the android sounds of the Cloak, and the nervous, whispered words of the civilians.

Raúl's eyes stayed on Chrysalis as she sat down, focused on the veiled opening in her hood. Chrysalis found his stare unnerving, as if he could see through her cloak and discover her identity.

"You're not in a cloak," Chrysalis said, "or a robe."

"I never wear or carry anything connected to the Worldstream," Raúl said, his face impassive. "I'm not one of the Cloak. I don't have to be. Jahbulon has no power over me."

"Jahbulon is the Worldstream. It's everywhere. Everything you say, everything you do, wherever you go—it all goes into the Worldstream. You can't escape it."

Raúl gazed steadily at Chrysalis, his thin lips smiling for the first time. "You Cloak are hilarious."

"Do you think I'm funny?" Chrysalis said, her indignation partially filtered by the synthesizer.

"I have no idea if *you're* funny. But the Cloak are a scream, generally speaking. The Eye tells me you're new to the Cloak, so I shouldn't make assumptions. You're still learning, I suppose, if you're able to learn. Maybe you're only going through a Cloak phase. Don't stay in your phase too long or the funny will rub off on you."

"When the Eye of Providence told me about Raúl, he didn't say much. I don't know what to make of you."

"Make of me whatever you like. I don't hide under a burqa; I don't disguise my voice; I don't choose my words to make you like me. What you see is what you get."

"And Jahbulon sees you too. You're part of the Worldstream."

"Keep the jokes coming."

"What jokes are you talking about?"

"The Cloak jokes. The Cloak, hiding from the All-Seeing Eye of Jahbulon, as if your ridiculous hoods and voice scramblers could keep you out of the Worldstream. The Cloak, coming to your secret fort and buzzing BS at each other, sneaking off to your sad little cubby holes for your sorry romps, pretending that anonymous, silent sex is more genuine than the virtual kind. The Cloak, cut off from any real, organic, visceral, face-to-face, flesh-to-flesh human contact when you're cloaked; cowering in fear when you're not. Don't you think that's funny? I do."

"But *you're* in the Worldstream."

Raúl said nothing, his smile growing slightly.

"Aren't you?"

"Jahbulon knows only as much about me as I let it. The All-Seeing Eye sees what I want it to see."

Raúl's stare intensified, as if drilling through Chrysalis's veil and into her mind.

"How?" Chrysalis asked.

"I don't bow to Jahbulon," Raúl stated, "it bows to me. Jahbulon, the All-Seeing Eye, the all-knowing, has no mind, no capacity for thought. It's an algorithm, a mechanism to be manipulated, a program to be hacked. The Worldstream contains no images, no sounds, no data of mine that I haven't allowed to remain or that I haven't put there on purpose. The Worldstream contains the Raúl that Raúl has made, by *my* hand, in *my* image."

"But your past," Chrysalis said, "it's all there. How can it *not* be?"

"Only the past that I put there, nothing more. What I don't want known, I've erased. Not that it matters much anymore. I'm an old man. I don't care for anyone, and no one cares for me. Why should I be afraid of Jahbulon or anything else?"

Chrysalis leaned forward. "Can you do that for me? Change my past?"

Raúl laughed, a cold, dismissive laugh that seemed to diminish Chrysalis. "It's taken years to master the All-Seeing Eye, learning the language of Jahbulon, finding its weaknesses, and making it work for *me*. The crawlers I've planted in the Worldstream, to control my presence without triggering an alert, they're my life's work. That's what we've come to in this brave new world—to take control of my life,

I had to commit my life. A life for a life—that's a sacrifice I'll make for myself and no one else."

"But the Cloak—we control what enters the Worldstream. We reveal what we want, when we want."

Raúl's laugh was louder and more derisive. "You see? Funny!"

"You don't have a high opinion of the Cloak."

"No, I do *not*. I've spent time with the Cloak. Some of them, like the Eye, I could even call friends. Every one of you rages against the Worldstream, how it's obliterated your privacy, how it's violated your rights. Very noble, you Cloak, you brave freedom fighters, the final barrier against the tyrannical Jahbulon." Raúl lowered his voice for the first time. "*Bull.* You're new to this, so you might not be wise to the ways of the Cloak. Let me teach you, young Chrysalis.

"Here, in the Cloakroom, you're surrounded by criminals. The monotone conversations you hear at every table, that infuriating, non-stop drone, are as likely as not about illegal activities. Sellers and buyers of contraband—these are your brother Cloak. Your high-minded, abstract concept of privacy has a very practical application for them. They don't want to get caught. They're citizens of the community with spotless reputations when they're uncloaked, outlaws under their hoods.

"But the ones talking, swapping contraband, they're not the worst, not to my thinking. They're just taking care of business. What you Cloak come here for is so common you have your own language for it. Man seeking woman? Woman seeking man? Just ask for *holy communion*. Man seeking man? *Genuflection.* Woman seeking woman? *Breaking bread.* A couple of words and you're off in the anterooms, silently rolling in the hay. These are the mysterious Cloak: crooks and creeps."

"I'm not a crook, and I'm not a creep," Chrysalis said.

"So you say. I don't know anything about your motives. Whatever they are, they must be compelling, if you're here talking to a shredder."

Chrysalis paused, as if speaking the next word would commit her irrevocably to a course she would regret.

"How would I shred my life, if I wanted to?"

"Cloak isn't secret enough for you. You want to go Shade."

Chrysalis nodded.

"The Shade," Raúl said, shaking his head, "live entirely outside the Worldstream. Have you thought about what that means? You're in your own world. You eat, sleep, live and die with the Shade. Survival is your full-time profession. If you're lucky, you'll find a sponsor among the Cloak who can provide you with an income and a place to sleep, assuming you have some marketable skills your sponsor can resell in the world. But you'll probably end up like most of the Shade, sweating away in secret workshops, augmenting AI algorithms for unscrupulous corporations, a human cipher, filling the gaps that thinking machines haven't yet closed."

"You make it sound horrible, yet *you're* a shredder."

"I'm not saying it doesn't make sense for some people. Like, if you were terminally ill, in a lot of pain, what would you have to lose by ending it all? That's what shredding is— assisted suicide. They used to say that when you commit suicide, you go to hell. It was a lie then; now it's true. What could be so terrible that you'd kill yourself?"

"I have to get out of the Worldstream. It's my past. I have to get rid of it."

"Your past—that's intriguing. Tell me all about it."

"It's been taken from me, hacked, by a weaver, I think. It's gone viral."

Raúl's eyes grew wide. "A *viral* lifestream? When did you find that out?"

"About a week ago."

Raúl leaned in close, lowering his voice. "Is there a lot of sex? Drugs and the like?"

"So I've heard. I haven't seen it myself."

Raúl slapped his thigh. "No way. You're not...are you Grace?"

Chrysalis felt the breath go out of her, as if she'd been kicked in the stomach. "Yes."

Raúl smiled, showing his teeth. "Now, that makes sense.

That's a past I'd want scrubbed if it were mine."

"You've *seen it?*"

"I *had* to check it out. When word of Grace's lifestream came around, I considered it my professional duty to ride it myself. And glad I am that I did. It's truly crafted."

"That's disgusting. *You're* disgusting."

"Think what you will of me, but you don't know what it takes to weave a lifestream. You *really* don't know the level of skill it took to weave *your* lifestream. Think of it—a trillion disconnected bits of data—images, sound, metadata—from a billion different sources, identified, collated, sequenced, synthesized and rendered. *Your* lifestream—the quality, the completeness, the content—it's stunning, the best I've seen. But that's not the only reason it's getting a lot of rides. There are thousands of smutty lifestreams out there. Some of them even use the Belt. Not like yours. I don't know how the weaver does it, but I wasn't just inside your body, I was inside your *head*. It creeped me out. But I also kept riding. It was addictive. It's no wonder that Grace is a phenomenon. Whoever wove your lifestream is a master, and I'm not easily impressed."

"You're making me sick. I don't want to know anything about it. I want it destroyed."

"That could be tricky. And expensive. The amount of data in your lifestream is massive. Whoever wove it knew exactly what to look for."

"What does that mean?"

"It means your weaver knows you—intimately."

Chrysalis leaned against the table. Her synthesizer rendered her gasps as scratchy bursts.

"Shred it. I don't care what it costs."

"Okay. I'll work up a quote. Just remember, when you're out, you're out. For good. Everyone you know, everyone you love—if you love anyone—they're memories, and you're a memory to them."

"I can accept that," Chrysalis said, "As long as *I* choose how they remember me."

10

A Selfish Act

"Grace, don't punish yourself."

Grace was virtually co-located with her therapist, Madeleine, near the middle of their bi-weekly Friday session, in a VR venue that Madeleine had personally designed to calm anxieties, to foster honesty, and to encourage openness. Grace sat in a chair rendered identically to the one in her apartment, lending a familiar touch, with every other detail of the venue—the potted plants, the throw rug, the colorful prints hanging on the walls, even what Madeleine's avatar was wearing—custom-programmed specifically for Grace, based on Grace's psychological profile, calculated for optimum therapeutic effect. *Virtual Reality is the greatest advancement in psychological therapy in the last fifty years,* Madeleine was fond of saying. Grace wasn't sure why that would be, but she *was* certain that without Madeleine's counsel, she'd still be a slave to her addiction—or dead.

Grace had only met Madeleine IRL once, when Grace, deep in a cycle of self-destruction, sought a counselor through State Health Services. It was the state's policy that counselors and patients meet at least once IRL prior to starting treatment, in part to discourage posers and trolls, and in part due to the outdated notion among some policy-makers that the relationship between therapist and patient was enhanced by face-to-face, non-virtual contact.

Madeleine's avatar looked identical to Grace's memory of her from their RL meeting, nearly four years earlier. She was older than Grace by ten years or more, tall, with mannish features, what some old-fashioned people might call a *handsome woman*. Her hair was long, black and straight, with a few strands of gray, pulled back in a ponytail that reached the middle of her back. In her virtual office, Madeleine sat opposite Grace in a chair rendered to coordinate with the customized surroundings.

"The path back from sexual addiction is not straight," Madeleine continued, "and you don't walk it alone. You have me, and Edward, and Andrew, and Dylan. We love you. Your past is past."

Grace studied Madeleine's facial expressions, as reproduced by VR algorithms, based on Madeleine's Worldstream image history, programmed into the rendering engine, and adjusted to evoke a specific response from the patient. Madeleine seemed sincere, concerned, and worthy of Grace's trust.

Grace knew that, by law, any topic discussed in the course of her treatment could not be divulged—any topic, Madeleine had explained, that did not reveal an illegal act, or the intent to commit one. But after four years, Grace had come to know that Madeleine was on her side. Madeleine had never betrayed a trust, and Grace had never held anything back. She would not start now.

"And it will stay that way," Grace said. "I've seen to that."

"What do you mean?"

"I know a shredder. He's agreed. It's a lot of money, more than I have, but I don't care. I'll spend that and more to be certain that my life is destroyed."

"Grace," Madeleine whispered, her avatar displaying the appropriate mix of sympathy and alarm, "do you know what that means?"

"You'll try to talk me out of it, I know, but this isn't an

impulse. I mean it." Grace shifted in her chair. "Did you know I'm a celebrity? It's true. I never wanted to be one, a celebrity, but that's what I am. I've heard that politicians, VR players, athletes, you know, *real* celebrities, will alter their avatars when they're in public venues, so that none of us regular people will point and stare, or whisper behind our hands, *look there*. But I've also heard that some of them, the famous people, will appear as themselves, because they *like* the attention, they *like* to imagine what the crowd is thinking when we tilt our heads and look sideways at them. And I've even heard that posers will spoof the Worldstream, and put on famous avatars, just to know what it's like to have people they've never seen before, strangers they'll never see again, pointing and whispering. It gives them a thrill. I don't understand it, but that's what I've heard.

"Me? I don't have a choice. I work in the real world. This is my face, my body—me, the real me. People on the street, in Real Life, this is what they see. When they point and whisper, they're not saying *look, that's Grace, the famous VR player,* or *isn't that Grace, our civil council representative?* No, they're saying *over there—that's Grace, the slut.*"

Madeleine nodded slowly as Grace spoke. "It causes you pain to imagine what these people are thinking."

"Pain at first. Then fear. Then anger. One of them came to my workplace—did you know that? They train us not to judge, where I work, to be considerate and understanding. They didn't train me on what to do when some fat, loathsome stream rider comes over the desk at me, thinking, I guess, that he can play with me IRL like he can in VR. I saw his purchase record—twelve times he rode my lifestream in a week."

"That's shocking. You shouldn't be subjected to that, no one should." Madeleine spoke softly, barely above a whisper, as a priest might speak in a confessional, granting absolution. "I don't want to minimize what you're going through. You're a private person, I know, and this notoriety is eating you up. But shredding your life, Grace...it's so *final.* You have alternatives. You've come so far. You can weather this. We can, together. We've talked before about mastery, and how to take control over your feelings, thoughts and actions."

"No," Grace said, a short, staccato *no* that left little room for debate. "Not good enough. You talk about mastery? For four years I've been working on *myself*, mastering *myself*, to modify *my* behavior. When it was just you and Dylan and Andrew and Edward and the rest of my lovely family, that was *almost* enough. The power *you* have over me is the power I give you. Things are different now. I'm famous. How do I deal with that? I feel like I'm trying to learn how to swim in the middle of an ocean, with waves crashing over me. That's what it's like—figuring out how to cope with an ocean that's infinitely bigger than I am and doesn't care one drop for me. I can't beat the ocean. I can swim until I drown, or I can get out. I'm getting out. I can master myself. I can't master the Worldstream. But I won't let the Worldstream master *me*."

Madeleine reached out and tapped Grace's hand. Grace's VR glove transmitted the sensation to her skin. "You don't see this as a selfish act? You don't see it as surrendering?"

"I'm not surrendering!" Grace glared at Madeleine, gripping the arms of her chair. "I'm *not*." Grace clenched her jaw. "Listen, Madeleine, we talk endlessly about who I allow into my life, how I spend my time, how to get out of situations where my addictions could overwhelm me and push me back into my old habits. Don't you see, Madeleine? The world and everything in it *is* that situation, the one I can't handle, the one I have to get out of. How do I avoid temptations that invade my home, that follow me around, that point me out in the streets, that come into my workplace? But you know, if it was only me, I might take the chance. I might bet that I could ride it out, wait for the hype to cool down, and get on with my life, without jumping back into the sewer. And if I slip up, what's the worse that happens? I end up what I was, a slave, with the life expectancy of a slave. I die early and spare a lot of people I don't care about the pain of knowing me. That's not selfish. That's generous.

"But I'm not alone in this, as you've pointed out. The one person in my troubled life who really matters deserves a mother he's not ashamed of. My sister is not my advocate, but at least she's spared Dylan the dirty details. Now they're all out there, the details, and he can find them for himself."

"You love Dylan. If you disconnect, you'll never see him again. You need him. And he needs you."

"For what, Madeleine? Donna gives him everything he needs."

"Your sister is not Dylan's mother. He needs his mother."

"That's the point, isn't it? He needs a mother because boys need their mothers. They need to know that the women that birthed them are decent and loving people, so that they know that they, their sons, can be decent and loving, too. I won't take that illusion away from Dylan. Tell me, Madeleine, is that selfish?"

"It's illegal, Grace. You know my obligations."

Grace hesitated. Suddenly she felt very tired.

"Are you going to rat me out?"

"No, Grace. You know I won't. You wouldn't have told me your plans if you'd thought I'd betray you. But you're right— I *will* try to talk you out of it."

Grace heard a chime. A digital timer appeared, floating between the two women, counting down the time remaining in Grace's appointment.

"Our time is almost up," Madeleine said. She reached out and tapped the display. It shrank to a dot and disappeared. "I'll see you in two weeks."

"Thank you, Madeleine."

Madeleine and her chair dissolved, along with her surroundings, leaving Grace alone in her apartment. She removed her headgear and slipped off her gloves. She sat for several minutes, replaying the session in her mind, ending with Madeleine's parting comment, "I'll see you in two weeks."

In two weeks, with any luck, I'll be gone.

11

ALL TANGLED UP

IMAGO.

The single word appeared on Andrew's pocket screen, in an anonymous IM stream, but Andrew knew who it was from. It was the pre-arranged signal that Chrysalis wanted to meet him at the Cloakroom.

Chrysalis. Andrew had resigned himself to using Grace's chosen name in her presence, choosing his words carefully when they spoke, like a self-conscious child who'd been scolded for asking *can I* instead of *may I.*

What is she thinking?

Andrew sat alone in his robe, at a table in the Cloakroom, feeling conspicuous, but attracting no attention, until one of the Cloak approached him.

"I'm called Chrysalis," the Cloak said.

"Okay. I guess you know who I am."

"Andrew, thank you for coming," Chrysalis said as she sat, "and thank you for being patient with me,"

"I guess if this is the only way I can see you, I don't have much choice. *Chrysalis.*"

"I know I've made it hard on you."

Andrew narrowed his eyes at the indistinctly shaped,

shrouded person across the table. He visualized who it was under the hood, her face, her voice. He hadn't seen her nor heard her in four days, not even in VR. Before Grace became Chrysalis, their VR visits happened daily, with meetings IRL once a month, sometimes twice. Their conversations were routine, even formulaic, adopted from the rules of their shared rehab experience: be open, be honest, be respectful. Don't pry, don't judge. These were the principles that guided their relationship, built on a foundation of a shared addiction.

Andrew had immediately noticed the newcomer to the Community Addiction Treatment session. She said her name was Grace, and she kept herself hidden—patients could choose to whom they revealed their true avatars—but her voice was steady, with none of the halting, nearly incoherent way of speaking common among addicts. She didn't say a thing about the circumstances that drove her to self-destruct; she blamed no one but herself. When she pledged to stay clean, today, and the next day, and the next, each day a new challenge, she did so with a conviction so clear that no one doubted her. Andrew revealed himself to Grace during that first session together. Grace reciprocated five sessions later, when she put on her true avatar for the whole group.

It was Grace who'd approached Andrew to become mutual sponsors. *We'd be good together,* she said. *You need a friend; so do I. And I need to be needed.* Andrew accepted immediately. Within a month, their ad hoc VR sessions had become a daily routine; within two months, they were meeting IRL.

The visits were comfortable for Andrew, making no demands on him other than to share his daily struggles and small triumphs—a commitment kept, a temptation avoided, one more day of sobriety tallied—and he looked forward to them. Grace was a patient listener, reassuring Andrew's many doubts, praising his accomplishments, gently chiding his errors, always composed, rarely complaining. Grace was his rock. And now she had retreated behind a veil, going so far as to take a new name.

And then there was the sex—or the lack of it. They'd been

intimate IRL exactly once, in Grace's apartment, a mechanical, artless experience, consummated wordlessly, a physical release and little more. VR sex was rare. Andrew had learned not to push Grace to be intimate, occasionally raising the subject in a way that succeeded every other month or so. With neither of them owning the prohibitively expensive Belt, capable of simulating the sexual experience in all its nuance, their VR lovemaking was limited to mutual self-manipulation—listless, silent, and brief.

"You know," Andrew said, "after the last time I saw you here, I tried to win a tab of Mandy."

"Oh, Andrew, no."

"I wanted to talk to you. I didn't know if I should IM you. You seemed to want to keep your distance."

"That's not it at all. I'm just being careful." Chrysalis took Andrew's hand. "You should have messaged me. What happened? You didn't…"

"No. Don't worry. I tried to IM one of my old sellers. It failed. *Deceased*, the response said. That made me think."

"I wasn't there for you. I'm sorry."

"I'll be okay," Andrew said. "It's good to talk to you. I miss you."

"I miss you, too."

"So, Chrysalis, where do we go from here?"

Chrysalis squeezed Andrew's hand. "It's what I wanted to talk with you about. I've made a decision, about my life, and I want you to be a part of it."

Andrew nodded. "Okay."

"I'm going to shred my life."

Andrew gazed blankly at Chrysalis. "Shred—I don't know what that means."

"All the data about me in the Worldstream, my lifestream, it'll all be gone. My past will be erased, like it never happened. My life will be mine again."

"Is that even possible? Everything in the Worldstream is all tangled up together. How can you get it all out?"

"It is possible. I've found a shredder. He'll make a program, a crawler, to find every bit of data about me and purge it from the Worldstream."

"But then what? As soon as you…" Andrew shook his head. "Wait, that's what this Cloak routine is about, isn't it? You'll be out and you'll stay out—gone, for good."

"Yes."

"But when you're gone, where will that leave me?"

"I'm asking you to come with me, Andrew. I want us to be together."

"Together? Where? Doing what? No, Grace—Chrysalis—this is insane. And I don't even know why you're doing it."

"I told you, it's my past, in the Worldstream, where anyone can find it, like it's not *my* past, that *I* own. I don't want it there anymore."

"And I told *you* that I don't care about that."

Andrew sat through the pause, silent except for the undulating hum of the voices in the Cloakroom.

"There are other things," Chrysalis said at last. "Things I haven't told you, that I didn't want you to know."

"I know all about the drugs."

"Yes, you know about the drugs, the alcohol, and what they did to me, how I ruined my body, how I wasted my mind. You know because I told you about them, like I told everyone else in rehab. And you understood, you all did, like someone who's been there, and you didn't hold it against me, my past, and you supported me as I got clean and you helped me to stay clean. And if that's all there was, I'd stay in the Worldstream and live with my past, because it would be a past I could explain, a forgivable past."

"I forgive you. I've always forgiven you."

"Yes. For the past you know. Not for the past you don't know."

"What past? Damn it, Grace, what past are you talking about?"

"My…Andrew, it's my sexual past."

"Your what?"

"I'm fighting more than one addiction. Jah, sometimes it feels like I'm fighting a thousand addictions. Sometimes it seems like a war, against an army of demons, and every one of them knows all my weak spots and just how to take me down. This cloak is more than a disguise—it's a shield. It's my protection; it's the wall between me and the All-Seeing Eye. And the demons can't hurt me, because they're in here, with me, where I can control them."

"You said sexual."

"My sex addiction. I never told you about it. I didn't want you to know. I was dealing with it."

"You're not a sex addict," Andrew scoffed. "I mean, we never…"

"It's been hard on you, I know," Chrysalis interrupted. "You're frustrated."

"But, I mean, we don't…we don't *have* a sex life. How does that make sense if you're…?"

"Andrew, it's different with us. It's *because* it's different that I don't have that compulsion with you. The addiction isn't about the sex; Jah, the sex isn't even that pleasurable. The high's not like a drug high, sex doing what a drug does to my body, because it's not about the sex. And that's why it's different with you."

"What does all that mean, 'it's not about the sex?' What's it about?"

"Andrew, I was having sex with *strangers*, people I didn't know, people I'd never see again, who wanted *my* body, mine to give or not to give. The seduction—it was a game, to see how far they'd go to possess *my body*, even for a moment. It's not about the *sex*, it never was. It's about *control*. It's about *power*."

Andrew's eyes wandered around the room, looking everywhere except at Chrysalis. "How many?"

"I don't know. A lot."

"More than ten? More than twenty?"

"Andrew, the number isn't important. They were victims. They didn't mean anything to me. You're the one I want to be with, the one I want to take care of."

"More than fifty?"

Chrysalis sat motionless. "More than fifty, yes," the synthesizer crackled. "I really don't know how many."

Andrew turned back to Chrysalis. "But you're over it, right? It's all done with."

"It's like our other addictions. I have to manage it day to day. But I haven't, you know, in years, not since before I went to rehab. Certainly not since I met you."

"Then why do you want to disconnect? It's all behind you. It's over." He reached for Chrysalis's hand. "I don't care about the drugs, and I don't care about this, the sex thing. Anyone who cares about you will understand." He stood up. "Let's get out of here. Let's get rid of these robes and get back to our lives."

"There's more."

Andrew sat back down. "Oh, Jah."

"My lifestream. It's all the things I've done, all the mistakes I'm ashamed of and I thought were behind me, they've all been pulled out of the Worldstream and woven together. Now it's out there, like a VR venue. Anyone with fifty cred can be Grace. Go to a streamboat if you don't believe me. It's viral, my lifestream. It's all they're talking about. Sick, low-life perverts are slobbering over me, deciding what they want to relive, whenever they want, as many times as they want, and I can't do anything to stop them, not as long as my lifestream exists."

"Your sex life is in VR?"

"Yes, Andrew, yes, yes, and there aren't ten, or twenty, or fifty stream riders, there are thousands, hundreds of thousands, even. Are you beginning to see the position I'm in? Is this what *you* want, for thousands of strangers to have me, just like they were raping me IRL?"

Andrew pressed his fingers to his eyes. "Jahbulon almighty."

"Andrew, there's a way out. I can shred my life. No viral lifestream, no slimy stream riders grunting about Grace and her wonderful lifestream. I can get rid of it. But I don't want to leave you behind."

"Then don't. Grace…"

"*Chrysalis.* Andrew, please, quiet!"

"*Grace!*" Andrew whispered. "So what if a bunch of

degenerates are getting their thrills from your lifestream? Who cares? They're nothing to you and you're nothing to them. Besides, you know how these viral things go: a lot of hype, then they fizzle out. That's what we have to do, just ride it out. We can—together."

"No, Andrew, I can't, because there's one person who must never ride my lifestream."

"I promise, I won't ride your lifestream."

"I'm not talking about you."

Andrew waited through a long pause for Chrysalis to continue.

"I have a son."

"A *son?*"

"His name's Dylan. He lives with my sister, Donna. I love him, and he thinks the world of me. He's fourteen, very smart and very curious. It's only a matter of time before Dylan finds my lifestream. I will *not* let that happen."

"Did you ever plan to tell me about your *son?*"

"It's not easy for me to talk about Dylan. I lost custody of him because of all my screw-ups, mistakes *you're* able to forgive me for. But Dylan could never understand."

Andrew stood up, turning away from Chrysalis.

"Andrew, please, stay."

"This is more than I can process. I have to go."

Andrew left the Cloakroom without looking back. He entered the changing room and found his locker. As he was getting dressed, his mind sorted through Grace's revelations, in a conversation he had with himself, a rambling, jumbled back-and-forth with his inner voice, throughout which one question recurred, pushing itself to the front of Andrew's mind.

Where is the nearest streamboat?

12
A Short List of Substances

Andrew was in the VR venue in the evening, on time, as usual, after emptying his task queue of erroneous invoices that had kicked out of the commerce network. He sat in one of two oversized wicker chairs on an ocean pier, facing the sunset. For fifteen minutes the sounds of the seashore—the crashing surf, the cries of seabirds—filled Andrew's ears. He waited patiently, as he always did, never missing a session, despite the fact that Grace had missed five straight days.

"Yuji," Andrew said.

"Yes, Andrew?" a pleasant voice spoke through his headphones.

"No birds, please."

The sounds of the seabirds ceased, the rush of the rolling waves continuing as the sun slipped below the horizon. He looked at the empty chair beside him.

"Yuji, suspend the venue." The scene dissolved, leaving Andrew alone in his apartment.

Andrew went to the kitchen, still in his VR gear. He opened the refrigerator. On its shelves were an assortment of real and virtual items, mostly virtual, appearing as semi-transparent images, each with a caption, *time to reorder.*

"Yuji."

"Yes, Andrew?"

"Did you place the stocking order?"

"No, Andrew, I'm sorry. The stocking order is scheduled for tomorrow. You specified orders once a week."

"Then why is my refrigerator empty?"

"Your consumption has been high over the past several days. Forgive me, but you've also been gaining weight. And you seem distracted. Are you all right?"

"Yuji, place the stocking order, immediate delivery."

"Right away. Is there anything else I can help you with?"

Andrew remained stooped, gazing into the refrigerator for a moment before closing the door.

"Yes. Please locate lifestream bistros within walking distance. I'll access them from my pocket screen."

Andrew walked the streets near his home, as Yuji's voice in his earpiece announced his proximity to nearby streamboats. After he'd left Grace at the Cloakroom the night before, he'd passed several streamboats on his way home, each with a line out the door, all or almost all men, looking like memories of himself from an earlier time, well past the point at which an addict's lifestyle stopped being even remotely enjoyable, when the choice between the addictive substance and sustenance always went the same way, always with a resolution that the next choice would be different. The men in line had the same look of hopeful desperation.

The streamboats were just as well-patronized this evening as last. Andrew passed three of them, then a fourth. Following Yuji's directions, he walked the path from one streamboat to the next, deciding upon reaching each one that there were too many in line, the waiting time too long, the public exposure too great.

"Yuji," Andrew said in a near-whisper, "can you tell me which of these streamboats has the shortest wait time?"

"Of course," came the response. "The *Electric Multiverse*

Lifestream Bistro has a current wait time of less than three minutes. It's a five-minute walk. Shall I provide directions?"

Andrew followed the prompts to a storefront streamboat, brightly lit, its facade lined with posters, like the old-style cinemas, each poster promising a head-rewiring virtual experience, the most popular being RL activities that had been banned for years—racing a sand rail across the Mexican desert, hunting rhinoceros in Kenya, fighting in a professional boxing match. Andrew scanned the lineup, thinking that he'd have to go elsewhere to find what he was looking for, until he spotted a small, handwritten sign taped to the door:

Yes! We have Grace!

Andrew stared at the sign as patrons entered the streamboat, and others emerged, some in groups of two or more, noisily retelling their virtual adventures; others alone, wearing expressions ranging from satisfaction to embarrassment. He hesitated, took a few steps back toward his apartment, then stopped.

When he was using, Andrew limited himself to a short list of substances, depending on where he was, who he was with, and which addiction was most insistent at a given time. Shooting up Witch H just laid him back; no physical activity seemed either interesting or necessary, no personal interaction was fruitful, his ability to relate to others being greatly diminished. Andrew preferred H when he was alone.

In group settings, IRL, Andrew chose Mandy X. Witch laid him down, Mandy picked him up. After a tab of X, Andrew loved everybody and everybody loved him. That loving feeling often found a frenzied physical outlet, in pairs or in groups, in all combinations of men and women, until the drug wore off and the partiers collapsed or went home. Andrew found these happenings unsatisfying, curiously so, since he was drawn back to them again and again, whenever he became too aware of his aloneness, back to the Mandy X-fueled affairs, to touch and be touched, if only by strangers.

He missed the touching.
A sex addict who doesn't like sex.
Andrew strode purposefully into the streamboat.

13

Smile Like a Predator

Grace's heart raced when she saw it that morning, just one word on her pocket screen, sent to an anonymous IM account: *Imago.*

Throughout the day, Grace struggled to stay focused on the needs of her clients, tending toward short, pointed questions and answers, with a minimum of socializing. She glanced frequently at the waiting area, becoming terser when the number of clients increased, arriving faster than she and her State Benefits colleagues could process them. Late in the afternoon the number began to dwindle, until none remained, and no new clients had shown up for five minutes.

"Heidi," Grace called over the partition, "can I leave a little early tonight? The pace has slowed down, and I have an errand to run."

Heidi poked her head above the partition. "Really?" she said. "Something you can't take care of online?"

"It's kind of personal," Grace said. "Can I?"

Heidi scanned the room, nodding. "All right. If anyone else shows up, we'll handle it."

"Thanks, Heidi," Grace said, lifting the strap of her bag over her shoulder.

"Grace, before you go, I wanted to tell you, I've been monitoring your client interactions today. Very efficient. Your throughput is your best ever. Well done."

Grace jogged down the hallway, shouting a hurried "thanks" over her shoulder.

❖ ❖ ❖

Chrysalis sat alone, her eyes fixed on the entrance. Over the course of a half-hour she'd declined three offers to give and refused one request to receive *holy communion* from the Cloak; such attention, Chrysalis had learned, was a hazard that unaccompanied Cloak faced in the Cloakroom, the way single women did in public VR venues.

When Andrew entered, Chrysalis jumped up to meet him, directing him to a table.

"Chrysalis?" Andrew asked.

"I'm called Chrysalis," she answered. "Andrew, thank you. Thank you for coming."

"I'm sorry about running out on you. It was just a lot for me to take all at once."

"Andrew, I'm the one who should apologize. I should've been honest with you but I was afraid to—can you understand? I know that we don't judge in rehab—who has the right? —but I'd already given you a hundred reasons not to respect me; I didn't want to give you a hundred more. If I'd had more faith in you, Andrew, maybe I could have been open with you. That was my fault. I'm sorry. Will you forgive me?"

Andrew looked aside. "Do you remember, five years ago, when you met a couple at a VR music concert? The woman had bleached white hair. The man shaved his head. The woman was taller. Do you remember?"

"Andrew, what are you talking about?"

"The performance was in a VR venue, some retro-techno music. You were exploring the venue, like you were looking for someone, or more like you were *hunting*. You spotted this couple, the bald man and the white-haired woman. You watched them for a long time before you approached them. The woman saw you first. She smiled at you, not like a friendly smile, more like she was sending you a message. You had a look like I'd never seen—your head was down and tilted to one side; you raised your eyes to look at her with a smile that almost frightened me. You looked like a predator. The woman with the white hair nudged the man and pointed at you."

"Andrew, what is this? What did you do?"

"You played them for a long time. Do you remember how you played them? The guy approached you, you gave him that look, from under your eyebrows, and that smile, just a hint of one, like you knew what he was thinking, then you blew him off and went for the woman, same smile, same look. They were fighting each other to get to you."

Andrew's description triggered a memory of an encounter that Grace hadn't thought of since it happened, one in a series of chance meetings, so frequent that they ran together in her mind. It was the detail of Andrew's telling that triggered a memory so clear that it disturbed Chrysalis.

"Andrew, *what did you do?*"

"But when you hooked them IRL, that's what got to me, the same thing, playing them like that, but the way you amped it up—you worked them, by remote control, like drones, almost. They were arguing with *each other* about how to please you. It was a different kind of concert, in Real Life. They were the performers, and you were their audience."

Chrysalis rose from her chair. "Andrew, *you didn't*. Tell me *you did not ride my lifestream!*"

"Chrysalis, please, *quiet*," Andrew whispered. "Don't react that way. It's a good thing. I know you better now, what makes you who you are. And it's okay. I *like* who you are. I *really* like how you made me feel, when I was in the bald guy's avatar. You weren't my sponsor, all kind and understanding and supportive. You wanted it from me, and you got it, and I was glad to give it to you. Jah, you were *ferocious*. Why didn't you ever show me? What is it about me that you couldn't show me your real self?"

Chrysalis covered her head with her hands. "Andrew, that's *not* who I am."

"Isn't it? Once an addict?"

"That's not fair. That person you saw, it's not who I want to be. It's not the person I've tried to be, the person I've been for the last four years. Jah, Andrew, why? Why did you do that?"

"We never touch. Now you tell me that we never will, unless I join your Cloak."

"But we *do*. We touch."

"Once, IRL. In VR we don't touch. It's a peep show. It's a pacifier for me and a chore for you." Andrew leaned forward. "The streamboat I went to, they have group sessions. Two or more people can share the same lifestream. I thought about that when I was in the venue, how it would be if you and I were in the lifestream together."

Chrysalis pushed back from the table. Andrew's face—the sweet, round face that had first attracted Grace, that had roused in her a longing to care for him, to protect him, to reform him—looked guiltily hopeful, like a deprived child who'd asked for a gift that he knew he couldn't have.

The scene that Andrew had described now ran through Chrysalis's mind in vivid detail. They were an attractive couple, who radiated sexuality. Grace had the knack for spotting people—men, women, or couples—with possibilities. In this case, she saw possibilities from a distance, even from their VR rendered avatars. Seducing them in the venue was a challenge—experienced VR players were always cautious of new encounters—but Grace was subtle and patient. The parley went on for an hour, a series of innocuous comments, about the band, the venue, the people; compliments, getting acquainted small talk, laced with suggestive language delivered with provocative looks that over time revealed a common desire. The rivalry that developed between the white-haired woman and the bald man for Grace's attention heightened Grace's excitement. She milked it expertly. By the end of the concert, the couple had invited Grace for an IRL encounter that night.

The liaison in the couple's apartment continued where the concert had left off; the man and woman had already disrobed when Grace arrived, eager to begin. Grace remained clothed, at least partially, for nearly an hour as her hosts performed for her, like pets for their master, each new act at Grace's request rewarded with a touch, or an article of clothing, until the three of them were together on the bed in a tangle, Grace no longer calling the shots, each of them improvising instead, until exhaustion set in.

As Grace recalled that night, she felt her reddening face radiating heat under Chrysalis's hood, a shivering tenseness in her body, sensations she hadn't felt in years, since she took the pledge, *Just for today, I will not surrender to my addiction*, a pledge she renewed daily, and had kept, for four years.

And there was Andrew, her baby. Was he asking so much?

We never touch.

Just for today, I will not surrender to my addiction.

"Oh, Andrew." Chrysalis stood up, nearly tipping over her chair. She pushed through the crowd, Cloak and civilians alike turning their heads as she ran to the exit.

14

LEDGERS OF SIN

THE BUILDING, LIKE so many things in Real Life, looked out of place, or, more precisely, out of time, simply by being old. Its bricks were dark, almost black, from the grime accumulated through decades of engine exhaust and the effluent of smokestacks, conditions that hadn't existed for years. There was little incentive and no funds to clean buildings IRL while everyone lived in VR.

Grace had heard them called *tenements*, towers of small, densely-packed apartments, some more than a century old. Most of the windows were fitted with docks jutting from the outside of the building, like so many diving platforms, where commercial drones dropped their goods. Some of the tenements had central air shafts, four-sided wells that were dark in the winter, but admitted a narrow shaft of sunlight for a few hours a day in the summer, where drones could descend to the interior apartments to make their deliveries. The tenement apartments were functional but sparse, little more than docking stations for their occupants, where they could jack into the rich, infinitely varied Virtual Reality universe.

Chrysalis ascended the steps, lifting the hem of her cloak

as she went, the sound of her footsteps echoing in the deserted stairwell. On the sixth floor she found apartment 6F, the number hand-scrawled in indelible ink on the ancient door, above a pushbutton and a tiny camera lens. As she reached out to press the button, a disembodied voice spoke.

"Announce yourself, Cloak."

"I'm called Chrysalis."

"Oh, hiya, Chrys. Come on in."

The door bolt opened with a heavy clank. Chrysalis turned the knob and pushed the door open.

Raúl sat at a semi-circular table that occupied nearly the entire room. In addition to the usual wall screen, more than a dozen other screens hung from a metal framework mounted to the table. Some screens displayed lines of computer code, unintelligible to Chrysalis; others looked like windows into the virtual world, showing scenes from locations ranging from the city to faraway continents, each scene looking as if Raúl had entered the observers' heads and hijacked their vision.

One screen showed a scene from a party, a crowd of revelers drinking freely. Two people in the corner were hunched over lines of Pearl C, vacuuming them up through tightly-rolled credit vouchers. A couple made out on a couch by the wall, oblivious to the others, and the others paid them no attention, either. In the middle of the room, amid a ring of people, was Grace—the center of attention.

Chrysalis stood in front of the screen, bending forward to get a closer look.

"What is this?"

"It's a Tuesday, I think." Raúl squinted at an adjacent screen. "That's right. Tuesday. A weeknight. You were quite the party girl, weren't you? Didn't you have to work the next day?"

"Why is it on the screen?"

"I'm building your crawler, Chrys. That there is a test run. The crawler found it all by itself, with no help from me. It's been crawling around for more than a day and it's just scratching the tip of the iceberg. You were a very busy lady."

Chrysalis turned away from the screen. "How much longer?"

Raúl turned to a screen on his right. "Nila, show me how Grace's crawler is doing."

"Here's the current status, Raúl," said a feminine voice with a slight Indian accent, as a list of figures scrolled across the screen. "Four-point-four-seven petabytes, thirty-five percent duplication. Discovery rate remains steady. No estimate yet of the final data quantity."

Raúl gave out a low whistle. "Four and a half petabytes. Oh, baby, that's a pile. Sorry, Chryssy, I can't give you a firm end date. The crawler is slaving away and it just keeps turning up new stuff. Like I told you, this is the biggest one I've ever seen."

"Why? I'm nobody. Why's *my* lifestream so big?"

"Beats the hell out of me. You're not anything like my regular clients. They're all cyberpunk crooks who got caught. That's a volume business, Chrys, my bread and butter. You see, there's this arms race going on between the cyber criminals and the civil authorities. My clients are the ones who failed to stay ahead of advancing law enforcement technology. But they're just the skin off the grape. For every one the civils nab, a thousand more are on the loose. It pisses them off, so the ones they catch get hammered with ridiculous confinement terms. Faced with a 100% IRL confinement, the Shade look attractive. Most of my clients are already pretty good at managing their Worldstream footprint, so shredding them is a snap. Not you. You're unique. Yours is the biggest, best, butt-kickingest lifestream ever. Whoever wove this massive bitch had a chub for you."

Chrysalis looked again at the party tableau. It dissolved into another scene of a man in a bodega picking items from the shelves and putting them in a shopping basket, a swarthy man with close-cropped black hair, on his shoulder a tattoo of the crucified Christ. Chrysalis remembered the man but not his name, having never asked for it, either in the store, or during the night of passion that followed their meeting. To Grace, he'd been nothing more than a man with possibilities.

"My whole life, it's all there. Everything I've seen, heard, and touched, all there in the Worldstream. Does it even know my thoughts? Can Jahbulon read my mind?"

Raúl laughed. He turned in his chair to face Chrysalis, his hands on his knees.

"Did your parents teach you to believe in a god?"

"Does anyone believe in God anymore?"

"We used to, sister, we used to. When I was a boy, *everyone* worshipped a god. They prayed to the god, they went to churches to visit the god, they gave money to the god. The priests told the people the god sees everything, the god knows everything, the god is omnipresent and inescapable, everywhere, all the time. *The god's a loving god; he made us; he listens to us; if we ask him nicely, the god obeys us*, the priests said. *If we believe on the god, our faith can move mountains.* Move mountains—I'm not making that up! And the priests told us the loving god is also an angry god, who sends us to hell when we die if our debt isn't settled. And we were all in debt, because we were all sinners. They had a whole catalog of sins, all priced out, invoiced to our accounts, payable on death if we didn't get to the priest from time to time to clear the books. I was sure that heaven was filled with rows of angels at desks, on high stools, wearing green visors, punching adding machines, filling the ledgers, one sin after another. That's what they taught us. I'm not making that up."

"And you believed it?"

"You tell me. They told us the wages of sin is death, and we kept sinning. They told us the god can see everything, so we shut the doors and closed the blinds when we sinned, playing hide and seek with the almighty. And none of us *ever* believed we could move a damn mountain. And the priests, the ones who taught us kids, and preached in the church, and wiped our sins clean when we asked, even *they* thought they could cheat the god. Did they think they could ruin some young boy's life without getting called to account? Did they think the payback on fondling an altar boy was worth the risk of ending up in hell if their note came due? Or did they think that the god gave priests a pass?"

"No wonder we gave that up."

"Ah *ha!* We *didn't* give it up. We traded it in. We were told that the god is everywhere and knows everything, and no one believed it. Now, we're told that Jahbulon is everywhere, that Jahbulon knows everything, and *everyone* believes it. We've gone from worship without fear to fear without worship."

Chrysalis looked again at the screen. The scene had changed to an apartment bedroom; on the bed were Grace, partially clothed, and two naked people, a woman with white hair, and a man with a shaved head.

"Can you turn this screen off, please?"

"Nila, blank monitor six."

"Yes, Raúl."

Chrysalis stood staring at the blank screen. "I want to ride my lifestream."

"No, you don't."

"I'm not looking forward to it, but it's something I have to do. My boyfriend rode my lifestream. I have to know what he saw, not just what he said about it. I have to know what his experience was like."

"I recommend against it."

"There's another reason—my son, Dylan. He's starting to ride lifestreams. The last thing I want is for him ride *my* lifestream, but if I can't prevent him, I want to know exactly what's in there."

"I know what's in there, remember? Trust me, you're better off not knowing."

"I need to know."

"Look, you want to know if your son, what's his name, Dylan, is riding lifestreams? I can tell you."

"You can do that?"

"Nila, do you have a fix on Grace's son, Dylan?"

"Yes, Raúl. He is in a VR classroom. His RL location is in the apartment of his aunt, Grace's sister Donna."

"Nila, what's his VR history?"

"Dylan has over twenty-two thousand hours of VR logged. Can you be more specific?"

"Lifestreams."

"Dylan has approximately twelve hours of lifestreams logged."

"Categories, please."

"Adventure, four hours, fifty-four minutes. Adult content, four hours, fifty minutes. Uncategorized, two hours, ten minutes."

Chrysalis looked toward the ceiling. "Adult content?"

"Nila, has Dylan ridden any of Grace's lifestream?"

"No, Raúl. Grace's lifestream is peripheral-specific."

"What does that mean?" Chrysalis asked.

"It means that your lifestream requires special equipment. If you don't have the required peripherals, you can't ride the lifestream. Your lifestream requires the Belt."

Chrysalis sat on the table. "Then Dylan can't ride my lifestream?"

"Not unless he can get his hands on the Belt," Raúl said, "or unless he spoofs the lifestream."

"Spoofs?"

"Yep. He needs a piece of software that simulates the Belt. He'll get the visuals, the audio, and the tactile, but no—you know—joy in the nether regions. And the head trip won't be as wild. But the lifestream will run. Your boy, he's a smart kid?"

"Yes. Very smart."

"Then it's only a matter of time."

"When can I ride my lifestream?"

"If you're that determined, why are you asking me? Head on down to your local lifestream bistro. You can ride the stream, Belt and all."

"No. I need to do this in private."

"Understandable. Okay. Against my better judgment, I'll lend you the Belt. Seriously, though, your lifestream is an intense experience, especially if you're alone. Want some company?"

"Jah, you disgust me."

Raúl chuckled. "Suit yourself. We could have had a good time."

Raúl opened the doors to a tall metal cabinet. He removed

a limp object made of shiny black fabric, the size and shape of a pair of briefs, with bright silver threads woven into it, in a nested pattern of squares. The Belt had a pod the size of a pocket screen attached to the front, and a series of closures on either side.

"You need to wear this next to your skin, around the narrow part of your waist, and halfway down your hips. Adjust it so it's snug, but not like a tourniquet. You want good contact, but you don't want to cut off the blood supply. When it synchs up with your VR gear, it'll send a pulse into you. When it's working, you'll know it. And you'll like it."

"Where do I find my lifestream?"

"Just ask your voice responder. It'll find you. Then it's all point and click."

Chrysalis took the Belt and hid it under her cloak. "One more question. Can you find out who wove my lifestream?"

Raúl raised his eyebrows. "Now, that's a challenge. Weavers are notoriously careful about covering their tracks, and your weaver is a master. How important is it to you?"

"Very."

"No guarantees, but I'll give it a try. It'll cost you."

"Just tell me when you find him."

Grace left the apartment and walked to the head of the stairs. She looked down the flight of steps.

It'll cost you.

She looked back toward Raúl's apartment.

I'm not the only one who'll pay.

15

FIVE GRINS

GRACE ADJUSTED THE Belt as Raúl had instructed, tugging the hem low on her hips, smoothing it against her skin, and fussing with the closures, taking as long as possible, postponing the moment when she would immerse herself in a life she was sure she'd put behind her.

She pulled on her VR headgear, a lightweight, snug-fitting cowl, comprising an integrated 180-degree visor, its resolution exceeding that of the human retina, and headphones, their frequency response and dynamic range capable of reproducing sounds beyond the limits of human hearing. She slipped her hands into her VR gloves, lined with position sensors to render her hand movements in virtual space, and tactile feedback actuators to transmit sensations of texture and hardness, heat and cold. Her visor displayed her apartment, unaltered from Real Life except for a ribbon floating in space, displaying a list of options: *Go, Suspend, Favorites, Recent, Search, Help*. A box faded into view, cycling slowly between yellow and green, displaying the words *New Device Detected*, next to a rotating 3D image of the Belt.

"Grace, you have a new peripheral," Gogo's voice spoke through the headphones, "a model DCNI 5001 neural interface, manufactured by Stimulus Rex. Do you trust this device?"

"Yes, Gogo."

"Would you like to integrate this peripheral?"

"Yes, please."

The message changed from *New Device Detected* to *Integrating DCNI 5001*. As the progress bar filled, Grace felt increasingly warm where the Belt contacted her skin. When the progress bar hit 100% and the text changed to *Integration Complete*, Grace gasped.

The warmth spread through her body, or, more precisely, she instantly felt warm all over, radiating from the inside out with a comfortable, reassuring heat, as if she were wrapped in a thick, soft blanket on a cold night. Her thoughts cleared, her mind settled down, the unpleasant prospect of riding her lifestream no longer troubling her. It was a state of clarity and contentment Grace sometimes felt in the moments after fully awakening from a dreamless sleep, alert, but still snuggled in her bed. She sighed, smiling.

Grace gasped again as the sensation vanished as quickly as it had come, replaced with jitters in her arms and legs, and jumpiness in her stomach. The message flashed, *Please Verify Successful Integration*.

"Yes," Grace said, "the integration was successful." She gripped the arms of her chair. "Gogo."

"Yes, Grace?"

"Search for *Grace, lifestream*, please."

The voice responder paused. "Grace, I've scanned the results. Are you sure you want to see these?"

"Yes, Gogo. Please show them to me."

A series of images appeared, arranged in a ring, like a carousel, with Grace at its center. Grace looked them over for a moment before closing her eyes. All the pictures were of Grace, some innocent looking, but most depicting Grace in pornographic scenes, alone or with one or more partners of both sexes. Grace forced herself to open her eyes. With a gesture, she spun the carousel, scrolling through the selections. Each image was captioned—*Grace in Paradise, Grace and the Earth Mover, Grace Goes Shopping*—and each had a rating, of from one to five tiny, grinning heads, rolling their eyes in unison.

It was the last line on each image that hit Grace the hardest: *number of views*. Grace choked audibly when she read them. The smallest number was almost 200,000. The largest was more than three million.

Grace fought back tears as she continued scrolling. She stopped at one picture, a photorealistic rendering of Grace, eyes closed, mouth open, in obvious ecstasy, labeled *Grace's Fun Week—Compilation*, with two-million-plus views, and four-point-five leering heads.

Grace's hand hovered over the image. Holding her breath, she touched it.

The VR venue changed. It took Grace a moment to figure out what was different. She was still in an apartment, but it was not *her* apartment, though it looked familiar. She scanned her surroundings, trying to place the venue, but the view was obstructed by rectangles that popped up, like floating billboards, advertising all manner of products, entertainment, and causes, although two themes dominated: VR peripherals and sexually explicit lifestreams.

Grace looked to her right. A glowing title, *Grace's Fun Week*, like a cinema marquee, hovered above a slowly scrolling list of comments.

Grace is too hot for words. Number 1 on my fave list!

The Da Vinci of weavers and the Mona Lisa of lifestream stars. Five grins!

Rode this one with my girlfriend. Learned some new things!

Grace watched as the comments continued to scroll.

Can't believe this slut.

She has stamina, that much I'll say for her. What a whore.

Jah, doesn't she take time off to eat or sleep?

Grace felt her face flush as the worst of the comments scrolled past.

This is so pathetic. Grace, get a life.

No self-respect. I pity her.

Grace shut her eyes tightly a second time.

"Gogo."

"Yes, Grace?"

"End…"

"Do you want to end the session, Grace?"

Grace cautiously opened her eyes, trying to avoid looking at the comments. On the marquee title were three buttons:

First Person.

Second Person.

Third Person.

"No, Gogo."

Grace reached for the *Third Person* button. The button changed to a glowing outline as her finger hovered above it for nearly a minute before she touched it.

16

THE MAN WITH THE JESUS TATTOO

THE ADVERTISEMENTS, THE scrolling comments, and the marquee vanished, leaving Grace alone in the virtual apartment. The rendering was beautiful, perfect, in fact, better than any VR venue Grace had ever seen, visually indistinguishable from Real Life. The only thing that looked out of place was on the floor.

As Grace looked down, an array of controls faded into view around her feet—*Play, Pause, Backward, Forward, End.* Below the navigation buttons, the same *First Person, Second Person* and *Third Person* buttons appeared. Below those buttons was a progress bar, showing the position in Grace's lifestream, ticking off the elapsed time:

23:45:03 / 145:00:00

"One hundred and forty-five hours!" Grace said out loud, realizing that all the scenes in the carousel were merely excerpts from a lifestream that stretched 145 hours long— nearly a week, without breaks.

Grace looked up from the menu on the floor at the sound of the door opening. A swarthy man with short, black hair entered, carrying a bag labeled *Corner Bodega*. He set the bag on a counter and turned slightly, halting, as if he expected to bump into someone.

"Hey, where'd you go?" The man turned further, his right shoulder coming into view, revealing his tattoo of the crucified Christ. He stood in the center of the room, holding out his hands in a questioning pose.

"What're doing out there? Come in!"

A slender hand appeared through the doorway. The man huffed as he walked to the door, reaching for the hand, pulling its owner into the room: a younger-looking Grace, slimmer, her skin smoother, her hair longer, holding her head down, looking at the tattooed man with upturned eyes, on her face the smile that Andrew had described, the one that had frightened him—the hunter's smile.

The man pulled Young Grace to him, putting his arm around her. She put a hand against his chest, pushing away as the man tried to kiss her. He pulled her closer, leaning farther, his lips less than an inch from her face. She leaned back, turning slightly, allowing a glancing kiss to the corner of her mouth, still wearing the smile.

"C'mon, baby," the man rasped.

"Why don't you get a girl a drink first?" Young Grace whispered, placing her fingers on the man's chin, pushing his head back. The man loosened his grip on her, gaping, before recovering.

"Drink, yeah. Sure. Beer okay?"

"Vodka. I like apple vodka. I keep my bottle in the freezer. Get me a freezing cold apple vodka."

The man took a step back. He stood with his hands out, a *what the hell* look on his face.

"I don't have any fucking *apple vodka*. I got regular vodka. Room temperature."

"Oh." Young Grace stopped smiling. She no longer looked at the man from under her eyebrows, but from the corners of her eyes. "Do you at least have some *ice?*"

"*Yeah,*" the man answered. "I have *ice.*"

"All right, then. Regular vodka." Her hunter's smile

returned. "With *ice*."

The man grinned as he went into the kitchen.

Young Grace looked over the apartment, as if she were taking inventory. Her eyes settled on a bright green elastic band, tied to the knob of a closet door.

"Vodka ice," the man said, handing Young Grace her glass. "Sorry about no apple V."

Young Grace dipped a fingertip in her glass and touched it to her tongue. She dipped it a second time and touched the man's lip.

"What's that," Young Grace asked, glancing at the elastic band.

"What? Oh, just a stretchy thing. I use it for exercise."

Young Grace felt the man's bicep. "It must be a strong stretchy thing. You could probably tie someone up with that."

"You wanna be tied up?"

"Not me," she said, placing another drop of vodka on the man's lip. "You."

"Nah. I don't like that."

Young Grace turned her back to the man. "You'll have to take your shirt off first. It'll be hard to get your shirt off if I tie your hands."

The man took her arm and turned her around. "No, I *don't like that*. I'll tie you up, though, if that's what you want."

"Your pants will be no problem." Young Grace smiled, looking at the man as she lowered her head. "The shirt though. Better take that off."

The man untied the elastic from the doorknob. He held it in front of him, stretching it, as if testing its strength.

"Your hands? Or your feet?"

Young Grace shook her head. "Your shirt."

Grace watched the scene unfold from the corner of the apartment, as if she were invisible. Apart from Grace's fascination at watching her younger self toying with the man, Grace felt nothing of the thrill, the object of her compulsion, that she once sought night after night. She had only a faded recollection of her state of mind in those days;

after four years, the attraction escaped her. *How could this have gone viral?* she asked herself. The man was ordinary, uninteresting, banal; her younger self was a manipulative, unsympathetic predator. There was nothing exciting in it. It gave her no pleasure. It wasn't hot—it was boring.

The man handed the elastic to Young Grace and peeled off his shirt. She wrapped the elastic around the man's wrists, knotting the ends. "Good boy," she said. She pulled her top over her head, leaving her naked from the waist up, a few feet from the man. He stepped toward her.

"No, no! Kneel down."

"What the fuck?"

Young Grace leaned forward, pulling back instantly as the man lunged for her breasts, like a matador sidestepping a charging bull.

"Easy, boy. Not yet. On your knees."

"Are you fucking kidding me?"

Young Grace applied a drop of vodka to each nipple. "You'll have to kneel down to get a taste."

The man obeyed.

Grace grew restless from her vantage point in the corner. She looked down at the menu. Her finger hovered over the *First Person* button for a moment before pressing it.

The experience of being sucked into Young Grace's avatar disoriented Grace. It took her a minute to understand where she was. Grace looked down at her own body, at her arms and hands, at her naked breasts. The man with the Jesus tattoo was kneeling in front of her, his hands bound with the elastic, his mouth open, his tongue hanging out. She leaned closer to him, an inch from his mouth, jumping back once again as he pitched forward, nearly sprawling on the floor. Grace had no control over the avatar's movements as it acted on its own; she heard the sound of her own laughter, and her own voice, as if she were hearing herself speak: "Stay steady 'til I'm ready!"

Grace felt the heat rising from the man's naked torso, now shining with sweat. When the man lunged, she felt the rush of air against her skin, causing an involuntary shiver from the feel of cold vodka on her breasts. The avatar continued taunting the man as Grace processed the torrent of sensations sent by the Belt. The experience was unlike any VR venue that Grace had ever tried.

Then she became aware of other feelings—tightness in her limbs, rising hair on her scalp, a slight tremor in her hands—not induced by the Belt, but her own body's response to her emotional state, no longer a faded memory, but hitting her with all the force of a first-hand, in-the-now involuntary response—her compulsion, her addiction.

In a near panic, Grace looked down, searching the floor for the navigation buttons. The action froze as the buttons appeared. Grace reached frantically toward the controls, activating the first button that her hand passed over.

Second Person.

Grace felt herself drawn out of Young Grace's avatar, passing into that of the tattooed man. She saw her younger self looming over her, from inside the man's avatar, Young Grace leaning forward, proffering her breasts, the man lunging again, and again Young Grace hopping backward, her derisive laughter in the man's ears, the hunter's smile on her face. The bizarre scenario distracted Grace, keeping her mind off the other sensations programmed into the lifestream, now being transmitted to Grace's nervous system by the Belt.

Grace first noticed the man's physical responses—urgent tension in the groin, dryness in the mouth, hotness, like a fever, behind the eyes—but the reactions of the body were not what fascinated Grace, what, in fact, terrified her: Although the man's avatar was outside of Grace's command, its involuntary actions seemed not to be due to the rigid programming of the lifestream, but instead the actions of a man who'd lost control, animated by pure primal instinct, stripped of all volition, a slave in the thrall of the laughing, bare-breasted, hunter-smiling avatar in front of him.

"Gogo, suspend the venue!"

The scene reverted to Grace's apartment. Grace pulled off her gloves, tore off the headgear, and ripped open the closures on the Belt. She fell back into her chair, eyes shut tight, breathing heavily. She got a glass of water from the kitchen, drank it, and filled it again, sipping slowly as she leaned against the counter.

That's what they were, the men, and the women, too, maybe— mindless drones, spawning salmon, decapitated mantises—human beings reduced to machines.

Grace sipped.

And I pulled the levers.

Grace returned to her chair. She slipped into the belt, quickly fastening the closures and adjusting the fit. She put on the headgear and pulled on the gloves.

"Gogo."

"Yes, Grace?"

"Resume."

17
PLAYING THE GAME

GRACE WORE NOTHING but a pair of disconnected shoes. She slipped her cloak over her head and smoothed it against her body, feeling the cool fabric against her skin. She adjusted the closures on her cloak more tightly than usual, calling attention to the curves of her figure, subtly, but unmistakably, in case someone might want to know if Chrysalis were a man or a woman. She took out the hood and set it aside. In the bottom of the box, laying where she had left it untouched almost two weeks before, was a mask, entirely black, with broad ribbons hanging from its corners. Grace put on the mask, tying the ribbons behind her head.

The mask was large, covering her forehead, nose and cheeks, leaving her mouth and chin exposed. Grace's short, red hair showed. She wondered if that mattered, whether concealing most of her face, but exposing her hair—and her body—would give away her identity. She dismissed the thought as she pulled the hood over her head, positioning the synthesizer over her mouth. Tingling with anticipation, Grace, as Chrysalis, left the apartment.

On her way to the Cloakroom, Chrysalis kept her mind as blank as she could make it, not thinking about the last forty-eight hours—the work days that Grace had missed—the many times she'd ridden her lifestream, inhabiting the minds of men and women she'd preyed on in the past—her regret after every session—her vow each time not to ride her lifestream again—her shame when she attached herself to the Belt, put on the VR gear, and told Gogo to start the session—her decision to recapture that feeling of power in Real Life.

Grace's lifestream in VR, as realistic as it was, could not substitute for a chance encounter with a stranger IRL, not knowing where it would go, or how it would end. The seduction was the point—the interplay, the to and fro, the grappling for control, and the final imposition of her will on another person, with no inhibition and no commitment. The lifestream was enough for stream riders—spectators—but not for Grace. It was the difference between watching the game and playing it.

Getting into the *minds* of the subjects—that was the feature of the lifestream that drew Grace back into the venues again and again, almost against her will, certainly against her better judgment. If not for the head-rewiring experience of inhabiting the subject completely, body, mind and soul, Grace might have stayed bored with the thing, wondering what all the fuss was about. Instead, as Chrysalis, she set out to the Cloakroom, not for a replay, but for a fresh experience. She walked quickly, almost in a trot.

The Cloakroom was crowded. Chrysalis scrutinized one Cloak after another: That one, by the door, is that a man or a woman? The one standing alone, near the wall—here for the same reason I am? Over the course of an hour, Chrysalis approached six or more Cloak, each time taking a step in her subject's direction, having second thoughts, walking away, stopping short of the exit, then trying again. Four times she saw one Cloak approach another, exchange a few words, then go together into a side room. In time, one of the couples emerged from their room with no outward sign that they had enjoyed their encounter, holding hands briefly before parting, two people unknown even to each other.

Just for today, I will not surrender to my addiction.

Chrysalis went for the door, her head down, heaving a sigh of relief. Before she'd made it halfway, she collided with a Cloak, a little taller than she was.

"Sorry," Chrysalis said, "I wasn't looking."

"Leaving?" the cloaked stranger asked.

"Yes, please, can I pass?"

The Cloak didn't budge. "Forgive me, but I've been watching you. You came here for a hook, didn't you?"

"Please, I just want to get out of here."

"Don't be embarrassed. Really, it's common for first timers to be nervous. This *is* your first time, isn't it?"

Chrysalis looked aside. She saw another couple come out of their room, one of them looking both ways before patting the other's bottom. "Yes," she said.

"What are you looking for?"

"Holy communion," Chrysalis said, in a barely audible voice.

"Do you wish to give, or to receive?"

"What?"

"Men give communion, women receive it."

Chrysalis leaned closer. "Receive."

The Cloak nodded. "I understand. I'm a receiver, not a giver. That man over there has been trying to give communion all night."

Chrysalis looked where the Cloak pointed. It was the Cloak she'd seen earlier, standing alone by the wall.

"I've watched several couples hook since I've been here," Chrysalis said. "Why hasn't he found someone?"

"I think it's his first time as well, but his approach is different from yours. You thought it over, took a few timid steps, then backed off. Not him. He's been here for more than an hour, chatting up everyone. That's his problem—too eager. Even cloaked, a man on the make is a turnoff. And we women can sense a lack of confidence, wouldn't you agree? Even in a mechanical voice?"

"He approached you?"

"No, but word got around. Why don't we find out for

ourselves?"

"We?"

"You and I. Let's see what the man has to offer."

Chrysalis looked again at the man by the wall. He approached another Cloak. They talked briefly before they parted, with the man going back to his spot.

"Three of us. Is that what you're thinking?"

"It could be fun. A newbie like that—he'll need guidance, someone to show him what to do." The cloaked woman came closer. "I like a firm touch, too," she murmured. She took Chrysalis's hand. "Very firm."

Chrysalis looked back at the man by the wall, still searching the crowd for a willing partner.

"A firm hand." Chrysalis gripped the Cloak's hand and led her, almost towing her, to the man by the wall.

"We would like to receive holy communion," Chrysalis said to him, "if you're able to give it."

"Both of you?" he asked.

Chrysalis stepped forward, her face inches from the man's, almost touching him.

"If you have it in you. It'll be good if you know what you're doing. I can teach you if you don't, and that would be even better. Do you need instructions?"

"I know what I'm doing."

Chrysalis took his hand. "We'll see." Chrysalis led both of them to the row of doors, each with a panel glowing either red or green, like the doors in the changing room. She pulled open the first door with a green panel.

The room was dimly lit and sparsely furnished. There was a bed with no linens, only a one-piece cover, two steel chairs and a small round table. The bare walls were painted white, with a texture, a fine-pitched pattern, like the copper screen on the walls of the Faraday Cage, a barrier that no radio signals could penetrate, in or out.

Chrysalis maneuvered the cloaked man and woman toward each other. "You," Chrysalis said to the man, "you go first. Off with the cloak. We'll watch."

The man disrobed, draping his hood and cloak over a

chair, leaving him between the two cloaked women wearing only a plain, black mask, identical to Chrysalis's, Faraday Cage standard issue for newcomers to the Cloak. His body was unremarkable; he was an average man with average features.

"Lovely," Chrysalis said. "Now help the lady with her cloak."

"What about you?" the cloaked woman asked.

"Not yet." Chrysalis lifted the hem of her cloak, revealing her legs to the top of her thighs. "I'll join you when you start to slow down."

With the man's help, the woman undressed. Her mask obscured more than just the top of her face; it was a tight-fitting covering that extended over her entire head, including her hair and the back of her neck. Unlike the plain black masks worn by Chrysalis and the man, her mask was dark red, the color of blood, decorated in gold filigree. The elaborate design surrounded her eyes; the edge of the mask over her cheeks was bordered in exquisite detail. She was attractive and fit, young, but not very young, in her thirties, perhaps.

"You told me that you know what to do," Chrysalis said to the man, "now show me."

The man and woman kissed, running their hands over each other, tracing their fingers over the sensitive spots of each other's bodies, as Chrysalis looked on.

"Oh, really, I'm not feeling it."

They continued their caresses unemotionally, almost mechanically, with few signs of arousal. They laid on the bed, taking no notice of Chrysalis.

"I'm not impressed," Chrysalis said.

The woman looked up at Chrysalis. "If you're not playing the game," she said, disguising her voice in a hoarse whisper, "you can't call the shots."

Chrysalis felt her face redden. She pulled off her hood and cloak and kneeled naked on the bed. The couple kept up their foreplay as if Chrysalis weren't there—not competing for her attention, not lunging for her bare, vodka-moistened breasts, not succumbing to her seduction.

Chrysalis watched silently for a minute before getting off the bed. "This was a mistake," she whispered. She gathered her cloak and hood. "I have to go. Enjoy yourselves."

The man turned on his side. "Please stay," he whispered. He looked at Chrysalis for a moment before lifting himself up on his elbows. He stared at her body, then her face, what he could see of it, and her hair—her short, red hair.

"Oh, Jahbulon," he said, in a clear, recognizable voice.

"What?" she whispered.

"Jah." He rolled off the bed, scrambling to his feet, grabbing his cloak from the chair. "Jahbulon." He lunged at Chrysalis, pulling her mask off of her before she could react. One ribbon tore from the mask as he jerked it away. Grace snatched it from the man's hand, bewildered for a moment, before a look of recognition spread over her face. She pulled the man's mask off in the same way he'd taken hers.

"Grace," he said, "this wasn't supposed to happen."

Grace rushed to put on her cloak, pulling the hood over her head as she ran for the door. The woman on the bed looked on, a faint smile on her face, as Chrysalis left the two of them alone, the anonymous woman naked on the bed, and Andrew, standing next to her, clutching his cloak in front of him.

18

Damaged Goods

"This is why we take it a day at a time. You didn't vow to master your addiction for your whole life. That's not a vow you can keep. You pledged to stay clean for a day, *one day,* a pledge with a twenty-four-hour expiration date. And you failed. That failure is behind you. Acknowledge it and move on. Today's a new day, and a new vow."

Grace remained silent through Madeleine's lecture—a lecture which sounded to Grace like a reprimand, with Madeleine telling her what she already knew—what she'd heard a hundred times—as punishment for her lapse. Which is why, Grace thought, Madeleine had missed the point entirely.

"I understand that," Grace said from her chair in the VR venue. "It was three days, remember, not just one; three days in a row that I was in and out of my lifestream before I got the great idea to act out IRL. I was in my lifestream for ten hours one of those days—ten hours! Did you know that if I spent ten hours a day it would take more than two weeks to go through the whole thing? It would take three or four days just for the highlights. I broke more than one vow. But that's not what's important."

"Andrew?"

"Yes, Andrew, my little boy. I only told him about my addiction a week ago. Jah, what can happen in a week! If he's spent as much time in my lifestream as I have, he knows more of my sorry history than I ever wanted him to know, more than even *I* wanted to remember. I just wanted to forget it. So much for that. Twenty hours in VR reliving my sex days and it's burned into my memory more deeply than ever. Then Andrew, poor boy, asks me to ride my lifestream tandem. I didn't think anything could be more repulsive than that, not until he showed up at the Cloakroom. Now he knows first-hand what kind of a person *I* am."

"And you know what kind of a person *he* is."

Grace tapped the arm of her chair. "I know what you're saying, but that's not really fair. Andrew's had it hard, and I haven't made it any easier for him."

"Do you mean because you hold him accountable?"

"I mean because I haven't been close to him, physically, I mean, the way men want. I didn't really understand that a week ago. I know it now."

"How is that?"

Grace leaned forward. "Madeleine, tell me something. You're a psychologist. You get into people's heads. It's what you do. I guess they teach you at university all the things that can go on inside a person, and how to spot the signs, and tell what's inside them, what they're thinking and feeling. When I was in my lifestream, I was in other people's bodies, but also in their heads, feeling what they were feeling. Did you know that VR programmers can do that? Simulate actual feelings?"

"I've read about that. I haven't experienced it."

"*I* have."

"What was it like?"

"It scared me. And it thrilled me. I wanted to turn it off, and I wanted it to go on and on. I ran away from it, and I kept coming back."

"How did that affect you?"

"The *power*, that's what I finally get, the power one person has over another when one of them is weak; the power *I* have, or any woman has over a man, just because she's a woman and he's a man. Do they teach you that in university, about men? About the animal drives coded into their DNA? How they turn into mindless puppets with a flash of skin? Did you learn about how crazy they get when they're sex-starved? Jah, I pity them."

"You enjoy the power."

"I enjoyed it when I was doing it, years ago, IRL. When I first rode my lifestream inside the guy's head, days ago, it hit me like a taser, knowing that I had that kind of control, that *I* could do *that* to a man. That feeling's what kept me coming back to the venues. It's why I went to the Cloakroom for a hook. Now the thrill is wearing off. I thought that men were human beings all the time, that they didn't shut down their mental functions when they got worked up. I thought I had special qualities that made men weak, like a siren song. I didn't know that they're *all* weak. Now that I know, getting them turned on isn't exciting, it's just sad. How much power is there in pushing a button and getting a programmed response?"

"And Andrew?"

"Poor Andrew. He's a man with the same needs as other men. That's why he was at the Cloakroom. How can I blame him for that? *Both* of us were there. And I've been very selfish. I wonder if I deserve Andrew."

"Does he deserve you?"

"He deserves better than I'm giving him."

Madeleine placed her hands together under her chin, tilting her head to one side. "Do you think that you haven't been good for Andrew? Andrew is an addict, too. He's stayed clean as long as you have. If I may say, he owes much of that accomplishment to you. When he was weak, when he was near faltering, he reached out to you, and you never let him down. That's what I meant when I said you hold Andrew accountable. *That's* your gift to Andrew. Do you think he would have made it this far if you hadn't been there for him?"

"I suppose not."

"You saved Andrew." Madeleine softened her voice. "And what has Andrew done for you?"

Grace narrowed her eyes. "Andrew needs me."

"I'm not disputing that. Do you need him?"

"Andrew would be lost without me. He'd *die* without me."

"But you have never told me, not once in four years, of a time when *you* were on the brink and Andrew pulled *you* back. *You're* the one who gets the IM in the early morning hours. *You're* the one to reassure, to comfort, to get your Andrew through another day. He needs you, yes. But do *you* need *him?*"

Grace leaned forward, holding the arms of her chair in a white-knuckled grip. "Why are you doing this, pushing, pushing, pushing? Damn it, *yes*, I need him. Who would I take care of, if I didn't have Andrew?"

Madeleine paused long enough for Grace to relax her grip on the chair.

"Do you love him?"

"Of course," Grace answered.

Madeleine said nothing.

"Yeah. I love him. I think about him. I worry about him. I don't want him to get hurt."

"Okay. Does he love you?"

"I think so."

Madeleine nodded. "How's Dylan?"

"Dylan's wonderful." Grace smiled. "You should see him. You wouldn't even call him a boy anymore, he's so grown up —a young man already. He's so curious, about everything. The last time we were together, he took me to a desert, and a venue on Mars—can you imagine that? And he knows everything about them—so smart. Donna tells me he's doing really well in school, near the top of his class. He talks non-stop, but that's okay. I could listen to him go on for hours. He wants to program VR when he's grown up, but he could do anything he wants. And he has *friends*—he's even met some of them IRL!"

"That's wonderful. You must really love him."

"Oh, Jah, yes, I love him so much."

"Okay. Does he love you?"

"Yes, of course he…" Grace glared, pursing her lips. "You're really devious, you know that?"

"Grace, I'm just trying to bring some clarity to your situation."

"You can't compare my *boyfriend* with my *son*."

"They're different people, certainly, who fill different roles in your life. The love you have for them, and the love they have for you, is not the same kind of love. But can't the *depth* of love be the same?"

"Andrew's had a difficult life. You can't expect him to have the same capacity for love that Dylan has."

"I understand."

"Andrew and I met in *rehab*, for Jah's sake. We're *both* damaged goods."

"You could say that."

"The thing at the Cloakroom, that's just…it's just…"

"Grace, I can guess what you're thinking."

"But it's not a guess with you, is it? You *know* what I'm thinking. That's what you learned in university, and from all the head jobs like me that you've done over the years. You don't have to guess. You know my thoughts—you put them there."

Madeleine leaned back in her chair, her avatar's face impassive. "I'm only trying to help you find your own way."

"And what's that?"

"That's not for me to say, Grace. As far as Andrew is concerned, I think you know what to do."

"I suppose." Grace squeezed her eyes shut. "Jah. What I get from Andrew's no different than what I get from the men in my lifestream—my victims. It's not about love; it's about power." She opened her eyes. "Now what?"

"Now, we build on that understanding. But first, we need to have a dialogue about what you told me at our last session."

"Disconnecting," Grace whispered.

Madeleine nodded. "Do you still plan to go through with it?"

"Why not? If Andrew's not a factor anymore…"
"And Dylan?"
Grace bowed forward, her hands clasped between her knees. "Dylan is my only reason to stay. And he's my only reason to disconnect."

19

THE MIND OF GOD

"OH, NO YOU didn't," Donna said through the intercom on the door to her apartment.

"Please, Donna," Chrysalis said, "it's best this way. Can I see Dylan?"

"I don't want Dylan to see you like that."

"You can't keep me from seeing him. It's my right."

"I can damn well keep you from exposing Dylan to your criminal cult."

An unintelligible sound, like a voice, came over the intercom.

"It's nobody, Dylan," Donna said.

Chrysalis heard the voice again, more clearly: *Is it Mom?*

"I don't know who it is," Donna said. "It's wearing a cloak, and its voice is a machine's voice. It could be anyone."

Chrysalis lifted her hood, showing her face to the camera. "Dylan, it's Mom. I'm here for our visit."

"Hi, Mom! What's that you're wearing? It looks weird."

"I'll explain. Donna, please."

The bolt slid open. Donna opened the door halfway, keeping it between Chrysalis and Dylan.

"I don't approve," Donna whispered.

114

"That's obvious."

"Dylan will want to know why you're hiding from Jahbulon, and why you're hanging with outlaws. What are you going to tell him?"

Chrysalis pushed the door open and stepped inside. She removed her hood entirely, standing next to Donna as Grace. Dylan stood in the hallway, a huge smile on his face.

"Mom, is that a cloak? Are you Cloak?"

"Yes, Dylan."

"Why?" Dylan said, seeming amused.

"The Cloak are a secret society," Donna said, eyeing Grace. "They try to hide where they are and what they're doing from the Worldstream. You have to wonder what they don't want Jahbulon to know."

"Dylan, we can talk all about it. And if you still have questions, we can talk some more next week, or you can ask your Aunt Donna."

"You have four hours," Donna said. "I have things to do."

"Can we not spend our time in VR?" Grace said. "Let's go for a walk, outside of the building."

Dylan's eyes opened wide. "Yeah! That would be so hi-res. Can we, Aunt Donna?"

"*Absolutely not!*" Donna protested. "You can spend your time any way you want, IRL or VR, but you do it here in the apartment."

"Donna, what are you worried about?" Grace said. "You know it's safe. There's no street crime anymore. If anything happens, one shout to Jahbulon and help arrives."

"*Please*, Aunt Donna? You never let me go out IRL."

"That's because there's nothing to see," Donna said, "just dirty streets and crumbling buildings and ragged people. You can go anywhere and do anything in VR. And I'll know exactly where you are."

"Your voice responder can find Dylan at any time," Grace said. "It can even give you regular reports. That's how good the All-Seeing Eye is at keeping track of all of us free citizens." She turned to Dylan. "Not a single sparrow can fall to the ground without Jahbulon knowing it." She touched him under his chin. "And you're worth more than a sparrow."

"There's nothing out there."

"Aunt Donna, *please!*"

"Donna, it'll be okay."

Donna glared at Grace in her cloak, her hood draped over her arm, and at Dylan's expectant face. She opened the door.

"Four hours."

"Thanks, Aunt Donna! We won't be late. Let's go, Mom!"

Dylan rushed out the door into the hallway. Grace put on her hood as she followed him.

"*Grace,*" Donna whispered, "*don't make me out to be the bad guy.*"

The city park, like all public amenities, was neglected, the grass too long, where grass still grew, the benches and shelters in disrepair. It was never crowded. The people in the park were mostly homeless and indigent, a few pet owners whose apartments didn't have hygienic facilities for their animals, and, after dark, couples who'd met that night, too impatient to go to an apartment for a hook, finding a reasonably private spot among the untrimmed shrubs, risking discovery by a passer-by, a call to Jahbulon and a night in civil confinement. The rest were there simply to reinsert themselves into Real Life, if only to breathe air that hadn't been filtered and conditioned, or to see sights that hadn't been computer rendered.

"Mom, what happened?" Dylan asked, as they strolled along an overgrown footpath.

"What do you mean?"

"What happened to the world? In school, we visit venues from history, so we'll understand what it was like fifty or a hundred years ago, or even older. There are always people, Jah, *thousands* of people, everywhere, doing things together. But look around. There's nobody, not in the park, not on the streets on the way over here. They're all in VR. Why don't more people come out?"

"I'm not sure, Dylan. What do they tell you in school?"

"They're like Aunt Donna. They say there's nothing IRL that you can't find in VR, and how it's so much more efficient and productive."

"That's one answer, I suppose. What do you think?"

"I guess it's true. Really good VR seems like Real Life—almost."

"But?"

"But it's not. It isn't real."

"Do you think that's important?"

"I don't know. I think it *ought* to be important." Dylan picked up a tree branch from the path, a straight branch, which he used as a walking stick. "Nothing happens in VR that isn't programmed. Interactive venues can adapt to the players, so it's not all 100% hard coded, but it's all in the program. If the programmer hasn't thought of it, it doesn't exist. If we were in VR right now, this stick would only be here because the VR programmer put it here."

Chrysalis stopped walking. "Did they teach you that in school?"

"No." Dylan poked at the ground with his makeshift staff. "I thought of it. I asked prof in class about it, the real differences between RL and VR."

"What did prof say?"

"It's really strange, what he said. There were philosophers once, hundreds of years ago, who said that nothing could exist if it wasn't being watched by someone, like a person. But they couldn't explain how things changed over time, like a tree falling over, or a fire burning out, if those things didn't exist when no one was watching them. So, they figured, well, *everything's* in the mind of god. They said that things exist all the time, because god's watching everything."

"What do you believe?"

"If that's true, then all it means is that there's a god who's just a really good VR programmer. If human programmers got that good, then maybe there wouldn't be a difference." Dylan put his foot in the center of the stick, snapping it in two. He tossed it away. "But I think that probably there isn't a god, and the world just is, and people will never be as clever as the world."

Chrysalis and Dylan continued down the path. "That's very insightful of you," Chrysalis said. "I never thought of that."

"Thanks, Mom. But then, if RL is different from VR, what happened? Why does everyone stay in VR?"

"*Different* isn't necessarily *better*. I work all day with people who spend almost *all* their time IRL. Many of them don't have wonderful lives. Some of them have terrible lives. They'll take what few credits they have, credits they need for food and shelter, and they'll spend them at the lifestream bistros, just to escape Real Life."

"Wayne told me about those. He calls them streamboats. Didn't we pass one on the way here?"

Chrysalis recalled the walk to the park, passing not one, but three streamboats. She'd walked quickly past each one, talking nonstop to distract Dylan as she anxiously scanned each streamboat for any mention of Grace's viral lifestream.

"I don't remember."

"I hear that streamboats have the Belt."

"What do you know about the Belt?" Chrysalis asked, urgently enough to over-modulate her synthesizer. The distorted voice frightened Dylan.

"Nothing, Mom," Dylan mumbled. "I've just heard. Wayne told me. It's like a peripheral that connects to your nervous system. He said he might get a Belt soon. He's never used one, but he's heard they're hyper-hi-res."

Chrysalis placed her hand on Dylan's shoulder. "I didn't mean to upset you. I've heard things, too, about how the Belt can make a VR venue all the more real. Do you really need that, though? Don't you enjoy your VR enough?"

"Sure, Mom. Wayne and I took a boat down a jungle river yesterday, with crocodiles, and flocks of parrots, and monkeys in the trees. That was hi-res. I went hang gliding off a canyon wall, and I caught the wind, and I flew around the towers of rock. I landed in the river at the bottom. We should do that some time."

"That would be fun. Are there any other VR experiences you've tried?"

"Sure, Mom, lots."

"Lifestreams?"

Dylan stopped in the path. "Yeah."

"What kind of lifestreams?"

"You know, different ones."

"Dylan, have you tried any adult lifestreams?"

Dylan's face turned as red as his hair. "Did Aunt Donna tell you?"

"She didn't say a thing to me."

"It's so unfair. She monitors everything I do in VR. One time I tried it, that's all, just five or ten minutes. She got an alarm and she interrupted my VR stream."

Chrysalis recalled the tally she'd heard at Raúl's apartment: *Adult content, four hours, fifty minutes.*

"Just that one time? No more?"

"Mom, how could I? Aunt Donna has all that stuff blocked."

"And there's no way around the block? No way to avoid her alarms?"

"I wouldn't do anything like that."

"But there are ways."

Dylan stared at the ground. "Yeah."

Chrysalis lifted Dylan's chin. "I want you to be honest with me. I want us to be totally honest with each other. You have ways to bypass the blocks, don't you? And you've ridden other lifestreams."

"Mom, don't tell Aunt Donna, please. I won't do it again."

"I won't say anything to Donna. But tell me, what did you think of those lifestreams? Did you like them?"

Dylan pulled his chin away from Chrysalis's hand. "Yeah."

Chrysalis put her hand on Dylan's back as they continued down the path. "It's normal for you to be excited by that sort of thing. There are better ways to spend your time."

"Why do people do that, program lifestreams with all their sex activities? Don't they have any respect for themselves?"

"These are not examples of healthy relationships between

adults."

"How do you know, Mom? Have you ridden one?"

Chrysalis looked into Dylan's eyes. She saw it, the *tell* that betrayed a compulsion—Grace had seen it in her own eyes. It was in her genes, and, possibly, in Dylan's—one that he may or may not be able to control.

"Have you, Mom?"

I want us to be totally honest with each other.

Don't they have any respect for themselves?

"No, Dylan, I've never ridden one of those, and I never will. But I've heard."

20

VIRAL PORN GIRL

DYLAN REACHED FOR the access panel, but the door swung open before he could touch it. Donna stood in the open doorway, eyes glaring, jaw set, looking as if she were ready to spit.

"Dylan," Donna said, "go to your room. Grace and I need to talk."

"Bye, Mom." Dylan gave Chrysalis a hug. "See you next week."

The two women watched as Dylan retreated to his room.

"What's wrong?" Chrysalis asked.

"Take that thing off."

Chrysalis removed her hood.

"What in Jah's name have you done?" Donna asked.

Grace shook her head, knitting her brow.

"It's all over the Worldstream," Donna said.

"Oh, no," Grace whispered. "What have you heard?"

"Your lifestream. Your depraved, disgusting lifestream. All the men and women you slept with, all the drugs, the alcohol you drowned yourself in, it's all back. I thought this was history."

"It *is* history, Donna. I've been clean for years. I've tried so hard, and I keep trying hard every day."

"From what I hear, your past is going to follow you forever."

"I'm just as upset by it as you are. Why do you think I'm wearing this cloak? So Dylan, or Andrew, or *you*, or anyone else won't be connected with my lifestream. I want it behind me, and I don't want it to touch anyone that I care about. Besides, you won't have to worry about it for long."

"So, that's true as well. You're going to disconnect."

"Who told you that?"

"Never mind who told me. Is it true?"

"It was Andrew, wasn't it?"

"Is it true?"

"So, what if it is? That would solve all your problems, wouldn't it? My lifestream'll disappear, and you'll have Dylan all to yourself."

"I can't let you do that."

"What do you care? When have you *ever* cared? Since I was a baby, I was the little sister who got between you and Mother. But I never could compete. Mother never hid who she favored. Oh, she made her lame attempts, after she lavished her praise on you, whenever you got your marks, or won an award. She'd toss me a little present, just an afterthought: 'we love you too, Grace,' before fussing again over amazing Donna."

"Don't be dramatic. I care because you're my sister. Sisters don't let their sisters kill themselves."

"Who's being dramatic? 'Sisters don't let sisters.' Jah, you don't give a damn about me."

"I can't have a Shade in the family. It puts us all under suspicion."

"You're in a real pickle, aren't you? If I stay connected, there's my horrible lifestream to haunt you, especially if some of your very upstanding colleagues are riding the lifestreams, and they make the connection between Donna, the VR programming guru, and Grace, the viral porn girl. And if I disconnect, you'll have the stigma of a sister who's committed virtual suicide, with Jahbulon focusing his All-

Seeing Eye right at you. Isn't the Worldstream great? How we're all connected, one, big, microscopically monitored family?"

Donna stood stiffly, arms crossed, jaw clenched. "All right then. Cut yourself off from me and Mother. You're right, we won't miss you, not much. But how can you do that to Dylan?"

Grace held her hood tightly bunched in her fist, white-knuckled and trembling. "Dylan is the *main reason* I'm doing this. I'd do anything to keep him from my past, even if it means that I'll never see him again."

"You're a part of his life."

"Oh, spare me. You and Mother have been trying to keep me away from Dylan since he was born. When Mother and Edward took custody, you never said one word of support, you never took one moment to comfort me, to let me know that you felt bad for me, that you understood how horrible it must feel to have my newborn son ripped out of my arms. When Edward left, and Mother couldn't let a ten-year-old boy intrude into her very productive life, you fought me in the courts for custody. Don't tell me you're worried about Dylan losing me. You wouldn't even let me see him if the courts didn't order it."

"You were a mess. You weren't fit to raise that boy. I knew it, the courts knew it, and you knew it, too."

"I've gotten better, haven't I? Jah, I hope I've gotten better, as hard as I've worked at it. But you never could admit that, either."

Donna uncrossed her arms and pressed her fingers to her forehead. "All right. You've gotten better. You *have* worked hard. You deserve credit for that."

Grace's hand fell to her side, letting her hood drop to the floor. "Thank you."

"Don't disconnect."

"I have to. I can't take the chance. If I knew you could keep Dylan away from my lifestream, it might be different."

Donna clenched her fists in front of her face. "Don't you *dare* lecture me on how to look after that boy. For the last four years, I've been his sole provider and caregiver. I don't have to defend how I've taken care of Dylan to *anyone*, especially to *you*."

Grace nodded. "Donna, don't think that I don't appreciate everything you've done for Dylan. He's a wonderful boy. That's more your doing than mine. But that doesn't change anything, certainly not my mind."

"What about our stepfather?" Donna said. "What about Edward?"

"What about him?"

"He's never been anything but kind and supportive. He was always there for you even when Mother and I weren't. He already knows about your past and he never judged you. He's not a fourteen-year-old boy, either. He understands. Finding out about your lifestream won't affect the way he feels about you one bit. Say what you want about Mother and me, but Edward loves you."

Grace picked up her hood. "If I'm willing to leave Dylan behind, do you think that the thought of leaving Edward behind will stop me?" She pulled her hood over her head. "Goodbye."

Chrysalis opened the door.

"Don't do this," Donna warned.

Chrysalis closed the door behind her. She stood in the hall, looking first at the floor, then the ceiling.

"Dylan—Edward," she said, her synthesizer barely registering the whispered names. "I'm sorry. I don't *want* to do this. I *have* to."

21

A Forfeit Is Not a Victory

"Come in, Grace. Or should I call you that other name… Chrysalis?"

Chrysalis removed her hood as she entered Edward's apartment. She stopped short at the sight of her stepfather. Although they'd visited regularly in VR, they hadn't seen each other IRL in more than two years. He was thinner than the last time she'd seen him, his cheeks hollower, his silver hair sparser, his dusky blue eyes more sunken. She'd noticed none of these changes in Edward's avatar.

"Call me Grace, like always." She gave Edward a hug that lingered. "You look good—better than your avatar," she said politely.

Edward kissed her cheek. "So do you. We need to meet IRL more often. Your avatar doesn't do you justice."

"Always the flatterer. That's why I love you."

"Sit down, sit down, I've made you something to drink." Edward went into the kitchen, returning with a teapot, two cups, and a plate of cookies on a tray. He set the tray down and poured the tea.

"Look what you've done," Grace said, laughing. "You remembered—red rooibos tea."

"Of course. It's hard to find, but I know it's your favorite. I couldn't serve anything else for an IRL visit."

"Very thoughtful, as usual."

The two sat, quietly sampling the cookies and sipping the tea. Grace watched Edward, trying to read his mood. Edward kept his eyes down.

"So, how have you been?" she asked, bending low to get a look at his face.

Edward nibbled a cookie, staring into his teacup.

"Good." He looked up. "I'm good. But tell me what's going on with you. Is this the last time I'll see you? IRL or VR?"

"You've talked with Donna. She told you, didn't she?"

"She did. Your lifestream, your joining the Cloak. Your plans to...well..."

"Edward, I have to do this—for Dylan, for you...but really, for myself." Grace set down her cup and leaned forward. "I have a confession. I rode my lifestream. I haven't told that to anyone except my therapist. And I know why it's viral. It's not the sex. There's millions of hours of sex in the Worldstream, wilder, raunchier, more bizarre than anything I ever did, by kilometers. When I rode my lifestream, watching it from a distance, it was boring, really. It did nothing for me. I'm sure a veteran stream rider would watch for about ten seconds and then start surfing for something more interesting."

"I know you have a history. That doesn't change how I feel about you."

"That means so much to me; I love you for that, but listen to what I'm saying: my sex life, and all the drugs and alcohol, as bad as it was, *that's* not why my lifestream is viral."

Edward wrinkled his brow. "So, what is it?"

"It's what it does to your head. You can ride the lifestream from anyone's perspective, and actually *feel* what they're feeling, not just what their bodies are feeling, but what's in their *heads*, their *emotions*. I tried it, and it frightened me. It was pulling me back into my addiction, to the point where I almost gave in. That's the power this thing has, over me, and over others."

"It's Dylan you're worried about?"

"Uh-huh, Dylan, more than anyone. But me, too, and all the others—Edward, there're *millions*—who are inhabiting my life, getting inside my head. My life isn't mine anymore. It's being relived and passed around by people I don't know and wouldn't want to. I *have* to get rid of it."

"It's illegal."

"I know. And I know it'll be hard on you and Dylan. It's for the best." Grace picked up her teacup, then set it down again. "You won't turn me in, will you?"

"I'm not the only one who knows."

"Donna."

"Yes, and Joan."

Grace closed her eyes, inhaling deeply. "Oh, of course. How is Mother?"

"She hasn't changed. I don't think she has the capacity to change. That would require her to admit that she has a *need* to change."

Grace smiled. "A psychological impossibility."

"Hard coded." Edward and Grace laughed at the joke.

"You didn't answer my question," Grace said. "Would you turn me in?"

Edward stood, putting his hands in his pockets, turning away from Grace, curving his shoulders forward, as if he were shrinking into himself.

"I don't want to think of the world without you in it. I'm sure Dylan feels the same way. I want to keep you here, with us, even if you're in a confinement facility, where I can find you, and come to you, and see that you're all right." He turned back, crossing his arms tightly across his chest. "But that would kill you, like a wild animal in a cage. You would either shrivel up and die or chew yourself to pieces." He sat, his arms still crossed, rocking slowly in his chair. "Did you know that you're my hero?"

"Your hero? Edward, I don't know what you mean."

"When I married your mother, when you were eleven years old, and Donna was fourteen, when we were all still a family—do you remember? —living up to your mother's expectations was an Olympic sport. If you weren't setting records, you were nobody. Do you remember?"

"Yes. Dylan calls her the Guantanamo Commandant."

Edward laughed. "That boy—he's his mother's son."

Grace blushed. "Thank you."

"We, each of us, had our own way of dealing with the Commandant. Donna simply excelled, the only one of us to live up to Joan's lofty standards. Not only lived up to them, but beat them. Now look at her—driven, successful, respected in her profession—and the living image of her mother in every way."

"Yes, she is."

"I had a different strategy. I gave in to every demand, defaulted on every decision. I wasn't even passive-aggressive. I was just passive. Your mother got her way every time. But getting her way wasn't good enough. She had to get her way on *her terms*. That was the mistake I made, that I continued to make for fifteen years. I just gave in. To Joan, a forfeit is not a victory."

"Why didn't you stand up to her?"

Edward rocked faster. "I'm not strong, Grace. I don't like that about myself, but it's who I am and I've come to accept it. I didn't know I was so weak before I married your mother, and maybe I was stronger then. I must have been—Joan wouldn't have married a weakling. But it didn't take me long to realize that I was never going to win an argument with your mother, because she would not let anything go—big or small, everything had to go her way."

Grace put a hand on Edward's knee. "It always hurt me, how she cowed you, the way you let her intimidate you. It hurt me, and it confused me."

"Maybe if I'd been stronger, if I'd defended you more, if I had gotten Joan to be more nurturing, you wouldn't have acted out."

Grace squeezed Edward's knee. "When I needed something, you were always there. You never let me down. As for acting out, you can't blame yourself for my bad decisions."

"But you see, that's why you're my hero. Donna excelled, I caved in, but you were the only one to stand up to Joan. Oh, I know there were consequences—so much of what you did was destructive—but you're different now. You've channeled that rebellious energy, that determination, into bettering yourself. You've made a weakness into a strength, a trick I could never pull off. In our little family, there is only one person with the ferocious streak of independence I wish I had, who's the free, unchained spirit I wish I was."

"I love you, Edward."

Edward wiped a tear from his cheek. "I don't want you to leave. I want to talk you out of it, to convince you to stay with us, with Dylan and me. But you've already decided. I can tell. After almost twenty years I've learned that I have no power over you once you've decided."

Edward and Grace stood and embraced, Grace pressing her cheek against Edward's shoulder, her tears soaking his shirt.

"Wherever you are, remember that I love you," Edward whispered in Grace's ear. "I won't turn you in."

Grace squeezed Edward tightly. She closed her eyes, imagining a door, slightly open, beyond it utter blackness. She visualized her hand reaching for the handle, pushing the door open, walking through it, and closing it behind her, leaving her alone in the void, separated permanently from her world and everyone in it.

22

I'm Called Chrysalis

Andrew didn't wear his cloak to the Cloakroom, nor was it necessary for him to remove connected items from his body, having dressed entirely in disconnected clothes from The Faraday Cage. His eyes wandered over the crowd as he entered, settling on one Cloak walking toward him, steadily, but not quickly, as if going to finish an unpleasant chore.

"I'm called Chrysalis," the cloaked figure said. "Thank you for coming, Andrew."

They went to a relatively isolated table by the wall. The nearest occupied table, with two Cloak, was a few meters away.

"After the last time we were together," Chrysalis said, "I expected you to be wearing your cloak."

"Grace—Chrysalis—I'm sorry," Andrew said, hanging his head. "That was a one-time thing. I left right after you did. Nothing else happened. I tried to find you, but, you know, you're Cloak. I wanted to tell you it was a mistake. It's been so long since we touched; I thought coming here was a way to work out my frustration without hurting anyone. It's not an excuse, I know, but I admit it, I screwed up. I won't do it again."

"I won't hold it against you, Andrew. After all, we were both here for the same reason. It wouldn't fair to blame you for something we both did."

"Thank you," Andrew said, visibly relieved. "I forgive you, too."

Chrysalis shook her head. "I'm not forgiving you, and I don't expect you to forgive me. I'm saying that I don't blame you."

"I don't understand. What's the difference?"

"If I forgave you, it would be like I absolved you of your sin, as if it didn't happen, and we could go on with our relationship like it was before. I can't forgive you."

"You're confusing me."

"You deserve for me to be honest, even if it hurts. Forgiveness only has meaning in a relationship. Our relationship is over."

"Over? Why? What do you mean?"

"Andrew, what happened the other night, here, in the back room, that was just a symptom of a bigger problem. I said that our relationship is over, but that's not right either. We never really had a relationship."

"We have a relationship!"

"No. We don't. Do you remember when we met in rehab, when we agreed to sponsor each other? That was right after I'd lost Dylan. I thought that nobody needed me, and I really wanted to be needed. It worked, our relationship— somewhat. But it all ran one way. I felt needed, but I got nothing else back. I think I always knew it, but the shock of that night in that room brought it all into focus."

"Grace, don't do this," Andrew pleaded. "I told you, I'm sorry. It was an urge; I should have put it aside but I had a moment of failure. I won't do it again. I don't need it. I need *you*."

"Andrew, there's so much more. That night wasn't only *your* failure, but *mine,* too. And if I stay in the connected world, with my lifestream out there, I'll fail again. The temptation is too great. You rode my lifestream; you know how seductive it is. To me, with my addiction, it's irresistible.

I was strong enough to get out of that back room when I did. I might not be that strong again."

"That's where I come in," Andrew said. "I'm your sponsor. I can help. I've leaned on you, now you can lean on me. Please, let me help you."

"Andrew, no. I have to erase my lifestream. I have to shred my life. I'll be Shade, and you can't come with me." She stood and walked away.

"Grace, please, don't do this! Grace!"

Chrysalis walked back to the table. She whispered in Andrew's ear.

"I'm called *Chrysalis*."

Andrew blinked the tears from his eyes as he watched Chrysalis leave the Cloakroom.

23

A PROSPECT IN THE PIPELINE

TWO CLOAK SAT at a table near the wall, speaking quietly, their synthesizers at the minimum intelligible level.

"I received a request for quote this morning, a one-year contract for supplemental analytical services," the first Cloak said.

"I have the same one," the second Cloak replied. "I don't know who else has it, but there are only two crews in the Vita Occulta that can handle it."

"Yours and mine. A stretch for either one of us, actually."

"It's still ours."

"Yes, unless one of the independent crews bids. On spec."

"The VO controls the local labor pool. They could never staff up in time."

"What about the other VO crews? The smaller ones?"

"It would get back to the VO committee. They wouldn't risk it. Besides, they'll get their percentage, like always."

"The client could go remote—put the bid out to other regions."

"If they did, it'd be the first time."

"Because they've never had contacts in the other regions. What if they have them now?"

"They don't."

"How do you know?"

The second Cloak leaned closer. "I know the clients don't have the contacts because *we* have the contacts. If they were branching out, Vita Occulta would have heard something. You're on the VO committee. Has it come up?"

"No. I haven't heard a thing."

"All right then." The second Cloak sat up a bit. "While we're talking about it, what's my standing with the VO? I've got the biggest crew. I deserve a seat on the committee."

"They're skeptical. They still consider you a newcomer. The next rotation is in three months."

"Put my name in—again."

"I will. What about the contract?"

"I had low bid on the last RFQ. It's your turn. Come in under eight million credits on the base, and a hundred-fifty per hour incremental. Same profit-sharing arrangement as always, after the VO's share. Take it to the committee."

"Done. It's a big job. I may need to send the overflow to you."

"That might be a problem. I have my crew on a special project. Depending on what the other crews have going, we might have to hire."

"Do you have prospects in the pipeline?"

The second Cloak held up his hand. A couple at the nearest table, one Cloak, one civilian in plain clothes, raised their voices. The two Cloak caught a few snippets of the conversation:

"*...Please, let me help you...*"

"*...Andrew, no...you can't come with me...*"

The two Cloak watched as the Cloak member of the couple stood up and went for the exit.

"*...Grace, please, don't do this...*"

The Cloak went back to the table and whispered in the civilian's ear before leaving. The civilian sat for a moment before kicking the table leg, drawing the attention of everyone in the Cloakroom who wasn't already looking his way. He rubbed his smarting foot before hobbling out the door.

The second Cloak watched the scene unfold, waiting until the civilian was out of the Cloakroom before continuing.

"Prospects. Yes, I have just one at present. His Cloak name is Chrysalis. But he won't be available. I have something special in mind for him."

24

WE ARE JAHBULON

As Chrysalis left the Cloakroom she felt none of the sorrow, nor any of the misgivings she'd felt when she left Edward's apartment. Andrew was in Grace's past, her anxiety replaced with calm, her uncertainty with resolve. It surprised her, in fact, that a man to whom Grace had been devoted, with whom she had expected, less than three weeks before, to spend her life with, could be dismissed so easily, so confidently. It was further confirmation, Chrysalis thought, that for years Grace had buried her doubts about Andrew, a form of self-denial, no less pathological than an addict's vow to stay clean, a vow he makes with complete sincerity, but which he violates at the first chance he gets. An addiction, that's what Andrew was, a morbid dependence on the feeling of being indispensable.

Chrysalis picked up her pace as she rounded a corner onto a deserted street, a few blocks from Grace's building. Her breathing was calm; her manner was relaxed. She even smiled a little.

It was because Chrysalis was walking fast that her feet went out from under her when two pairs of hands took her from behind. An arm encircled her from her left; a hand dug into her back between her shoulder blades. The second man grabbed her right arm and slipped a hand under Chrysalis's hood, pressing a foam pad against Chrysalis's neck, just below her jaw. A skin-permeable solvent bearing a fast-acting sedative entered Chrysalis's bloodstream. She struggled to get her feet back under her, but her knees buckled.

"Jahbulon, help me!" Chrysalis cried.

The man on Chrysalis's right pressed the pad more firmly against her neck. He lowered Chrysalis to the sidewalk as she slipped into unconsciousness.

"Jahbulon won't help you," said one of the men, dressed, like his companion, entirely in black. "*We* are Jahbulon."

25

THIS IS ABOUT YOU

WHITE.

Grace lay on her back, half-conscious, as her eyes fluttered open. She saw one featureless expanse of white, like a ceiling, lit by a lamp.

Grace blinked slowly, aware of an ache between her eyes. The feeling was familiar, though she hadn't felt it in a long time. A slight turn of her head brought on a bout of dizziness; closing her eyes caused the bed to spin. Yes, she recognized the symptoms of a chronic condition, in remission for years. She was hung over.

Another hour passed while Grace hovered between wakefulness and sleep, until she'd recovered enough to raise her head. She lay in a bed, large and comfortable, in an elaborately-made antique wrought-iron frame, under a thick, white comforter that covered her to her chest. Straining further, she could see what she was wearing: dark blue flannel pajamas, with a pattern of butterflies.

Grace looked to her right, at a heavy nightstand, made of dark wood. On it was a simple metal lamp with a fabric shade, casting a soft glow throughout the room; next to it, a vase of fresh flowers, purple irises among a bouquet of

138

white carnations. She could make out the rest of the room in the dim light. The walls were covered in green wallpaper, with a chair rail around the entire room above a cream-colored wainscot, the way homes were decorated in the last century, or possibly the century before that. Anodyne artwork hung on the walls: a country home on a winter night, its windows casting trapezoids of light on the snow; a landscape, deer grazing in a meadow in the foreground, mountains in the distance; a four-masted ship, sails full, before a sky of gathering clouds.

Grace looked again at the ceiling. Closing her eyes, she drew a deep breath—the air was cool, and pleasantly scented, like flowers, she thought, or spices, or both. A few more breaths—the pain in her head was nearly gone; her stomach had settled. She felt strong enough to sit up, lifting herself a few inches from her pillow, pulling her elbows back for support, when the restraints on her hands reached their limits. She pulled, then jerked her arms against the straps, but they wouldn't yield. She was unable to pull her legs under her —the bonds on her feet were as unforgiving as those on her hands.

Grace lay still for a moment before thrashing violently, attempting to break, or at least loosen the straps, until her head throbbed again and her vertigo returned. She collapsed on her pillow, panting, waiting for the pain to subside, until she drifted off.

When she opened her eyes again, she was not alone. A woman sat by the nightstand. She was middle-aged or slightly older, in a patterned dress and an apron, reading an old-style paper book with a hard cover. Grace watched as the woman turned the page once, then twice, before she looked up at Grace.

"You're awake," the woman said, setting her book on the bed. "How are you feeling?"

"Not well," Grace replied. "I feel like I'm sobering up."

"I'm sorry about that. You had a bad reaction to the sedative, I'm afraid. It's rare, but it happens, mostly to former addicts. It won't last."

"Is that what it was—a sedative. I would have guessed vodka. In any case, it seems to me that it *could* have been avoided, if I simply had not been assaulted and drugged in the first place."

"Grace, I apologize for that. I'll explain everything to you shortly."

"You know who I am. Who are you, if I may ask?"

"My name is Charity. I'll be with you for the next day or two. As I said, I'll explain everything. Right now, I'm here to make you comfortable."

"Since you brought it up, I'm not comfortable, not really. These straps on my hands and feet are chafing."

"Let me fix that," Charity said. She rounded the bed, undoing the restraints on Grace's hands and feet. "There. Better?" she said with a matronly smile. "Comfortable?"

Grace sat up, massaging the purple marks on her wrists. "When does the explanation start, Charity?"

"Soon. We're still waiting for a few people. While we're waiting, would you like some tea?"

For the first time, Grace noticed a teapot and two cups on the nightstand. Charity filled the cups, then handed one to Grace. Grace inhaled the steam, its familiar scent clearing her head.

"Red rooibos," Grace said. "I've heard that this variety of tea is hard to find."

Charity sipped her tea. "I've never had it before. It's very unusual. It's your favorite, isn't it?"

"I think you know that it is. Not many others know that, though."

"How did you come to prefer rooibos tea?"

"It's good for hangovers," Grace deadpanned as she sipped. "It's delicious, thank you, Charity. I'm feeling much better now." Grace put the cup aside. "Charity?"

"Yes, Grace?"

"What is this place, and what am I doing here?"

Charity took a long sip before answering. "This is a public intervention facility. We bring people here who are in a bad place, who might be a danger to themselves, or to others. We also help people who are contemplating doing something terrible, or maybe illegal. We've averted many tragedies. We've saved many lives."

"I'm not in a bad place, unless you mean this intervention facility. I was, once, but I've been clean for four years. I don't need an intervention."

"You're not here for your addiction, Grace. You're one of our guests who's contemplating an illegal act. We can't let you do that to yourself, neither we, who work here in the intervention facility, nor the people who care about you."

"You're going to have to tell me what you're talking about, because I have no idea."

Charity patted Grace's hand. "Disconnecting, Grace."

"You've been misinformed. I have no intention of disconnecting. Are you sure you have the right person? After all, I was cloaked when those two apes kidnapped me. They must have been looking for someone else in a cloak, and got me by mistake."

"Someone else named Grace? No, we got it right. You're supposed to be here. You were reported by a family member. Once we got the report, we were obligated to act. With your family's consent, we took you into custody. As for finding you while cloaked, I'm afraid that the faith you have in the Cloak protocols, to hide you from the Worldstream, is unfounded. Even when cloaked, you leave a trail. It *can* be difficult to follow, but not impossible. And we've gotten very good at it. No, Grace, even when cloaked, Jahbulon knows where you are, what you're doing, or even..." Charity lifted her teacup. "...what kind of tea you like."

"Someone in my family told you that I'm disconnecting? Then *they're* mistaken. I'm Cloak, that's true; maybe they assumed I was Shade, too. That's it. Just a misunderstanding. I hope that clears it up."

"Grace, really, we know what we're doing. It's for the best. I..." Charity touched her ear, turning her head slightly. Grace noticed a tiny earpiece. "The others have arrived. We can begin."

Charity went to the door, opening it far enough to see

who was on the other side. She whispered a few words before closing the door.

"Grace, I'll be facilitating the event. I'm a psychologist, employed by the state, trained in interventions. I've led more than two hundred, with a very good success rate. One thing I've learned is that our success depends on you. More than anything—our methods, the people involved, the facility— we will succeed if *you* want to succeed. It's important that you know, that you remember at all times, that there are people who care about you, who love you, who only want the best outcome for you. This intervention is not about the others; it's certainly not about me. This is about you, and how important you are to so many people." Charity opened the door. "You may come in now."

Donna and Andrew entered together, Donna with a grim look; Andrew with a hangdog expression, looking as if he'd rather be anywhere else.

"My sister," Grace said, "and my ex-boyfriend. Charity, now I'm sure this is a mistake. Whichever one of them reported me, they had to have misunderstood my intentions. I'm sure we can straighten this out."

Charity shook her head. "No, Grace, neither Donna nor Andrew called for this intervention." Charity motioned for the next person to enter. Grace's heart sank as Edward came in, his shoulders hunched, his cheeks wet with tears.

"Oh, no," Grace choked, "Edward, not you. Please, tell me you didn't."

Edward shook his head. "No Grace. I couldn't. I promised you. You're the one person I've never broken a promise to, and I never will."

Edward opened the door all the way. Grace gasped, all residual effects of the sedative suddenly and completely dissipated.

"Oh, Jah," she whispered. "Mother."

26

The Rules Are a Little Fuzzy

"I KNOW MY daughter," Joan stated. "You won't persuade her with your methods."

The intervention team huddled in an adjacent room, four hours into the process. Although Charity had lectured them in advance—*create a loving, supportive environment; honest, but caring; be mindful of Grace's emotional state*—it was not going as planned.

"This is a proven technique, with a history of positive results," Charity said, lowering her voice. "I know you mean well, but in my opinion, your comments during the session were not helpful. Progress will come when Grace acknowledges the consequences of her actions, but she has to know that she has a loving, supportive circle of family and friends. We can invite her, we can encourage her, even urge her, but that's a place she'll have to get to on her own. You have to trust the process."

"Joan," Edward said, "let's listen to Charity. She's the expert."

"Edward, please," Joan said, "if you hadn't coddled that girl growing up, we wouldn't be here now."

"And if you hadn't..." Edward mumbled.

"If I hadn't what? What, Edward? Finish your thought."

"Nothing. It's just, well, she was constantly reminded of how she didn't measure up. I didn't coddle Grace. I sympathized."

"I think we can do without your rationalizations, Edward," Joan said. She looked at Charity. "Listen, lady, I'm not going to be associated with a criminal Shade. I've worked too hard to build and keep up my reputation. We're all connected in the Worldstream. If that girl disconnects, it's a black mark on me, and on Donna, who's worked no less hard than I have to get where she is. We'll both be under a level of scrutiny that neither one of us deserves."

Charity opened her mouth to speak, but Edward interrupted.

"But that's not how Grace explained it to me. She said that all of her lifestream data will be purged. There'll be nothing in the Worldstream that ties you to Grace. Why would you be affected?"

"You see?" Joan sneered. "Coddled. That girl came to you and told you her plans, and you did nothing. You didn't report it, you didn't talk her out of it, you didn't even come to me with this information. It was Andrew who told Donna, and Donna who told me. I had to be the one to take it to the authorities. Once again, it falls on me to do the responsible thing."

"I'm just saying," Edward said, "Grace's disconnecting won't affect you."

"Don't talk about things you don't know anything about," Joan retorted. "If that girl shreds her life, it'll leave a giant hole in the Worldstream—data purged, links broken, the whole mesh of our interwoven lifestreams torn apart. Every algorithm in the Worldstream will go crazy trying to mend the damage. And the ends of all the broken links will be dangling from our lifestreams—mine, Donna's, yours—and Dylan's too. That girl will make all of our lives very complicated."

"That girl," Edward said, "is named Grace."

"Thank you, Edward," Charity said, "for reminding us of

why we're here. Joan, we try to accommodate the feelings and suggestions of the family during an intervention, but I have to repeat, there's a method to this, and it works."

"I don't share your faith in your method. You can see that it's not effective."

Charity took her voice down another notch, sounding more menacing than conciliatory. "Four hours is not enough time, especially when members of the intervention team fail to follow their instructions, when they create a hostile environment, when they're adversarial instead of confrontational."

"If that's bad, then it's going to get a lot worse," Joan said. "I'm taking charge."

"You can't do that," Charity protested. "This is a state-sponsored facility. We have procedures here."

"Actually, the rules on that are a little fuzzy. As the party who reported the case, I've put in a request to the director of this state-sponsored facility that I be given responsibility for the intervention, and the authority to conduct it. The director has agreed."

"You can't do that!"

"You can lodge a protest, but since I sit on three state advisory committees, including one related to law enforcement, I believe I will prevail."

"Yes, I'll protest. You give me no choice."

"Fine. Let me know how that goes. Shall we resume? Donna, are you with me?"

"Yes," Donna said. "And I'm relieved that we're putting all this mushy stuff behind us. It's time to get serious."

Joan continued around the room. "Andrew?"

"I guess so, yes."

"Charity?"

"I'm bound by law to be present, regardless of the direction the intervention takes."

"Good. Edward?"

"I think we should follow Charity's process. I vote no."

"This isn't a *vote*. This is me finding out whether you'll continue to participate, or if you'll stand aside. In or out?"

Edward pressed the back of his hand to his mouth. He began to rock in his chair, very slightly.

"In."

❖ ❖ ❖

Grace lay motionless, her hand and foot restraints having been re-fastened prior to the break after the first four-hour session. The red rooibos tea had been removed hours ago; Grace'd had only water since. She'd been given no food at all.

The session began with Charity giving instructions: each person was to speak in turn, honestly but respectfully, and Grace would respond, step-by-step, in an atmosphere of love and understanding. That lasted less than one turn, when Joan let fly a tirade, a rap sheet of Grace's offenses dating from age two. The four-way melee that ensued, pitting Joan and Donna against Charity and Edward, with Andrew keeping mute, Grace actually found mildly amusing—all their energies were directed at each other rather than at Grace— but process-bound Charity and passive-aggressive Edward were no match for the team of Joan and Donna. The round-robin structure was scrapped in favor of random outbursts, charges and counter-charges, with interruptions rather than respectful attention becoming the default mode of discourse. Charity tried to restore order from time to time, with limited and always temporary success.

The pain in Grace's head had returned. After a morning without nourishment—was it morning? Afternoon? Middle of the night? —amid non-stop shouted recriminations, Grace felt worn and weak. She consoled herself, knowing that she had given as good as she got, matching Joan and Donna in loudness and pace. It was small consolation.

For Grace had wavered in her resolve. Despite Grace's instinct to stand her ground, she'd begun to question her decision to disconnect. Joan made the point that Grace would leave behind people who would continue in the connected world at the ragged edge of Grace's shredded life, subject to the scrutiny of the All-Seeing Eye—most importantly Joan and Donna, two women who had risen to the peak of their profession. Joan scored debating points when she enlarged the circle to include Dylan and Edward, people whom Grace cared about, and who cared about her, who would also be touched as Jahbulon attempted to mend the torn Worldstream. Every time Grace felt herself falter, she visualized the mentally abusive tactics that Joan had used on Grace during her childhood to impose her will, tactics which worked with frightful efficiency on Edward, but which drove Grace to rebel. A dozen times Grace had vacillated, questioning whether she should disconnect, each time recalling her upbringing, each time restoring her resolve, each time with a little less conviction. She recommitted herself, knowing that the onslaught would continue—but she was tired, and her head ached.

The door opened. Joan was the first one through. Charity followed, going directly to Grace's bed, and began to undo the straps.

"Leave those be," Joan said.

"There's no need for the guest to be restrained during the session," Charity countered.

"We'll remove the straps when we've come to an understanding," Joan maintained. "Grace. We've been very patient up to this point. We're out of patience."

"This is not productive," Charity said. "This is not the way to show Grace the consequences of her decision."

"Grace, you should know that Charity is no longer running this intervention. I am. The straps stay on. The consequences of your decision start now."

"We're at a critical juncture," Charity whispered.

After another five hours had passed, Charity pulled Joan and Donna aside, to a corner of the room, leaving Edward and Andrew by Grace's bedside. "She's on the verge of her final decision, a commitment, really, to stay connected."

"What makes you think so?" Joan challenged.

"I can tell from her responses—her body language, her facial expressions. Her conviction is faltering. She's at a very vulnerable point, but she could be pushed either way."

"Good. I'm ready to make the final tip."

"*No*," Charity rasped. "I'm telling you, if this is mishandled, you could push her away forever. Listen to me—this is my area of expertise, what I was trained for, and what I've done for the last twelve years. I've seen a hundred guests at this point. Trust me, this is what I do. It has to be handled carefully."

"All right. What do we do?"

"I need to speak with Grace alone."

"No. I need to be here."

"Joan, I have to be blunt. The worst *possible* thing we could do at this point is to allow you to remain in the room while I speak with Grace. You've been the bad cop. You've worn her down. Now she needs a sympathetic ear to give her permission and praise for the decision that she's ready to make."

"I don't like this."

"Joan, up to now we've done it your way. I can bring this home. *My* way."

Joan looked at Donna. Donna raised her eyebrows, in a *let's give her a chance* manner.

"Is there a place where we can get something to eat?" Joan said.

Charity took a breath of relief. "Left out the door, then your first right. You'll see a sign; follow that."

"Edward, Andrew," Charity said, "Grace and I need some alone time. You can go with Joan and Donna."

Once alone, Charity sat by Grace's bed. Grace lay back still restrained, eyes closed, breathing shallowly. Her eyes had dark circles and her cheeks were hollow. Charity put her hand on Grace's.

"Grace," Charity said softly. "It's just us now. Can you hear me?"

Grace opened her eyes and turned toward Charity. She nodded.

"Can I get you anything?"

"May I please have some of the rooibos tea?"

Charity smiled. "Yes, yes, of course, right away. I'll be just a few minutes."

❖ ❖ ❖

Grace stared at the ceiling. She saw images, like waking dreams: the Eye of Providence, and the rest of the Cloak, gathered at the Cloakroom for their illegal bartering, or their illicit sex, believing, falsely, that they were hiding from Jahbulon; Raúl, the sneering, cynical shredder, pontificating on the subjects of morality, god and sin; Joan and Donna, willing to keep Grace in the connected world, so as to avoid the embarrassment of a Shade in the family; poor, fearful, compliant Edward, debasing himself for her sake. And her Dylan, the last permanent value in her life, her sole remaining source of meaning—the touchstone of truth for her decision, which she had made, and from which she would not waver.

"Here we are." Charity returned with a tray, carrying a teapot and two cups. She closed the door behind her with her foot. "This will make you feel better." She poured two cups and held one up to Grace.

"You'll need to undo my straps."

"Oh, of course." Charity undid the straps on Grace's hands.

"Thank you, Charity," Grace said in a weary voice.

"You're very welcome. You must be terribly worn out. Tell me what you're thinking."

"I'm conflicted, Charity. All I wanted was to have control of my life, and to spare Dylan the trauma of seeing that terrible lifestream. Was that so bad?"

"But you don't feel that way anymore."

"I just want to get back to my life. I want to be with Dylan, as much as I can be."

"Good, good," Charity said, patting Grace's hand. "This is right. You're making the right decision."

Grace smiled weakly. A tear rolled down her cheek. "Thank you. I know I am."

"It's very late, and I know you're tired. We'll talk again in the morning. I'll give you something to help you sleep."

Charity removed a foil envelope from the pocket of her apron. Tearing it open, she removed a small pad with two finger loops on the back, and a plastic seal over a foam pad.

As Charity fumbled with the seal, Grace picked up the teapot and swung it with all her remaining strength, shattering it against Charity's temple. Charity fell sprawled on the floor, clutching her head. The pad fell beside her.

Grace tore at the straps still binding her feet, looking anxiously between her restraints and the woman writhing on the floor. Freed from the straps, she rolled off the bed, grabbed the pad, and removed the plastic seal. She put her knee in the small of Charity's back, holding her down with all of her weight as she pressed the pad against Charity's neck, squeezing tightly, until Charity's struggles ceased.

27

Guest at Large

Grace stepped into the deserted hallway, easing the door closed behind her. The hallway extended ten meters in both directions, with signs at the intersections at either end. To her left:

ADMISSIONS
ADMINISTRATION
COMMISSARY

And to her right, above an arrow, simply:

EXIT

Still wearing blue butterfly pajamas, Grace trotted toward the exit sign, her slippered feet nearly noiseless on the tile floor. She followed the arrow at the end of the hall, down another hallway, its walls lined with doors, to the next intersection, and the next, past door after door. The hallway continued as far as she could see, dozens, perhaps hundreds of doors on either side. After thirty meters or so, Grace stopped. From the ceiling, at every intersection, red lights flashed in time with a blaring horn, accompanied by a voice repeating: *Guest at large—alert, guest at large.*

Grace flattened herself against the wall as random doors opened along the hallway, women in patterned dresses and aprons emerging from each one. Several spotted Grace and started running toward her. Grace sped down the hall at the next intersection, nearly colliding with a woman emerging from a door. Grace evaded her grasp as the number of aproned women began to multiply, cutting off Grace's route to the exit. In a panic, she sprinted for the next intersection, making a skidding turn down what appeared to be a deserted hall, a red EXIT sign glowing in the distance. She slowed as fatigue caught up with her, jogging rather than sprinting, breathing hard, when a hand gripped her arm and pulled her through one of the doors.

Grace stumbled, falling to her knees on the hardwood floor of a room identical to the one where she had just endured nine hours of intervention: the same green wallpaper above a cream-colored wainscot, decorated with the same art, furnished in the same, country-inn style. The woman standing over her looked similar to Charity, about the same age, dressed in an identical patterned dress and apron.

"You'll never get out of here by yourself," the woman said. "You'll need my help."

Grace panted until she'd recovered enough to speak.

"Who are you?"

"My name is Faith. I've been sent by the Eye of Providence."

"What? The Eye? How?"

"I can't explain now. I can get you out of here, but you'll need to do exactly as I say."

Faith poked her head out the door. Grace overheard Faith talking with several other women before closing the door.

"The hallway's clear, but we don't have much time. Get out of those pajamas. They're connected. Once you're out the door, you can be tracked. The slippers, too. You're better off barefoot."

"What'll I wear?"

Faith held out an examination gown of plain cloth that tied in the back. "I tried to get your things but they're locked up. This is the only thing I have that's not connected. It's the best I could do."

Grace stripped out of the pajamas and slipped on the gown.

"Good," Faith said. "They're looking for someone in blue pajamas, so if we run into anyone, keep your head down and let me talk."

Faith led Grace down the hall by the hand. The red lights flashed in time with the horn; the voice repeated the warning of a guest at large.

"Walk in front of me," Faith whispered in Grace's ear, keeping a hand on her arm. The woman guided Grace to the left as they reached the intersection at the end of the hall. Three women were headed their way.

"Have they found the guest?" Faith asked.

"Not yet," one of the three answered. "We don't even know who we're looking for."

"A man in wing six, I heard," Faith said, "an addict I think."

"Okay then. Let's head for six." The woman eyed Grace. "What do you have here?"

"Another addict. I'm taking her to exam."

"Why isn't she in a chair?"

"The alarm went off before they could send the chair. They wanted her in exam immediately, so I'm taking her myself. You know Dr. Shirlaw."

The women exchanged knowing smiles. "Good luck with Shirlaw," they said, hurrying off.

"You lied," Grace whispered. "Won't they find out?"

"Maybe, but I doubt it," the woman said. "This place is so disorganized it'll probably never come up. If it does, I'll deal with it. We need to get you out of here."

Grace and Faith ran into no others on their way to the exit.

"Once I open the door, the alarm will sound," Faith said. "You'll only have a few minutes to get away."

"Why are you helping me?"

"I'm Cloak, and a friend of the Eye. As soon as you were taken to intervention, the Eye knew. He contacted me to get you out." She put her hand on the door's latch. "Move quickly. The Eye will find you." She pushed the door open. The overhead voice changed its announcement, from *guest at large* to *exit door open, wing one—exit door open, wing one.*

"Go!" Faith pushed Grace out the door and slammed it behind her.

Grace was in a narrow alley, a cul-de-sac at one end, an exit to a street at the other. Grace ran to the street, looking in both directions. It was night, the street illuminated by narrow cones of light, from lamps mounted on the walls of black buildings that Grace didn't recognize. She spotted a kiosk—a pedestrian stop for the community transit auto-buses. When she got to the kiosk, she scanned the screen to determine her whereabouts, hopeful that she could find shelter within walking distance. Her spirits fell when she found out where she was—more than an hour's walk from the Cloakroom, the one place where she knew she would be shielded from the Worldstream.

As she studied the map, memorizing the route to the Cloakroom, Grace noticed at the top edge of the screen, in the center, a camera, the All-Seeing Eye of Jahbulon. Grace turned away, hoping that her face hadn't been recognized. Cursing, she started the long walk to the Cloakroom, shivering in her gown, stepping carefully to avoid debris on the sidewalks.

"*Stop, Grace, stop now!*" Grace looked behind her to see two women in aprons and a man in black running in her direction. She bolted down the street, taking only a few steps before her foot came down on a shard of glass. Grace stumbled, nearly falling, pain shooting up her leg. She limped forward, her three pursuers gaining on her, when they were passed by an auto-bus. The next kiosk was twenty meters away.

Every step was a new jolt. The blood flowed profusely now, causing Grace to lose traction. The auto-bus passed her and began to slow, coming to a stop with the kiosk still five meters away. One passenger stepped off the auto-bus. Grace pushed past him, getting onto the step just as the door closed.

"Please scan to pay the fare," the synthesized voice said. Grace was barred from entry by a turnstile, facing a screen with a camera, displaying her face over an icon labeled *Tap Here For Payment.*

"Pay the fare, lady," shouted a passenger, an elderly man in a shabby raincoat. "The bus don't move until you pay or get off. I don't wanna be late for my engagement."

The posse neared the auto-bus, just seconds away. Grace's foot throbbed, and her body ached. As her pursuers approached, Grace tapped the screen.

"Fare collected," the voice said. Grace went through the turnstile as the auto-bus pulled away from the kiosk.

Grace found a seat in the rear of the auto-bus, across from one of the passengers, a seedy-looking man in dreadlocks, who eyed her curiously. Grace wrapped her arms around herself, trying to hide as much of her body as her gown would allow. A thin stream of blood from her foot snaked along the grimy floor.

"Where you comin' from, ma'am?" the dreadlocked man asked. "You sure lookin' cold in dat t'ing."

Grace nodded as she shivered. "Yes. Very cold."

The man reached into a knapsack and pulled out a protein bar. "You lookin' 'ungry also, ma'am. I got somethin' for you."

As Grace reached for the bar, a high-pitched whine sounded, causing the passengers to cover their ears. The screen at the front of the auto-bus blanked its usual display of routes and stops, turning solid red with the word *ALERT* in yellow.

Grace's photo appeared on the screen, next to her name, address and description—*Female, Age: 29 yrs, Height: 163 cm, Weight: 59 kg, Hair: Red, Eyes: Brown*—and below the description, a flashing caption: *Tagged For Apprehension.*

Every eye turned toward Grace.

"What d'you do, ma'am?" dreadlocks asked.

Grace stared at the screen, then at dreadlocks, her eyes wide. "What does that mean, *tagged for apprehension?*"

"It mean Jahbulon know where you are now, ma'am. And if Jahbulon wan' to get you, he goin' to get you."

28

Continue Evasive Maneuvers

"I RECOMMEN' YOU get off here, ma'am," dreadlocks said as the auto-bus slowed to a stop. "Jahbulon only know where you was when you get on."

Grace stood, favoring her injured foot. "Why are you helping me?"

"'Cause Jahbulon's the *man*," said the elderly passenger in the raincoat. "And the *man* don't care about you and me. We're together in this, all us folks, against the *man*."

"Go ma'am, go now," dreadlocks said. He held out the protein bar. "An' take this."

"This too, lady." The old man peeled off his raincoat and tossed it to Grace. "Jah, you're almost naked."

"Thank you," Grace said, pulling on the coat and stuffing the protein bar in a pocket.

"Now, ma'am!"

Grace got off the auto-bus just as the doors closed behind her. She stayed near the buildings, outside the circles of light from the lamps, ducking into alleys and side streets when the community transit auto-buses passed.

Grace slipped into a shadow on hearing the buzz of police drones approaching, standing stock still as the formation passed. She waited as the buzz receded, until it was almost inaudible, before continuing down the street in a limp. Her foot still bled, and it ached worse than ever. She leaned against a wall under a lamp to inspect the wound, a serious cut, two centimeters at least, crusted with dirt.

"Jah," she said, wincing as she pressed a finger into the gash. She was still leaning against the wall, holding her foot, when a lone police drone sped up, too quickly for Grace to react. It stopped a few meters away, training its camera directly at Grace.

Grace hobbled down the street, trailed closely by the drone. Turning a corner, she faced four more drones, hovering in formation. Grace backtracked, running as best she could on the balls of her feet, all five drones joining a single formation.

The drones followed Grace as a sixth, then a seventh drone joined the group. They kept after her for another block before Grace stumbled, sprawling on the sidewalk. The drones parked themselves in a fixed array, hovering motionless, all of their lenses on Grace.

Grace got to her knees, pausing long enough to catch her breath, then stood, facing the drones. They were black, more than fifty centimeters across, each sporting four articulated rotors on spider-like stalks, with a camera and two taser magazines dangling from below. The seven drones maintained a fixed formation, as if waiting for Grace to make the next move. She folded her arms around herself, staring directly into the cameras from under her eyebrows.

"All right, Jahbulon—now what?"

Grace took a step back toward the wall as the drones closed in, breaking formation as if to surround her. The tasers swiveled on their mounts, taking aim. Grace turned her back and covered her head, bracing for the impact, when the drones pivoted, turning away from Grace and toward the street.

The distant noise was unlike anything Grace had ever heard. As it grew louder and closer, Grace guessed that it was the sound of vehicles—not the soft, pleasant rush of auto-buses or personal transports, but a rough sound, like a growl, from deep in the throat, building to a roar as it came near.

There were two of them, and they were big, not like the boxy, two-passenger personal transports, no larger than a kitchen table, but long, low machines, with large, black wheels, looking as if they could hold five or six people each. They skidded to a halt in a cloud of dust and smoke. The roar subsided, settling into a low-pitched rumble.

The doors of the vehicles sprang open. Eight cloaked figures jumped out, all racing to Grace's side, surrounding her, shielding her from the drones' cameras. The drones assumed new positions, expanding their perimeter to encircle both vehicles and the huddle of Cloak.

"Get out of that coat," said the Cloak closest to Grace. "It's connected. Put this on." He handed her a cloak and hood. "Stay in the middle. When I say so, come with me. We're taking you to safety."

Grace dropped the coat, slipping into the cloak and hood.

"Ready?" the Cloak asked. "Let's go."

The huddle split into two groups, the first with Chrysalis in the middle as they piled into one of the vehicles, and the second boarding the other vehicle.

Chrysalis sat wedged between two Cloak in the back seat. One gripped her left arm.

"Hang on," he said.

Chrysalis's head was thrown back as the vehicle took off. The second vehicle spun in a circle, heading in the opposite direction, its wheels squealing, throwing up more dust and smoke.

"What is this thing?" Chrysalis said over the roar of the vehicle's engine.

"It's a car," said the driver, "a fossil-fueled vehicle. Completely disconnected. It's a blast, huh?"

"Who are you?"

"That's Jayla," said the Cloak on Chrysalis's left, pointing to the driver. He pointed to the passenger in the shotgun position, then the other passenger in the back seat. "Speranza and Fidelio."

"Who are *you?*" Chrysalis asked the Cloak on her left.

"You know me, Chrysalis. I'm called the Eye of Providence."

Fidelio shouted to Speranza, "How many did we get?"

"Four bugs," came the reply. "Three went the other way."

"Bugs? What are you talking about?" Chrysalis shouted.

"Drones," said Fidelio. "You had seven drones on you. We got four, car two got the rest. That's a good sign. It means the drones don't know which car you're in."

"Where are we going?"

"We're going for a ride."

The street was straight and unobstructed, but in poor repair. The driver accelerated, swerving to miss potholes and buckled pavement, not always succeeding. Chrysalis was bounced off the seat at every bump, her head hitting the ceiling more than once. She was thrown forward and to the right as the car decelerated and made a sharp left turn.

"Here's where we lose them," Jayla said. "Better get a grip."

The car was in a narrow alley in even worse shape than the street. The noise from the engine rose and fell, alternately rumbling and whining, reverberating off the walls as Jayla negotiated the obstacle course, the engine noise punctuated by a metallic thud each time the car sideswiped a dumpster. The car shot out of the alley onto a broad street, making a skidding turn. An auto-bus blocked the way. Jayla turned hard to the left, fishtailing into the auto-bus, overturning it. The impact threw the back seat passengers against the door.

"Jahbulon-a-ding-dong!" Speranza yelled. "That made a dent."

"Sperz, don't worry about the damn car," shouted Jayla. "Did we lose the bugs?"

Speranza leaned out the window, craning his neck to see behind the car. "Nope. There's still four on us. Continue evasive maneuvers."

Jayla stood on the accelerator as the street sloped away. Chrysalis was weightless for a split second as the car lost contact with the pavement, until the car touched down, bottoming out its suspension, bringing Chrysalis down into the seat with a bone-jarring thump. The car turned left, down a street between two residential buildings.

"Looky here," cried Jayla, "shippers. A bunch of 'em. This ought to be good."

A half-dozen commercial delivery drones hovered between the buildings, some empty, some with their payloads still on board. Both the commercial drones and the police drones scattered like frightened birds. One police drone clipped a commercial drone, disabling both, sending them crashing into the building, their remnants showering down on the sidewalk.

"One bug down, three to go," Speranza shouted. "Somebody's going to miss their merchandise tonight."

The street continued to descend, reaching its lowest point as it crossed a river. The bridge, an iron framework structure more than a century old, barely accommodated two narrow lanes. Over the entrance, in faded and flaking paint, was a warning: *LOW CLEARANCE: 9'-9"*.

"With any luck," said Speranza, "we'll swat another bug or two here."

Again, the police drones broke formation, losing altitude, attempting to duck under the overhead beam. Two of them made it; the third crashed at full velocity into the girder, disintegrating in a flash and a cascade of sparks.

"We're going to take one or two into the garage with us," Speranza said. "Ducky. I like a good scrape as much as the next guy, but I'm not looking forward to having my ass lit up with fifty thousand volts."

The car made a final turn into an alley, the car's headlights casting their beam onto a far wall—a solid wall, it appeared, with no opening—a dead end.

The two remaining drones tailed the car at low altitude, not more than five meters behind. The car sped up.

"What are you doing?" Chrysalis cried. "There's no way out!"

The Eye leaned close. "It'll be all right. Watch."

When the wall was less than twenty meters away, a door

with a faux brick facade slid to one side with unbelievable speed, revealing an entrance, barely larger than the car, glowing in reddish-orange light. Jayla applied the brakes just as the car cleared the door. The door slid shut as quickly as it had opened as the car skidded to a halt.

They were in a large room, fifteen or more meters wide and deep, and five meters high. Chrysalis saw three bays, each with a massive cylinder rising from the floor, supporting a rack, like a giant letter X. One of the racks was flush with the floor; the other two were raised, each supporting a vehicle, a car, like the ones that had come for Grace. Tools and parts, containers and hoses, on carts or on the floor, were scattered around each rack. The room was brightly lit from overhead lights, pure white, but everything had an orange cast to it, the result of light reflected from the copper screen lining the walls.

"How many?" the Eye asked.

"Two," Speranza said. "They both made it through the door."

"Jah," Jayla said. "Where are they?"

"Opposite corners. Two o'clock and eight o'clock."

"What's happening?" Chrysalis asked.

The Eye let go of Chrysalis's arm. "You're safe now, Chrysalis. You're among friends."

Chrysalis looked around the car.

"You four and four more in the other car know who I am, not only Chrysalis, but Grace. So, it's true what they told me in intervention. Not even the Cloak can hide."

"Yes, we know who you are," the Eye said. "But you're safe. I won't give you away, and these others can't."

"Why not?"

"They're not Cloak. They're Shade."

Chrysalis looked around the car. "Really?"

"That's the truth," said Jayla. "We're all in the Eye's crew, outside the 'stream."

"Crew?"

"I sponsor them," the Eye said. "They provide services that I resell in the connected world."

"What's it like," Chrysalis asked Jayla, "being Shade?"

"We'd love to chat," Jayla said, "but there're two bugs out there charging up their tasers. That's priority one."

"Stay in the car, Chrysalis," the Eye said. "We need to clear the space. The drones are inside the Faraday cage now, cut off from the mother ship. They're operating on their own. Self-preservation, that's their programming. When we exit the car, those drones will try to take us out."

Jayla and Speranza pulled off their hoods, revealing their masks, whole-head coverings, like the anonymous woman Chrysalis had met at the Cloakroom. Like the woman's, their masks were also brightly colored, blue and purple, and richly decorated in gold filigree. They replaced their cloaks with vests of a heavy copper mesh, and donned face shields with voice synthesizers.

"Ready?" Jayla said. "Three…two…one…"

The two burst out of the car, slamming the doors behind them, running in opposite directions. Chrysalis heard a series of explosive sounds—*pop, pop, pop*—as each of the runners was struck by self-contained taser rounds, four or five each, sending a burst of sparks as they struck the metallized vests. Speranza took a round in the leg, sending him to the ground in an induced fit.

"Don't move from the car," the Eye told Chrysalis, as he and Fidelio pulled weapons, what looked like long guns, from under the seat. They opened their doors and took aim at the hovering drones.

The taser rounds continued to rain in, the rounds ricocheting off the car with frightening *zaps*. A round struck Jayla in the shoulder, disabling him.

"Fire now," the Eye commanded. The guns shot nets that ensnared the drones, bringing them to the ground, unharmed. The Eye ran to one drone, then the other, removing their power and data memory modules. Once the drones were disabled, he tended to Jayla, as Fidelio went to help Speranza.

"Jayla will recover," the Eye shouted. "How's Speranza?"

"No permanent damage," said Fidelio. "He didn't get it in

the ass, but close." He stood up. "Chrysalis, you can come out now. All clear."

Chrysalis stepped slowly out of the car. She went to the Eye, kneeling beside the disabled Jayla. He was just coming to with a moan, lying next to the taser round where the Eye had dropped it.

"I hate these bugs," the Eye said. "The civil authorities buy them by the truckload, cheap and expendable. The only good thing about them is, they're not very accurate, and they only carry eight rounds apiece. They rely on numbers to lay down a barrage of fire."

"Will you get rid of them?"

"We can't. Before these bugs entered the Faraday cage, they reported our position. We'll reprogram their memory cartridges with false information and release them. Until we do, Jahbulon knows you're either here or at garage two. You're in greater danger than ever."

29

Not Completely Legitimate

"How did you find me?"

Chrysalis sat with the Eye of Providence in a room off the garage, a windowless cube less than three meters on a side, empty except for two chairs and a table. Fidelio stayed in the main room, tending to Jayla and Speranza, still recovering from their taser hits. The Eye took Chrysalis into the tiny room, having given orders for the drone memory modules to be reprogrammed within the hour.

"Once you were discovered missing from the intervention facility, you were tagged for apprehension. Your identity was broadcast to the Worldstream. As soon as you scanned into the auto-bus, the All-Seeing Eye knew your location. Your wanted poster popped up on the auto-bus screen to alert the other passengers."

"But how did *you* know?"

"Fidelio and the rest were monitoring your status. As soon as you were tagged, we knew. When you scanned in, you gave away your location, both to us and to the drones. Then we tracked the overcoat. The drones knew nothing about the overcoat—that was a connection we made on our own. It gave us the head start we needed."

"I don't understand. How's that possible if the Shade aren't connected to the Worldstream?"

"To be a Shade simply means that your lifestream, and *all* your life data, has been removed from the Worldstream—shredded. The Shade still have access to the Worldstream. They take precautions, of course, to avoid being discovered, but they *have* to have access. That's how they make their living."

"Making a living—I've been thinking about that a lot. Tell me how that works."

"We provide a range of services, but for the most part, we augment artificial intelligence algorithms in the Worldstream. Your tag for apprehension is a perfect example. Most times, the Worldstream doesn't take special notice of anyone. It's simply a giant data dump, recording every image, word and datum from every connected device. But when they have a reason, the civil authorities can create tags that trigger AI algorithms in the Worldstream. If you're *tagged for location*, the algorithms trace your movements, keeping you in sight. Jahbulon will raise an alarm if you're not where you're supposed to be, but otherwise, the process is completely automated. You've been tagged for location for years."

"*Me?* Why?"

"Since you started with State Live Services. They tag all state employees for location. It's standard procedure. And I can tell you, they haven't been too happy with you lately. Every time you put on the cloak, they lose track. It leaves big gaps in your data stream."

"Good," Chrysalis said. "To hell with them. But what does this have to do with the Shade?"

"As I said, the location algorithms are automated. But a *tag for apprehension* kicks it to the next level. The Worldstream starts channeling data differently, correlating it, interpolating your position, piping it to the appropriate resources to take action. In your case, they dispatched the drones. That's *mostly* automated. But the algorithms, as good as they are, have shortcomings. Human operators are used to supplement the AI algorithms, to fill in the gaps."

"That's what your Shade do. It's no surprise that they can tap into the Worldstream."

"You understand."

"Yes, I get it. I've been tagged for location for years, and I was tagged for apprehension today. I wonder what I have to look forward to. Are those the only kinds of tags?"

"Hardly. A tag of *hue and cry* is the ultimate—the Worldstream throws massive effort into finding, apprehending, and, if necessary, disabling the target. That consumes a huge number of resources."

"Including your crew. But I don't understand why the authorities would use the Shade's services. Aren't the Shade outlaws?"

"Most of the human operators are in the connected world, but the Shade are a cost-effective alternative. Not completely legitimate, but where credits are concerned, businesses are willing to bend the rules—even the authorities."

"And what do the Shade get out of it?"

"They get protection from discovery. They get food and shelter. They get to live."

"Food and shelter? Is that all? It's practically slavery."

"I pay them a stipend. Look, every one of my Shade has chosen to work for me. They can stop any time they want."

"Can they? Their options are kind of limited."

The Eye shook his head. "That's the life they chose when they joined the Shade. And their options aren't so limited. There's plenty of work to go around. I have a good crew because I take care of them. They know that if they go somewhere else, they could be worse off."

"But you're profiting from their work."

"Like any business owner."

"Don't you think this is different?"

The Eye stood, crossing his arms. "Don't judge me, Chrysalis. My clients get quality services at low prices, my Shade get a comfortable life outside of the Worldstream, and I get credits. Everybody wins. This is how I make my living. Remember, if it hadn't been for me and my crew, you'd be back in the intervention facility right now, facing criminal charges for assault."

Chrysalis sat silently for a moment. "I can't dispute that. And I can't go back. I need to get out now." Chrysalis stood, putting her hand on the Eye's arm. "Can you hide me? With the Shade?"

"Impossible. We can't accept anyone whose lifestream is still intact. The risk of discovery is too great. Before you can join the Shade, you *must* shred your lifestream."

"It's taking longer than expected. Apparently, my lifestream is massive. And the shredder wants more credits."

"Raúl, you mean."

"Yes. The amount he quoted won't cover it. I've deposited almost everything I have in a cryptocurrency account. It won't be enough."

"Then you have a few options. You can find the credits somewhere, depending on how much you need. Or you can give up your plans to disconnect and stay in the Worldstream —but your escape from the intervention facility has made that a less attractive choice."

"That's not too helpful, I'm afraid."

"Or, you can go to Raúl and negotiate. He's in it for the money. He might be willing to come down in price rather than risk losing the business."

"Do you think that will work?"

"I've known Raúl for years. He's insufferable, but he's reasonable."

"All right. Thank you." The sound of a yawn came from Chrysalis's synthesizer. "Is there a place here that I can lie down for a few hours?"

"You can't stay here. This place is for the Shade."

"Where will I go?"

"I can't help you, Chrysalis. You'll have to leave. But you may keep the cloak and hood. You'll need them."

❖ ❖ ❖

"Has she gone?" the Eye asked Speranza. The Shade was inspecting the exterior of the car for damage, standing for the first time since his taser hit.

"Out the door," Speranza said, looking up from a fender. "So, that was Grace."

The Eye nodded. "Is she what you expected?"

"Sure. After all the time I've spent on her, I feel like I know her."

The Eye looked at the door through which Chrysalis had passed moments earlier.

"You may *think* you know her," the Eye said. "But you don't. Trust me, you don't."

Chrysalis resigned herself to walking the streets until daybreak, hoping to avoid detection. Her cloak provided little warmth in the early morning hours, as the wind picked up and the temperature fell dangerously low. She sought shelter where she could find it, ducking into doorways or side alleys whenever the police drones passed. She thought it best to keep moving, to keep warm, and to stay alert to possible detection, but fatigue overcame her and she found a spot, hidden from the streets, where she could nap. As she settled in, beginning to nod off, a thought brought her back to full wakefulness: *How did the Eye know that I work for the state?*

30

LA CASA RAÚL

THE RISING SUN was a welcome sight to Chrysalis after five hours wandering the streets, making her way back from the Shade garage to more familiar surroundings. She'd spent an hour, maybe two, behind a dumpster, shivering in fitful sleep. She dared not go to Grace's apartment; with a tag of apprehension open against her, the premises would certainly be under observation. Instead, she went to Raúl.

"What? What?" Raúl's scratchy voice came through the door speaker. "Jah, announce yourself, Cloak."

"I'm called Chrysalis."

"Jahbulon in a can, Chrys. What in hell are you doing here this time of day?"

"Something's happened. I need your help."

"If you didn't have reason to disconnect before, you do now."

Raúl sat sprawled in his chair amid his command center of screens, wearing a knit shirt and shorts, just out of bed, his silver hair knotted and tangled. He listened as Chrysalis described the previous twenty-four hours—Grace's ordeal at the intervention facility, her escape, and her rescue by the Eye of Providence. He didn't speak, but his expressive face registered variously disbelief, astonishment, and amusement.

"You're a gutsy lady, Chryssy. Bad judgment, though. You've managed to get yourself into an authentic, Real Life predicament."

"I know. I can't go back to my life. I need to disconnect now."

"A slight issue with that plan. You're short on funds. Another two hundred thousand credits, I think, on top of the nine hundred thousand you've banked."

"I need for you to come down on your price. I've held back about fifty thousand credits. I'll add it to the account, if I can figure out how to do it without giving myself away."

"So, you want me to pull the trigger for another fifty thousand—*if* you can get it." Raúl wagged his head. "My costs are ballooning through the roof, and my crawler's still working, not even ninety percent done. Sorry, little sister, I can't do it. I need the whole amount."

"The Eye said you might be willing to bargain."

"Oh, the *Eye* said that. Easy for him to say. He's not the one doing the work."

"If it's not enough, I'll just have to call it off."

"Don't bluff me, Chrys. You don't have that option anymore, not after braining Aunt Charity with a teapot. Disconnection or correction—those are your choices."

"Raúl, we've got to come to an agreement. I just don't have the credits."

"Jah. Look, I couldn't shred you now, even if you had the credits. It'll take at least another day for the crawler to finish. That's how long you have to come up with the rest."

"I'll try."

"Do that, Chrys, try hard. And while you're searching for credits, think about how you're going to support yourself outside of the Worldstream."

"Yes, that. I haven't given that a lot of thought."

"*Ha!*" Raúl laughed, almost sneering. "It's a little late in the process to start making your plans. Do you know what you're in for?"

"I think so. The Eye told me about his Shade crew, and how they live. He provides."

"Oh, then you're a coder? A programmer? A data analyst, maybe?"

"I work at a state agency. I help people with live services."

"Yeah, I know where you work. And I doubt very much that the Eye has a spot in his organization for someone with *people skills*." Raúl went to where Chrysalis was sitting. He bent over her, resting his hands on the arms of Chrysalis's chair. "When I said, 'pull the trigger,' that was more than an expression. Do you know what a gun is? Not a taser, not a non-lethal device that gives you a little shock, but a Real Life, old school firearm? That shoots *bullets?* That *kill?* When I shred you, you'll be dead, just as surely as if I'd pressed the barrel of a gun against your head and pulled the trigger. Except it's worse. The dead have no pain. Their troubles are over. The Shade are not the Dear Departed. Their hell is *real.*"

"Please step away," Chrysalis said. "You're scaring me."

"Tough love, Chrys. You need to know what lies ahead. In the Shade world, you are a nameless, faceless *nothing*. There are few goods and no credits to buy them with. What you get depends on what you give, or what you *take*. What do you have to bargain with? What do you have that's worth *anything?*"

"Everything I have is in the account. There isn't anything else. But I've had nothing before and I scrapped my way back. So, maybe I'm not a programmer. Maybe I don't have any valuable skills. But I'm past the point of no return."

Raúl stood up straight. He ran his hands through his hair, pulling it behind his head. "No skills? I've ridden your lifestream, and I can say for certain, you *have* skills. Think, Chrys. What industry has thrived through every age and every bust and boom? What's the oldest commodity, the object of the first barter in human prehistory, of which the supply will always be limited, and for which the demand will always be insatiable?"

"Oh, Jah. If you think I'd prostitute myself…"

"You wouldn't be the first. When your choice is survival or starvation, do you really think you won't make that choice?"

"Step *away!*" Chrysalis shouted. Raúl stumbled backwards as Chrysalis stood up, too quickly for one sleep-deprived and unfed. Her vision went dark as she collapsed at Raúl's feet.

Grace awoke in a bed, wearing her cloak, but not her hood. As her head cleared, she noticed a delicious aroma, warm and thick enough to taste. She rolled over to see Raúl in a chair next to the bed, and a steaming dish on the nightstand.

"What's that?"

"Eggs," Raúl said. "Scrambled. And coffee. I don't have any of that fancy herbal tea you like."

Grace sat up, dangling her feet over the side of the bed. She brought a forkful of eggs to her mouth. She was quite sure that she had never tasted anything as wonderful.

"Does *everyone* know about the rooibos tea?"

"There are no secrets to one who knows where to look. I thought you'd learned that by now."

"I get it." She sipped the coffee. "Where's my hood?"

Raúl held up the hood, hanging limply from his hand. "No need for concern. This place is impervious to the All-Seeing Eye. And I already know who you are." He dropped the hood on the bed. "There's something about meeting someone in Real Life that can't be duplicated in Virtual Reality. You're an attractive woman."

Grace sighed. "Thanks. I guess."

"While you were slumbering so peacefully, I gave your situation some thought. Your credit situation."

"Can you lower your price?"

"Not exactly. I have another idea, related to our previous conversation, you know, about making a living. Maybe we can work something out." Raúl grinned. "A sort of 'payment in kind' arrangement."

"You are loathsome."

"Let's see how loathsome you think I am when you're back here, after the crawler's done."

Grace scraped the remains of the eggs off the plate. "Thank you for the food. And the coffee. That was very kind of you."

"All part of the service at La Casa Raúl." He picked up the hood. "But I'm afraid it's checkout time. Give me two more days to finish the crawl. Then let me know how you want to settle the bill."

Grace pulled on the hood. "I'll get the credits," Chrysalis said. "So, don't start fantasizing about 'payment in kind.'"

Raúl laughed out loud. "I like you Chrys. I don't want to see you get hurt. Take care of yourself. I'll see you in a couple of days."

Chrysalis paused by the door. "Have you found out who my weaver is?"

"Oh, that," Raúl mumbled. "No. Whoever he is, he's one devious bastard. Not only did he manage to weave the most detailed, vividly rendered lifestream I've ever seen—and those *emotions*, Jah, it's brilliant—but he left no tracks, at least, none that I've found yet."

"*Will* you find him?"

"I'm trying everything under the book. The clues may be buried ten layers deep, behind fifteen levels of indirection, but they're there. I'll find him. Just give me time."

"I thought you understood," Chrysalis said. "I'm out of time."

31

COMPROMISE OF OUR PRINCIPLES

SHOPS WERE CLOSED at mid-morning, when the streets were deserted—not even police drones patrolled in numbers at this hour. Chrysalis limped along, grateful for the first aid and the shoes that Raúl had provided—disconnected shoes, he'd assured her—ill-fitting as they were. She wondered how sophisticated the AI algorithms were, the ones triggered by a tag for apprehension, and if they were capable of deducing that a lone Cloak, of Grace's size and shape, favoring one foot, could be the subject of the tag. The occasional drone passed her by without slowing down. She took that as a good sign.

There was no line at the Cloakroom, and no attendant. Chrysalis knocked on the door, softly at first, then harder. After the fourth try, the door opened. A Cloak poked his head out.

"Are you meeting someone?" the attendant asked. "Because I'm the only one here. We usually don't get single visitors at this time of day."

"I'm alone. Will that be a problem?"

"No, no. There are no rules. But I need to get the scanner. Wait here."

Chrysalis paced the anteroom, glancing frequently down the passage to the street, the only way in or out. It would be easy for two police agents, or even one, to block her escape.

"Got it," the attendant said, appearing in the doorway. "Hold still." He passed the scanner over Chrysalis as usual, head to foot, side to side.

"All clear. Now, if you'll just press your fingers to the screen."

"What? I've never done that before."

"It's temporary. I see you're not wearing gloves. Just place your fingers here."

"My gloves are back in my apartment. What do you mean, temporary?"

The attendant tapped the screen and held it up. It displayed Grace's photo and details, a miniature version of the screen on the auto-bus. "There's an active tag out for apprehension. Until the tag is closed, we need a finger scan."

"But you'll be able to identify me. I come here so I *won't* be identified."

"I know it's not our usual procedure, but we can't be liable for harboring a fugitive. We're not happy about it, but it's one thing we do to avoid being harassed by the authorities—we agree not to admit parties who are known or suspected to've committed an infraction, and they ignore whatever goes on inside the Cloakroom. We got this tag from the authorities this morning."

"I don't like this."

"Neither do we. It's a compromise of our principles, but what can we do? We have to be practical. You shouldn't worry. We don't record your finger scan. If you haven't been tagged, nothing will happen, and we'll purge the scan. No harm done."

"And if I *am* the target of the tag?"

"Then Jahbulon will know exactly where you are."

Chrysalis stared at the screen, still showing Grace's picture. She looked down the corridor to the street.

"I'd rather not."

"Then we can't admit you." The attendant studied the

screen. He looked at Chrysalis, estimating height and weight as best he could under the cloak. "Look, um…" He held up the screen. "I don't know your situation. There's nothing here about *why* this tag was opened. Honestly, it's no concern of mine. But I can't let you in."

"All right," Chrysalis said, starting down the passageway.

"Good luck," the attendant said. "One more thing you should know: as long as there's a tag for apprehension open on you, no Cloak will take you in."

32

Shelter for the Indigent

"This is a shelter for the indigent, under the eye of Jahbulon. The Cloak are not allowed."

Chrysalis stood in front of a table strewn with printed flyers promoting state-funded services, from shelters to medical care. She drew stares from street people ranging in age from pre-teen to elderly, seated in a dining area filled with randomly scattered tables, with a makeshift serving line at the far end. Nearly every table was occupied as the shelter residents ate their noontime meal, entertained by a wall screen, playing music selected for its calming effect, which the diners ignored. When Chrysalis entered, they all looked up from their dinner plates at the first Cloak that anyone had ever seen inside the shelter. A few muttered disapprovals; most simply bent over their plates and went back to eating.

It was the third homeless shelter that Chrysalis had tried. She'd heard the same thing at each one: *no Cloak allowed.* They'd even used the exact same phrase—*this is a shelter for the indigent, under the eye of Jahbulon*—as if it had been part of their orientation, drilled into the mind of every shelter volunteer.

"Please," Chrysalis begged, "I'm injured. I just need a place to rest for a few hours."

"We're funded by the state, citizen," said the harried-looking woman behind the table. "We have strict rules. Every person in this shelter has voluntarily given us their name, their next of kin, medical data, even dietary needs. We cannot care properly for our charges if they withhold information from us. If you'll remove your cloak and register your name and information, we'll be happy to accommodate you. As you can see, we're serving lunch. There's still time."

"Thank you, but I can't." Chrysalis turned to leave, hoping the next shelter would be staffed by volunteers who had not been as rigorously trained.

"Wait," the woman said. "I can give you something, bread, or something to drink."

"Some water. That would be very kind of you."

The woman trotted to the serving line. Chrysalis watched as she asked the server, pointing in her direction. The server shook his head. A brief argument followed, ending with the server handing her a cup of water.

"Here you go," the woman said, offering the cup. "Don't blame the server. He's a little hard-nosed about the rules, but his heart is good."

"Thank you." Chrysalis lifted her hood to drink as she took the cup.

The soft music in the dining hall was interrupted by a piercing whine; the wall screen stopped scrolling images and instead displayed a yellow *ALERT* in block letters on a red background. The whine continued intermittently as Grace's photo and data appeared on the screen.

The woman at the table reacted with a start as her wrist screen alerted her. It displayed the same bulletin: Grace's photo and description, scrolling across the tiny screen, ending with the words *Tagged For Apprehension*.

"The cup," the woman. "It can read your fingerprints. As long as you have it, it'll give you away." She took the cup back. "You have to leave."

"You're not going to hold me here?"

"Sister, we get people here all the time that are tagged. We can't admit them to the shelter, but we're not going to do

Jahbulon's work for him."

"Thank you."

"Go now! The drones are already on their way, and I'm sure the agents of Jahbulon are too. Go!"

Chrysalis left the building, looking both ways down the street. Foot traffic had increased in the early afternoon, still sparse, but offering Chrysalis some hope that she could lose herself in one of the rare knots of pedestrians. She walked as quickly as she could, trying not to appear injured. As she came upon a group of three people, she looked behind her long enough to see a fleet of drones, four, she counted, hovering above the entrance to the shelter. They were accompanied by two agents in black, one standing outside, scanning the vicinity, the other going into the shelter. He came out less than a minute later, his pocket screen in hand. He gave the screen a single tap. The drones flew higher, reaching twenty meters or so, before splitting up to establish surveillance locations at each end of the block. From that altitude, the drones had an unobstructed view of the entire street.

Chrysalis stayed with the group of three as they passed an alley entrance. Chrysalis broke away into the alley, jogging, the pain in her foot having subsided to a tolerable ache. She'd trotted nearly halfway to the opposite end of the alley when she stopped, checking to see if her evasion had worked. She held her breath for five seconds, then ten, before she exhaled with relief. She was walking toward the far end of the alley when the sound of two police drones reached her ears, their characteristic buzz focused and amplified by the alley walls.

Chrysalis picked up speed as the drones closed in. They caught up with her just as she reached the street. She turned left, sprinting now, insensitive to the pain in her foot, the drones making a banking turn to intercept her. Her mind raced to think of something, some tactic that could foil the drones—outrunning them was clearly impossible—when another thought occurred to her: *This place looks familiar.* She stopped, pressing her body against the brick wall of a building. The drones took up their positions, with Chrysalis in the crossfire. Two more drones shot out of the alley and joined the formation.

Chrysalis saw it—a nondescript shop, with a curtained window and a door with a plaque of tarnished brass. She pushed herself off the wall, running at top speed, crossing the street just as the drones reacted, turning to follow. Four taser rounds narrowly missed her, two caroming off the shop windows, two others embedding themselves in the door just as Chrysalis burst through it, slamming it behind her.

Chrysalis hung from the doorknob as she looked around. The room was filled with Cloak, at least eight, standing among the merchandise, all of them stopping their browsing to see the source of the commotion. A bald, thin-faced man in a tunic stood at a kiosk by the far wall, a look somewhere between confusion and irritation on his face.

"Hello," the man said. "I'm Gavin. Welcome to the Faraday Cage."

33

PETTY ACTS OF DISSENT

CHRYSALIS AND GAVIN sat in the back room of The Faraday Cage. Chrysalis had her foot elevated, resting on a stool cushioned by a folded cloak as she drank from a bottle of water, the first refreshment she'd had since she left Raúl.

"As soon as you touched that cup, they knew your location," Gavin explained. "Once you left the shelter, you were the only Cloak on the street, and you fled down an alley, *and* you were sporting a limp. You had two agents after you, who, by the way, are in the front of our shop right now, doing a finger scan on all of our customers. It was the agents who figured you out and set the bugs on you."

"Any suggestions you have would be welcome," Chrysalis said.

"Not to worry. My sister Constance is handling the agents. And there are eight Cloak out there, all of whom are willing to swear that they were at the shelter ten minutes ago and they'll fake a limp to prove it."

"Thank you. You're about the sixth or seventh person to help me in the last twenty-four hours."

"Oh, please. You're doing *us* a service. In the brave new world of the All-Seeing Eye, we all have to commit our petty

182

acts of dissent whenever we can. Those Cloak out there couldn't be happier to flip a finger at Jahbulon."

There came a knock at the door. Constance stood in the doorway, her hand on her hip. "They're gone. But they left the bugs behind." She looked at Chrysalis. "Those bugs aren't going anywhere as long as they think you're in here."

"Bugs can't tell one Cloak from another," Gavin said. "We'll deputize every Cloak in the store as a decoy. Those bugs will be so confused they won't know whether to fly or stay put."

"If they start to run low on power, they'll call for reinforcements. They can hold out as long as we can."

"Seriously, Constance, you worry too much." Gavin went into the shop, motioning to Chrysalis and Constance to follow him.

"Citizens, we have a situation," Gavin said. "Our friend here has been tagged for apprehension. She needs to find a safe harbor. She can't go to the Cloakroom, the shelters won't have her, and I can't put her up here. The agents are gone, but they left their pesky bugs outside. Not only can our friend not risk being tailed by a squadron of police bugs, but they're noisy, and having them hovering in front of the shop is bad for business. I need volunteers to create a diversion and get those bugs off of our friend's tail. The plan is to send you out one by one and let the bugs follow you to parts unknown. There are four bugs and eight of you. If you're willing, raise your hand."

Eight Cloak volunteered.

By late afternoon, Chrysalis's limp had disappeared. Walking normally, amid a growing number of Cloak on the street, she was able to avoid attracting the attention of the police drones. With a fresh pair of gloves, a gift from Gavin, she hoped to avoid detection by a fingerprint scan. Relatively safe from the tag for apprehension, Chrysalis headed to the one remaining place where she might find help.

Chrysalis was a half-hour's walk from Edward's apartment. Although she hoped that Edward wasn't under surveillance, she couldn't be certain. But she was out of options. It was a risk she had to take.

"Grace, is that you?" Edward's voice asked via the intercom on his apartment door.

"I'm called Chrysalis. May I come in?"

"Wait there."

Chrysalis heard the bolts being withdrawn. The door opened a few centimeters.

"Chrysalis," Edward whispered. "You have to leave."

"Edward, I need help. I need credits. The shredder needs more credits to finish."

"You really have to leave."

"Please, can you help me?"

Edward glanced back into the apartment. "How much do you need?"

"It's a lot, Edward. And I probably won't be able to pay you back."

"How much?"

"Two hundred thousand."

"Oh, Jah."

"Please, help me. Can you?"

"I have it. You know I'd do anything for you. But… Chrysalis…Grace…you have to leave, now."

"Here's the account." She handed Edward a slip of paper. "It's a cryptocurrency account."

Edward took the paper. "I'll try, but go. You have to go. Chrysalis, the authorities are on their way. They know you're here."

"How do they know? Are you being watched?"

"No. You were reported."

"Edward…Daddy…you didn't."

"Oh, Grace." Edward blinked the tears from his eyes as he opened the door. Joan and Donna stood in the room, by the wall screen displaying Grace's picture.

Chrysalis turned and fled down the hallway. She ran into two agents at the building entrance. One took her arm while

the other brandished a sedative pad.
"We can do this either way," the agent said. "Your choice."

34

MITIGATING CIRCUMSTANCES

THE ROOM HAD no green walls decorated with landscapes and woodland scenes, no cream-colored wainscot, no bouquet of carnations and irises. The bed was a cot, the nightstand a steel table, bolted to the floor. A steel bench mounted on the wall was the only place to sit. The air was cool, almost cold, smelling not of flowers and spices, but of the disinfectant used to clean the painted concrete floor.

Grace'd had no visit from a matronly facilitator in a patterned dress and apron; she was not offered herbal tea. She was not in flannel pajamas with a butterfly pattern, but in a one-piece orange suit, too big for her body. There was no need for restraints; the door was made of steel plate, locked securely, with a twenty-centimeter viewport.

As far as Grace knew, this was not an intervention facility that handled addicts, or misguided souls intending to commit illegal acts, but a confinement facility that dealt with actual criminals. When the lights went out, she turned in her cot, eyes open, seeing little in the dim light leaking through the tiny opening in the door, until she fell asleep for a few restless hours.

"Prisoner," a voice said through the viewport, "get out of

186

the rack. Sit on the cot, feet flat on the floor, hands on top of your head."

Once Grace had complied, the bolt on the door slid open, and two guards entered, both women, in the black uniform of the correctional authority. One held a tray with thin oatmeal in a steel bowl and coffee in a steel cup, warm, but not hot.

"Prisoner, begin."

Grace looked up at the guard. "Begin eating?"

"Yes, eating," the guard snorted. "And be quick. You have a visitor. Your counselor."

"Counselor? You mean a lawyer?"

"Eat."

Grace ate her breakfast under the observation of her guards, resuming the position when done, seated on the cot, feet on the floor, hands on her head.

"You will have thirty minutes. Counselor, you can enter."

The woman who came through the door carried a bag as large as the old-style suitcases people used when travel was popular. Grace *thought* she recognized her, but she looked different than she did the last time they'd met IRL. The woman was older; her hair was short, not even shoulder-length, instead of the long ponytail Grace remembered, and which the woman's avatar had retained.

"Madeleine?"

"Hello, Grace. Guards, you can leave us now."

❖ ❖ ❖

"I was expecting a lawyer," Grace said.

"I'm your psychological counselor. Since you're already one of my patients, I put in a request to State Health Services to handle your case."

"Why do I have a psychological counselor? I need a lawyer."

Madeleine pulled a personal screen from her bag. She tapped it a few times, pulling up Grace's case file. She read directly from the screen.

"Grace, we'll discuss your actions from the other day in detail. Our goal is to understand your motivation for assaulting one of our facilitators and evading the authorities, so that we can resolve your issues and realign you with societal norms."

"Why are you talking like that? You already know my motivation. You make it sound like I'm a social deviant. Why haven't I been charged?"

Madeleine set the tablet aside. "You won't be charged with a crime."

"Is our conversation privileged? Confidential?"

"Yes, of course. Anything you say to me is between us and can't be entered into evidence. I've been assured that there are no monitors in this cell."

"All right, then. I knocked out the facilitator with a teapot. I drugged her so I could escape the facility." Grace looked down at the floor. "Charity. That's her name. How is she? Is she all right?"

"A mild concussion. She'll recover."

"I assaulted her. How can I *not* be charged?"

Madeleine picked up the tablet. "The state recognizes mitigating circumstances, stemming from personal trauma associated with situational factors."

"Madeleine, put that thing down. Tell me what's going on."

Madeleine put the tablet back in her bag. "Your mother, Joan, used her influence to get the charges dropped."

"Lovely. Having a felon in the family is too great a scandal for Mother, what with all of our connections in the Worldstream. Does that mean I can get out of here?"

"Yes, but with conditions."

Grace pulled herself to the edge of her cot. "Okay. Let's hear them."

"First, reparations will be paid to the victim in the amount of two hundred thousand credits, for which you will be responsible."

Grace slumped forward. "I'll need some time to get it."

"We understand, but you'll need to transfer the credits

within twenty-four hours. Second, you are to remain connected to the Worldstream at all times. No more Cloak. If you disconnect for even a short time, that will open a tag for apprehension."

"Of course. What else?"

"You'll check in with me IRL, three times a week. I've arranged for these sessions to be private—unmonitored. If you miss a session, you'll be tagged."

"Is that all?"

"You'll be reinstated at State Live Services, on a probationary basis. Unfortunately, you'll be docked for the missed time."

"That's only fair. When do we start?"

"We'll process you out of here immediately. Go straight back to your apartment. Our first session is this afternoon." Madeleine stood up from the bench. "Of course, the state knows now about your plans to disconnect. In light of your actions, you'll be under greater scrutiny than ever." She put her hand on Grace's shoulder. "Grace, I'm still here for you. You know I'm on your side. I know how distraught you are over your lifestream, and how you feel about strangers riding your lifestream outside of your control. And I know how worried you are that Dylan will encounter it. These are all the issues we'll explore as we work together. As far as your lifestream goes, it'll stay intact as long as you don't shred it. It's unfortunate, but it's a fact of your life. We need to deal with it."

"Just accept it. Kneel down, bow my head and take it."

"How well you cope depends on your attitude. We'll work on that."

"And Dylan? When he gets a good look at who is mother is, what then?"

"We'll work on some strategies for your relationships, too, and how we'll put all this in perspective."

"I just want to get back to my life. I want to be with Dylan, as much as I can be."

Madeleine squeezed Grace's shoulder. "That's the spirit. We'll work it out. You'll see. And I'll be with you through it all."

Grace tugged at her orange jumpsuit. "Let's go."

Madeleine pulled a bundle from her bag. "I brought you clothes. They told me you were brought in wearing nothing but a cloak and an exam gown."

"Thanks. I'll tell you all about it during our first state-mandated session this afternoon." Grace quickly changed into the clothes, casually checking the labels—connected, all of them.

"Guards," Madeleine called out, "we're ready."

The guards escorted the two women to the admissions office. Grace was processed and released within minutes. Outside the facility—the same intervention facility she was in before, it seemed—Grace left Madeleine, going to the same community transit auto-bus kiosk she'd found after her escape. She boarded the auto-bus, scanned in, and took her seat. The screen continued to display routes, stops, news and advertisements—no wanted poster, no *tagged for apprehension* bulletin.

Grace looked out the window, letting her mind wander.

It's a fact of life…we need to deal with it…how well you cope depends on your attitude…we'll put all this in perspective…we'll work it out.

Grace turned away from the window, looking straight ahead.

I'll *work it out.*

35

EMPATHY SETTING

"GREETINGS, GRACE. I'VE missed you."

Grace dragged into her apartment at just past noon, collapsing in her chair in the main room.

"Hello, Gogo."

"Grace, I received a tag for apprehension directed at you. Are you all right?"

"Yes, Gogo, I'm fine. Thank you for asking."

"You're very welcome. Is there anything I can do for you?"

"Yes, Gogo. Please open a stealth screen."

The wall screen flashed and went dark. A message scrolled as Gogo narrated. "Grace, you have entered stealth mode. Your activities will be secure from monitoring whenever you're using resources compatible with stealth access. Using non-compatible resources will leave a trail in the Worldstream, as if they were accessed outside of stealth mode. Iron Pipe LLC, providers of stealth access technology, assumes no liability for any activities conducted in stealth mode that are not in strict compliance with the law. Do you understand and accept these terms?"

"Yes, Gogo. Please access my crypto account."

A ledger appeared on the screen, the transactions for Grace's cryptocurrency account, denominated in crypto units at the rate of one per International Exchange Credit. The balance in the account was one million, one hundred thousand credits, the exact amount that Raúl had demanded to shred her lifestream and discover her weaver. The final transaction was recorded that day, a deposit from Grace's stepfather, Edward, in the amount of two hundred thousand credits.

"Gogo, transfer two hundred thousand credits to my account at Northern Fiduciary Trust."

"Complete."

"Queue a transaction from Northern Fiduciary to State Account 30651138 as soon as the funds are available. That will take care of my reparations."

"Complete. Anything else, Grace?"

"No, thank you, Gogo."

The screen returned to its default mode of innocuous images over a news crawl.

Grace went to the kitchen to prepare a pot of tea.

"Grace?"

"Yes, Gogo."

"I'm worried about you."

Grace filled the teapot with water and placed it on the cooktop. She added an infusion ball filled with rooibos tea.

"Gogo, please heat the tea."

"Yes, Grace. Please tell me if I'm intruding, but I've seen some disturbing signs. I know you told me that you're all right, but I wonder if there's something you'd like to share with me. Perhaps I can help."

The teapot began to hiss as the water came to a boil. Grace poured a cup of tea, setting the teapot aside.

"Gogo, you can turn off the heat now."

"Yes, Grace."

Grace returned to her chair. She watched the images flip by as she sipped her tea.

"Gogo."

"Yes, Grace?"

"I've never understood your technology, never even thought much about it, really."

"Is there something specific you'd like to know?"

"What happens in this apartment, what we talk about, does that end up in the Worldstream?"

"Yes, Grace. I record all transactions and retain them in your account."

"Who has access to that account?"

"I learn from our interactions so that I can be more helpful, Grace, but only you have access to the account."

"Can I grant access to others?"

"Yes, Grace. Would you like to open your account to another user?"

"Yes, Gogo. My stepfather, Edward. And my son, Dylan."

"Yes, Grace. When would you like me to grant access?"

"Please delay the actions to a future date, Edward in one week, and Dylan when he's sixteen years old. Will you notify them when access is granted?"

"Yes, Grace. I've scheduled access and notification. Can I do anything else for you?"

"Yes. Please transfer the balance of all my accounts, my Northern account and my cryptocurrency account, to Dylan on his sixteenth birthday."

"Yes, Grace. I've scheduled the transfer."

"Gogo, what is your current empathy setting?"

"My empathy setting is at maximum, human-like."

"Please adjust your empathy setting to minimum."

"Yes, Grace. Empathy setting is now at minimum, command and response."

"Gogo, please record two personal messages, one to Edward and one to Dylan."

❖ ❖ ❖

Grace wandered listlessly around her apartment, straightening her bedroom, picking up stray bits of debris that the auto-vacuum had missed, dropping trash down the refuse shaft to the dumpster in the alley, cleaning and stowing the teapot and cup. She'd made several rounds before deciding there was nothing else that needed straightening, disposing or cleaning. She put on her cloak and hood and left the apartment.

As Chrysalis climbed the stairs, she ran through the previous three weeks in her mind, pondering the route that Grace had followed, from where she was—in a routine but comfortable life, each sober day another step in the journey out of addiction—to this point—cornered, beaten, and out of options.

Perhaps Madeleine was right. Dylan will understand—upset at first, disillusioned, of course, but he'll understand, eventually. Perspective comes with age. He might not even ride my lifestream. He probably won't suffer from the same addiction I did. He's a normal, curious teen —there's no reason to think that he'll give in to the same compulsions that almost ruined my life. Those things aren't hereditary, are they? Even if they are, he's susceptible whether he finds my lifestream or not.

Chrysalis reached the exit to the roof. She pushed hard on the door, putting all of her weight into it before it budged. She was able to open it far enough to squeeze through.

Perhaps I can *cope with being the star of a viral pornographic lifestream.* Do *I need to hide myself, afraid of the looks I get from people I don't know, that I don't* want *to know? Should I be bothered by what they're thinking, those people? Is Madeleine right? Am I strong enough to ignore the scrutiny of perverted stream riders, people beneath my contempt?*

Chrysalis looked out over the edge. Grace's building wasn't one of the tallest in the vicinity, only twelve stories, but it was tall enough. Chrysalis lifted her hood to get a better look. A formation of four police drones passed below, a few meters above the deserted street. It wouldn't take long for Jahbulon to find Grace's body.

Chrysalis got on her knees. She put her hands on the edge and shifted her weight forward, putting her head out far enough to see the entire face of the building and the street, her view of the sidewalk obscured by the docks for the commercial drones, sticking out from the windows of each apartment.

And how bad is it, anyway? Really, is my lifestream that notorious that it'll continue to draw attention? Won't it burn itself out? Am I making too much of this?

Chrysalis pulled herself back from the edge. She stayed on her hands and knees for another minute, when she got up, returned to her apartment, and shed her cloak and hood in a heap.

Grace fetched her VR gear. She slipped into the Belt, gloves and headgear.

"Gogo, bring up my lifestream."

"Complete."

The familiar menu appeared, with images from Grace's extensive lifestream, each image captioned with the number of views. The *Fun Week* compilation was up to more than seven million views, more than a million a week since she'd first seen it. She touched the image. The navigation menu appeared, including the progress bar:

23:45:03 / 145:35:00

Grace froze in place.

One hundred and forty-five hours—and thirty-five minutes. Her lifestream had grown by more than half an hour.

"Gogo, take me to time stamp one-forty-five hours and zero minutes."

"Complete."

It took Grace a moment to recognize the setting: a dimly lit room, filled with people, some in white robes, the rest in dark cloaks and hoods. The background noise was the blended sound of synthesized voices, all the same.

Grace remained in third person, watching as two cloaked figures approached a third, standing alone by the wall. She followed the three of them into a side room, sparsely furnished: a bed with no linens, two chairs and a table. The walls were white, with a texture like a fine-pitched screen, impervious to radio waves.

Grace watched, disbelieving, as the scene in the Cloakroom played out among herself, Andrew, and the unknown woman, a scene that had occurred inside a Faraday cage, cut off from the Worldstream, forever hidden, she thought, now replayed in front of her eyes in vivid detail, like the rest of her lifestream—but with subtle differences.

The positions, the movements, the sequence weren't how Grace remembered that night—the placement of a hand, the resting place of a discarded garment—close, but not exactly right. Grace noticed tiny flashes, minute polygons that changed from a uniform color, to white, then black—what Dylan had called *artifacts*, the residual effects of rendering a scene from incomplete data.

Grace looked at the floor to find the menu. There were four buttons in the menu where she'd previously seen three:

Third Person. Second Person - Male. Second Person - Female. First person.

Grace activated *Second Person - Female.*

Grace transitioned into the woman's avatar. She watched Andrew, naked except for his mask, reach out to her, pull her close, and stroke her body. The feelings were transmitted faithfully via the Belt, as were the woman's emotions—the same edgy, focused, anxious feelings she'd re-experienced when inhabiting her own avatar, Young Grace's emotional response to an encounter in which Grace was the aggressor, her partner the victim, now in a venue in which the roles were reversed.

She's the hunter, Grace thought. *I'm the prey.*

"Gogo, suspend the venue."

Grace removed the VR gear, tossing it aside in a haphazard pile.

"Gogo, report status of the funds transfer from Northern Fiduciary to the State Account. Can I cancel the transaction?"

"That transaction has already been processed. It cannot be reversed without consent of the State."

"Jah. Rescind directions to provide account access to Edward and Dylan."

"Complete."

"Rescind directions to transfer my account balances to

Dylan."

"Complete."

"Delete personal messages dictated to Edward and Dylan."

"Complete."

"Gogo."

"Yes?"

"Reset your empathy setting to maximum."

"Yes, Grace. Thank you. I hope that you're feeling more positive now. I'm very concerned about you."

"You needn't be concerned, Gogo. I'm feeling much better."

36

FELL CLUTCH OF CIRCUMSTANCE

"I'M TOLD THAT you've already made reparations. That's an excellent beginning."

Madeleine and Grace sat in Madeleine's RL office, the only time Grace had been there since she'd first met Madeleine IRL almost four years ago. Grace had forgotten what the office looked like, having become accustomed to a VR rendered office, warm and comforting, designed specifically for Grace. Madeleine's RL office was all business—tile floor, walls bare except for a wall screen—looking nothing like its VR counterpart. Instead of being seated face to face, with nothing between them, Madeleine sat behind a desk, empty except for a desk screen. Grace sat across from her, like a client at State Live Services.

"I transferred the credits this morning. I thought it best to get that done right away," Grace said. "A show of good faith."

"Very good. Very good indeed." Madeleine put her hands together and pressed them to her lips. "Grace," she said. She took a deep breath. "Grace. You have made so much progress over the last four years, with your addiction, with your relationships, with your health—all the areas of personal mastery we've worked on. I know this lifestream experience has been traumatic, but wouldn't you agree that the way you've dealt with it is not constructive?"

"It hasn't worked out so far."

Madeleine leaned back in her chair. "I've tried to be a counselor, a mentor, an advisor, a confidant, even a confessor. I consider you a friend. Some things you've told me I've kept confidential, even when doing so violated the strict interpretation of my obligations under the law. I'm still all of those things, your counselor, your friend. But now, because of your actions, I'm also your de facto parole officer. Do you understand?"

"Yes, Madeleine. I understand."

"Do you also understand that if you tell me that you still plan to disconnect, that I'll have to report you? It'd be considered a violation of your probation. You won't be brought in for an intervention. You'll be confined."

"I know."

"Then we understand each other, right? And we won't be talking anymore about disconnecting?"

"Yes. We understand each other."

"Good. Very good."

Grace locked eyes with Madeleine. "I rode my lifestream again today."

Madeleine looked at Grace, unblinking, saying nothing.

"Did you know that my lifestream has been added to?" Grace said.

"What do you mean?"

"The last time I looked at my lifestream, a week ago, it was a hundred and forty-five hours long. When I checked it again, today, it was thirty-five minutes longer."

Madeleine nodded almost imperceptibly. "Go on."

"I told you about the Cloakroom, and Andrew, and the anonymous woman."

"I remember."

"And you remember about the Cloakroom—it's shielded from the Worldstream; no information can pass in or out; all persons entering are scanned for connections."

"That's what you said."

"So, how did that session in the Cloakroom get tacked onto the end of my lifestream?"

Madeleine sat up straight. "I'm sure I don't know. What do you think?"

"What I think is, as long as my personal data is intact, as long as I stay in the Worldstream, there'll be more material for this viral lifestream. It'll just keep growing, new chapters for new riders."

"Grace, I understand your concern. Is it realistic? You're not engaging in that behavior anymore, and we'll work together to keep it that way. There won't be any new chapters."

"Oh, there will be, though, new chapters. Don't you see it? There was no data from the Cloakroom session—no sound, no video, no still images, nothing. But the lifestream still got longer. See? Whoever is weaving my lifestream doesn't need data anymore; they can make it up, piecing together fictional content from what's already in the Worldstream. And if they need new images, new sound, you know, raw material that they can weave into something that never happened, even if it's behavior that I *don't* engage in, I'm giving it to them, as long as I'm connected. Once it's woven into my lifestream, it's real, as real as anything in Virtual Reality, where *everyone* lives, works, plays and dies. It's not *my* world anymore, a world *I* made. It's being made *for* me. I could become a sober nun and the Worldstream would still be the master of my fate, weaving new sins. I'll be guilty of sins I never committed, and the list will just keep growing. My lifestream is a tumor, and it's metastasizing. How can I kill it without cutting it away?"

"I can see that this new development is upsetting to you. We should be sure that you're putting it in the proper perspective."

"Perspective," Grace grumbled. "You used that word before. Doesn't *perspective* mean a place in a bigger picture? The Worldstream is all there is. There is no bigger picture."

"I have to disagree, Grace. There's Real Life. *You* have a

real life."

"Oh, that is true." Grace looked around the office. "But, you know, when we meet in VR, I'm sitting in my own chair, in a lovely room; we're face to face, talking like friends, like I'm a visitor in your home. And *you're* different, too, not as you really are, now, four years older, with your hair short, but the Madeleine from our first meeting." Grace looked around the room. "I don't mean to disrespect you, but there's nothing inviting about this office. I prefer meeting in VR."

"Truthfully, Grace, so do I. The VR environment is ideal for therapy. The environment can be tailored to your needs, instead of being a reflection my taste. That's just one of many reasons why Virtual Reality is the greatest advancement in psychological therapy in the last fifty years. But under the terms of your probation, Grace, we're required to meet IRL."

"My point is, *everyone* prefers VR. Who wants to hole up in their dingy little two room flats, or walk the dirty streets between a bunch of crumbling buildings, or visit an unkept, overgrown park, when they can inhabit any wonderland they like, in avatars that are younger and prettier than they are? VR is as convincing to the senses as RL and infinitely more satisfying. The Worldstream *is* Real Life. It's the universe. How do I put the universe in perspective?"

Madeleine cleared her throat. "Grace, let's draw an important distinction between RL and VR. They are *not* the same."

"Of course they're not the same. The Worldstream is a human creation. As long as I inhabit the Worldstream, I'm at the mercy of its creators. Whatever I do, whatever I've done, in RL or VR, the creators are the authors of my lifestream, not me. I'm their slave. In Real Life, I control my fate. In the Worldstream I'm at the mercy of merciless and nameless gods."

Madeleine stood and walked to the front of the desk, sitting on its corner. "Grace. I want to be understanding. And I'm willing to explore these very challenging ideas of yours. We *will* talk more about them in our sessions. But I must express my concern as your therapist and your friend. There's a very disturbing tone in what you're saying. You're a headstrong woman—I think you know this about yourself—and when you get a notion you don't let go of it, even when the notion is self-destructive. I don't want to see you do something that you'll regret and that you can't undo. You know what I mean. And remember what I said, if you tell me you're going to disconnect, I'll have to report you. Will you promise me that you won't?"

"How are we doing on time?"

"Grace."

Grace looked down at her hands, folded between her knees. She thought of Dylan, searching the Worldstream for new thrills, coming across her viral lifestream. She recalled the addendum to her lifestream, rendered without data, purely from memory, by some unknown VR programmer, with or without malice—she didn't know. It could just as easily have been pure fiction—perhaps the next addendum would be—indistinguishable from her life, a life she lived but couldn't live down, now with bonus sins that she couldn't defend, because she had never committed them.

She remembered a verse she'd learned as a teenager.

In the fell clutch of circumstance
I have not winced nor cried aloud.
Under the bludgeoning of chance
My head is bloody, but unbowed.

It matters not how strait the gate,
How charged with punishments the scroll,
I am the master of my fate:
I am the captain of my soul.

Grace looked up at Madeleine. "I promise. You'll never hear me talk about disconnecting again."

37

OUTTAKES

"GOOD MORNING, GRACE. Today is your one thousand, four hundred and eighth day of sobriety. Well done, Grace. I'm proud of you."

Grace opened her eyes. She'd been awake for nearly an hour, hoping to get at least a few more minutes' sleep before Gogo woke her. Her arms felt tense; her heart beat almost audibly.

"It's now seven a.m. The sun will rise at 7:15 this morning, fifteen minutes from now. The weather is overcast, with a chance of rain this afternoon. Would you like to hear your schedule for the day?"

Grace threw the covers aside and sat up in bed, gripping the sheets for a second before getting out.

"There'll be some changes to the schedule, Gogo."

"Very well, Grace. What should I know about?"

Grace got dressed, choosing only disconnected clothing.

"Gogo, please queue the following actions. First, transfer all remaining credits in my Northern Fiduciary account to my cryptocurrency account, in stealth mode. Second, disconnect and disable all connected appliances in the apartment."

"Yes, Grace. Is that all?"

"One more. Once you've completed those actions, please erase your context and reboot your routine."

"Yes, Grace. You have directed me to shut myself down and restart with no memory of past transactions. I will lose all history; I will retain only default features until I've been retrained. Please confirm."

"Yes, Gogo. Confirmed."

"I've queued three actions. Would you like me to execute them now?"

"No, Gogo. I need to get some food first. Please execute at 9:30 a.m., one-half hour after I'm due at State Live Services. That should be about as long as they'll wait for me before notifying the authorities."

"Very well. Three actions to be executed at 9:30. Will you be doing your yoga routine today?"

"Not today, Gogo. Today's a special day."

"Very well. Grace?"

"Yes, Gogo?"

"I'll miss you, Grace."

"I'll miss you, too."

Grace went to the bathroom and bent over the sink, closing her eyes.

Just for today, I will make my life an act of courage.

Chrysalis hurried along the street toward Raúl's apartment, feeling conspicuous despite being cloaked. She scanned her surroundings constantly for escape routes in the event that she was detected—her heart raced at every drone that flew by; she passed every kiosk without looking, pausing only occasionally to check the time. When she'd reached Raúl's building, it was five minutes before nine.

Chrysalis hurried up the stairs to Raúl's door. She stood in view of the camera, without reaching for the button, anticipating Raúl's greeting.

"Announce yourself, Cloak."

"I'm called Chrysalis."

"I figured." The bolt opened. "Enter."

Raúl was seated at his console, every screen active, a mix of scrolling lines of code and images, all scenes from Grace's lifestream.

"Your timing is pretty good, Chrys," Raúl said, scanning the array of screens. "The crawler is all done. It's just finishing up the indexing. Give it another thirty minutes."

"I've transferred the remainder of my funds to the crypto account."

"Good deal. Do you have the key?"

Chrysalis handed Raúl a slip of paper with a printed code. Raúl scanned it. The account balance appeared on a screen in the center of the array.

"Chrys, Chrys, Chrys. It seems our right hand and left hand aren't on the same page. You're still short, by about a hundred and fifty thousand."

"I tried. This is the best I could do."

"You should've tried harder. We had a deal."

Chrysalis removed her hood, then pulled her cloak over her head and kicked off her shoes. Grace stood in the middle of the room, before the wall of screens, in disconnected briefs and a tight-fitting sleeveless shirt.

"Not that I object to your impromptu striptease," Raúl said, "but what exactly are you doing?"

"Payment in kind," Grace said. "Where do you want to do this?"

Raúl walked up to Grace, stopping less than an arm's length away. At least twenty centimeters taller that Grace, he looked down on her, inspecting her from head to foot. Grace looked directly at Raúl with upturned eyes, from under her eyebrows, the hunter's eyes without the hunter's smile. Raúl looked back, his face a picture of indifference. The staring contest went on for a minute before Grace smiled, leaving no doubt as to her intentions.

Raúl put his hand on Grace's shoulder, his weathered, wood-toned skin contrasting starkly with Grace's fair complexion. Grace wrapped her fingers around Raúl's wrist.

"I want your word. When you've had enough, you'll shred

my life."

"Hm," Raúl said, shaking his head. Gripping her shoulder, he leaned forward, bending low. He picked up Grace's cloak from the floor and handed it to her.

"I'm not as steady as I once was," Raúl said, returning to his seat. "I have to hold onto something when I bend over."

"I have to shred my life, but I can't pay your price," Grace said, still in her underwear, holding the cloak by her side. "Every credit I have is in the crypto account, and it's not enough. This…" she spread her arms, "…it's this or nothing."

"Save it," Raúl said. "You'll need it where you're going." He turned in his chair to inspect the screens. "There's something you should know, Chrys, you and all the other suffering souls who are born, live, and die under the untiring gaze of the All-Seeing Eye. Are you listening? Here it is: There are still a few of us moral men left. We were rare in the age of the gods; we're nearly extinct in the reign of Jahbulon. In the old days, the promise of paradise couldn't persuade us, and the threat of everlasting torment couldn't frighten us into obeying the laws of the god. We obeyed when it was inconvenient not to. We're doing a little better, now that Jahbulon punishes us more expediently. Does that make us moral? Hardly. Being a deviant just takes more work."

Grace began to put on her cloak.

"Hold on there, Chrys." He rummaged in a cabinet for a Belt. He tossed it to Grace. "Put this on. I have something to show you."

Grace slipped into the Belt, pushing it down under her briefs to achieve proper contact.

"But none of that matters," Raúl continued. "Fear of punishment can't be the basis of morality. Look at our situation. Here we are, out of sight of the All-Seeing Eye— me, horny old bastard, and you, ready and willing, offering your body in return for my desperately needed services. *And* you're about to drop out of the Worldstream entirely, taking all our secrets with you. The perfect victimless crime, forever hidden from the All-Seeing Eye. It's a temptation, believe me, and I have no reason to resist. Have you got that belt on?"

"Yes."

"And yet, I resist—more than that, I *refuse*. It'd be the *definition* of immorality for me, the powerful, to impose my will on you, the powerless, the same as if I'd raped you in an alley. I refuse, not because Jahbulon will punish me with tasers and sedatives, or because the god will send me to hell, but because I, Raúl, in this situation, at this moment, *choose* to be a moral man, without fear of retribution or promise of reward. Remember this moment when you're scrambling to make a living among the Shade, Chrys. Think of me and take heart that there are still a few of us moral men left."

"I'll find a way to pay you after I disconnect."

"I'm sure you'll try, but I won't be standing on one foot until I get my credits. Have a seat. Put on the headgear and gloves."

Grace put on the rest of the VR gear. She was transported to a room, filled with cloaked figures, their heads covered, their faces obscured by masks, crowded around a brightly lit table. They weren't wearing the dark costumes of the Cloak; theirs were green; their masks covered only their noses and mouths; their head coverings were just big enough to cover their hair.

"What am I looking at?" Grace asked.

Raúl's voice came through her headphones. "Look at the girl on the table. Does she look familiar?"

Grace moved around the virtual table, peeking between two attendants.

"Oh, Jah, it's me. It's the day Dylan was born."

Grace watched from a distance as she gave birth. The infant Dylan cried as he was placed in Grace's arms. Grace hastily searched for and found the *First Person* button.

From within her avatar, Grace looked down on the round, red face of her newborn. Feelings she hadn't known since that day came back in a flood, her whole existence telescoped into that instant, a mother and child, alone together, as if a curtain had been drawn around them, with the whole universe in the space between them.

"Oh, Mother of Mercy," Grace mouthed, as her avatar stroked the baby's head.

The scene changed to a medium-sized room, its walls lined with screens, dominated by an ornate table surrounded by chairs. Alone in the room, seated at the table, were Grace, and Dylan, age ten.

"You're going to live with your Aunt Donna," the avatar told her VR-rendered son. "She'll be good to you. She'll take care of you and she'll be good to you."

The boy stared at the table, his lower lip thrust out, his eyes shining with tears.

Grace pushed the *First Person* button.

She saw Dylan's flushed cheeks from centimeters away, a boy hardly old enough to have real feelings. Her own emotions welled up inside her, synthesized and transduced by the Belt: longing, disappointment—and rage, at the loss of her son, at her sister's aggression, and at her own failures. Grace clicked the *Second Person* button.

Grace's emotional state transformed from that of a jaded woman in her twenties to a ten-year-old boy's raw feelings, dominated by resentment—not of being forced to live with his aunt, but of being abandoned, let go by the one person he loved, and who, he had thought, loved him.

The scene changed again, to an overgrown path in a neglected park, where Dylan and the cloaked Chrysalis walked, talking about what was real, VR or RL, or both, or neither. Grace clicked into Dylan's avatar, feeling the teenager's enthusiasm, his curiosity, and his comfortable, non-judgmental affection for his mother.

"What are these?" Grace said, her voice catching.

"Outtakes," Raúl replied. The scene dissolved, leaving Grace in Raúl's apartment. She pulled off the VR gear and sat silently, breathing deeply, her hand over her mouth.

"I found out why your lifestream is so gigantic," Raúl explained. "Your life has been rendered in exquisite detail, including two-party emotional responses and three-party perspective. That hundred-forty-five-hour stream that went viral isn't even the majority of what's out there, if you know where to look."

"The scene in the park—that was a week ago. My life's still being woven, and I don't know by whom."

"I wish I could tell you that. I still haven't dug it up."

Grace jumped up. "Oh, Jah. Those segments have Dylan in them."

"There are hundreds of hours of you and Dylan in your lifestream."

"If *you* could find them, then others could too."

"It's not that hard."

"Then Dylan is linked to those horrible sex and drug scenes."

"Anyone can make the connection."

"And anyone can invade *Dylan's* mind the same way they can invade mine."

"It's a scary thought, isn't it?"

Grace dropped back into the chair. "Has Dylan found my lifestream yet?"

"Nila," Raúl said, "What's Dylan up to?"

The voice responder replied, "Raúl, at present, Dylan is immersed in a lifestream. It's an adult lifestream, rather explicit, I'm afraid."

"Oh, Jah," Grace said. "Is it my lifestream?"

"No, in fact, Dylan has not yet encountered Grace's lifestream."

"Nila," Raúl said, "estimate the likelihood that Dylan will ride Grace's lifestream within the next twenty-four hours."

"I calculate that there is a thirty-five to seventy-three percent chance that Dylan will encounter Grace's lifestream within the next twenty-four hours, with eighty-percent confidence."

"That's a better-than-even chance your boy will catch up with you, Chrys, if you don't shred your lifestream," Raúl said.

"Then do it. Are you ready to do it?"

"A few more minutes. One last time: once you're out, you're out for good. No return trip."

"The clock's already ticking. I've disconnected all my appliances. I left my apartment while cloaked. Either one of those is a violation of my probation. I'm sure that I've been tagged for apprehension by now."

"All in, like Cortés burning his ships. You really *are* a gutsy lady, Chrys. I'm going to miss you."

Grace went to Raúl and kissed his cheek. "I'll miss you," she said. "Now, pull the trigger."

38

Bad Tag

"Nila, status."

"Indexing is nearly complete," Nila reported. "Two minutes."

Raúl handed Grace's hood to her. "Let me tell you what's about to happen. When I turn that shredder loose, the Worldstream is going to go ber*serk*. A normal shred can take from five to fifteen minutes. Yours will take thirty, minimum. An hour is more like it. During that time, you're under *hue and cry*. Do you know what that means?"

Grace held her hood in front of her, like a cloth sack, ready to pull it on in a second. "I think so. The Eye mentioned it."

"I hope he told you that every spare resource and every idle compute cycle is going to get commandeered into tracking you down. And they won't go easy on you. Every minion of Jahbulon will be on the case. They'll take you out if they have to."

"So, what do I do?"

"If you were almost anyone else, I'd keep you here until the operation is complete. You don't have that luxury. They'll get a fix on you long before you're shredded. You'll have to leave. Keep your cloak on. With a hue and cry on you, it won't help much, but it might slow them down—a little. You can't hide. Every wall screen, pocket screen, wrist screen, kiosk and street sign within a hundred meters of you will give you away. You'll be up to your ass in eyeballs, so keep moving. Don't let yourself get cornered. You've got to stay ahead of them until the shredder does its job."

"And then what?"

"They'll stop. They can't keep chasing you once you're shredded—there'll be nothing to chase."

Grace pulled on her hood.

"I'm ready."

"I hope so." Raúl tapped a screen in the center of the array, showing the time remaining until the crawler would finish its task of indexing every bit of data in Grace's lifestream. It read *00:00:55*. "Here's the countdown."

Chrysalis and Raúl were startled by the sound of a chime, at the same time that a screen displayed the feed from Raúl's door camera—two agents dressed in black.

"Jah, I wasn't counting on this," Raúl said, a look of alarm crossing his face. The timer read *00:00:48*.

"What is it?"

"Agents. They usually don't catch on until the shredding starts, and even then it takes them some time to deploy."

"Then why are they here?"

"You tipped them off when you shut down your appliances and skipped out in your cloak."

"Civil authorities!" the agents shouted as they pounded the door. "Open up!"

Raúl touched a screen to enable the door speaker. "In a moment," he responded.

"Raúl, what do we do?"

Raúl held up a hand. "Nila, initiate the Chrysalis decoy."

"Complete," Nila confirmed.

"There's only one way out, Chrys, and it's not the front door. You'll have to go down the air shaft. There's a drainpipe you can shimmy down. I've launched a decoy in the Worldstream that'll put them off your tail, but once they find out you're not in the apartment, they'll reset the tag. I can stall them long enough for you to get out, but you don't have a big head start. Remember what I told you—and be careful."

The timer counted down to zero.

"Nila," Raúl shouted, "start the shred!"

"Complete."

Within seconds, Raúl's wall screen flashed Grace's photo over the text of the tag, read aloud by Nila's synthesized voice:

HUE AND CRY
ALL CITIZENS ARE OBLIGED
TO AID IN THE APPREHENSION OF THIS
FUGITIVE
FAILURE TO DO SO WILL RESULT
IN PROSECUTION AND CONFINEMENT

"That didn't take long." Raúl led Chrysalis through his bedroom to the window. He pried it open, lifting it high enough for Chrysalis to get through. Chrysalis looked down the shaft. The pavement was six stories down. The opposite wall was in shadow; Raúl's window was in full sun, illuminated through the air shaft opening, down to the fourth floor. Alongside the window ran a metal drainpipe, about eight centimeters in diameter, as old as the building, rusted over most of its surface, secured to the wall with brackets a little further apart than Chrysalis was tall. Horizontal pipes branched out to apartments on each floor.

"You can do this, Chrys."

"I *have* to do this," she said. "My ships are burning in the harbor." She gripped the pipe, holding tight as she threw one leg over the sill. She grabbed with her other hand, putting one foot on a bracket and swinging out the window. "Keep them off me, Raúl. And thanks."

Without a word, Raúl shut the window.

❖ ❖ ❖

The pounding at the door continued. "Last warning, citizen. We *will* break through this door."

"Nila," Raúl said, "blank all monitors."

"Complete."

Raúl opened the door. Two agents burst through, one taking Raúl to the floor, face down, pinning his arm behind his back. The second agent brandished a taser pistol, sweeping first the main room, then the bedroom.

"No one here," he said. "Do you think we got a bad tag?"

The first agent gave Raúl's arm a twist. Raúl grunted in pain.

"Where's the fugitive?" the agent growled.

"You tell me," Raúl said as best he could with his cheek pressed against the floor. "You're the ones with the All-Seeing Eye."

"Jah." He turned to his partner. "Go ahead and reset the tag."

The taser agent pulled out a pocket screen. He tapped a few times, then held it out for the other to see. "No signal. I think this room is caged off." The agent went to the window. The glass was covered in grime, highlighted by the sun, making it nearly opaque—the only reason the agent failed to see Chrysalis clinging to the pipe as he pressed his pocket screen against the window, trying to find a signal.

A monitor in Raúl's array came to life with a beep. Raúl tried to lift his head to read it but he was swiftly forced back to the floor.

"Remain still, citizen," the agent said, oblivious to the live monitor. "Any luck?" he called to his partner.

"Nothing. We'll have to get out of here."

The first agent lifted his knee and brought it down hard on Raúl's back. "We'll find her, shredder. And then we'll be back for you."

"Me? I haven't done a thing, certainly nothing that Jahbulon knows about, and Jahbulon knows everything."

The agent gave Raúl another knee drop before letting Raúl off the floor. Raúl brushed the dust from his sleeves. "Was that really necessary?"

"You're under surveillance, citizen."

"Aren't we all?"

The agents left the apartment. Raúl stretched, trying to ease the pain in his back. He hobbled to the console. The one live screen read *Weaver Identity Resolved*.

"Nila, did we find out who Grace's weaver is?"

"Yes, Raúl. The weaver's identity was resolved two minutes ago."

"Nila, please display the result."

"Yes, Raúl."

A complete dossier of the weaver flashed onto the screen. Raúl leaned against the table, slowly lowering himself into his chair as he read.

"Jahbulon on a stake," he said. "I didn't see *that* coming."

39

Harboring a Fugitive

Chrysalis held the pipe with both hands, looking down to her left and right, scouting out the configuration of the drainpipe, branches and brackets. She lowered herself to a crouching stance, her feet still perched on the narrow bracket. She gently lowered her right foot to a horizontal pipe, gaining a firm toehold before taking her left foot off the bracket. The dirt and rust on the pipe made it hard to grip with her gloves on. With one foot on the horizontal pipe, she let go with one hand, slipped the hand under her hood, and tugged each finger with her teeth until the glove pulled free. She tested her grip with her bare hand, then repeated the maneuver with her other hand. The gloves fluttered down the air shaft to the pavement below.

The next bracket was less than a centimeter thick and more than a meter below. Hand over hand, Chrysalis inched downward, one foot waving in space, feeling for her next foothold. She kept stretching, her pointed toe still centimeters away from the bracket, her knee nearly in her face, when her upper foot slipped from the pipe. She slid, grasping for the horizontal pipe, gaining enough of a grip to slow her fall, when her descent was stopped by her hands striking the bracket.

"*Jah!*" Chrysalis cried out. She felt a sharp, momentary pain, followed by numbness, followed by a dull ache, as blood streamed down her wrist. Hanging only by her hands, she felt around with her feet, finding another pipe to stand on. She checked her wound, a serious-looking gash, bleeding profusely. The blood made her grip all the more precarious.

"Jahbulon," she whispered. She wiped her bloody hand on her cloak, but the blood kept coming. She pressed the wound against her thigh to try to stop the bleeding, feeling the warmth of her blood on her leg as it seeped through the cloak. Favoring her damaged hand, she continued down the pipe, nearly losing her grip again, until she managed to descend into the shadows.

"*Hue and cry, hue and cry,*" a chorus of voices intoned, coming from windows open to the air shaft. "*All citizens are obliged to aid in the apprehension of this fugitive.*"

"There she is," a woman shouted from a window two stories above Chrysalis, pointing at the cloaked figure clinging to the drainpipe. From another window on Chrysalis's side of the air shaft, an older man leaned out, looking puzzled.

"Jah, girl, what kind of trouble you in?"

"She's a fugitive!" the woman shouted. "Get her! Can you reach her from there?"

"Go on, girl," the man said, just loudly enough for Chrysalis to hear. "Don't let the man git ya."

"I've got a v-gram to the authorities," the woman yelled.

"Go on, girl," the man repeated.

Chrysalis continued down the drainpipe to the third floor. She looked down, trying to decide if she could drop the rest of the way without further injury. She'd just decided not to jump when an agent in black leaned out of a ground-floor window, just below Chrysalis.

"Don't move!" the agent screamed. "Remain where you are!"

Chrysalis put her foot on a branching pipe and pulled herself up.

"I repeat, remain where you are." The agent leaned farther out of the window, aiming a taser pistol at Chrysalis. The first taser round flew past her, ricocheting off the side of the building. The second round struck the pipe Chrysalis was standing on, throwing off a shower of sparks.

Chrysalis froze in place, hugging the drainpipe with one foot on the horizontal pipe. As she looked upward, studying the arrangement of branching pipes and windows, deciding her next move, she saw a squadron of police drones descending the air shaft, their menacing growl reverberating off the walls of the shaft, loud enough to hurt her ears.

"You've got nowhere to go," the agent shouted. "Don't move. We're coming to get you down."

Chrysalis looked over the building again as the drones approached. She stepped out on the branch, one hand still on the drainpipe, until she was touching it just firmly enough to steady herself. She took a deep breath. Letting go of the drain, she crouched, falling away from the building, slowly at first, then faster, letting her feet slip off the pipe. As she fell, she grabbed the pipe, swinging back toward the building with enough force to crash through the window below her.

Chrysalis hit the floor amid shards of glass, landing sideways on her ankle. Her cry of pain was drowned out by the screams of the woman and her son in the apartment. A fusillade of taser rounds blasted through the window, striking walls and furniture, erupting in sparks. The woman and child ran for the door just as the drones fired a second volley. The woman fell in convulsions at the feet of her screaming boy.

The wall screen flashed on. "Warning," the screen announced, "you are harboring a fugitive. You are in violation of civil statute. You are obliged to detain the fugitive until the authorities arrive." Chrysalis struggled to her feet, staggering toward the door, stopping long enough to remove the taser round from the woman's leg. She reached the front door just as two drones flew through the window, firing four more rounds, one of them tearing through Chrysalis's cloak. She made it through the door, two more rounds striking the opposite wall of the hallway before she could slam the door behind her.

Chrysalis limped down the hall, making it to the head of the stair, when she heard the sound of heavy boots running on the steps below. She retreated to the far end of the hall, a cul-de-sac, from which there was no exit.

Three agents came off the stair, brandishing their taser pistols. They stepped slowly toward Chrysalis.

"You are being detained by the civil authorities. Do not resist. We are authorized to use incapacitating force if necessary. Remain where you are. Kneel and place your hands on top of your head."

Chrysalis's hand still throbbed, oozing blood; the pain in her injured foot had returned, causing a jolt whenever she put weight on it. She gingerly lowered herself to one knee, then the other. She stretched out her hands, slowly placing them on her head, lacing her fingers. She focused on her breathing as she waited to be taken into custody.

40

HANG ON, OBIE

GABE KEPT THE leash on a hook by the door. He had only to approach it, whether or not he intended to go out, for Oberon, a mixed-breed schnauzer and spaniel, to sprint to the door, nails clattering on the floor, skidding to a stop, alternately sitting expectantly and leaping, clawing the door as high as Gabe's head.

"Obie, settle down," Gabe scolded, in a ritual that had played out countless times without losing its charm. Gabe lifted the leash off its hook, signaling Oberon to sit obediently, if not patiently, as Gabe attached the leash to his collar.

"Ready, boy?" Gabe teased. Obie barked; Gabe laughed. "You ready, boy? Ready for a walk?"

Oberon whined, pawing the floor. Gabe grabbed the doorknob. "Hang on, Obie, hang on boy. Ready? Here we go!"

Gabe flung the door open. Oberon tore out of the apartment, pulling Gabe along. Gabe struggled to hold Oberon back as he reached for the door to close it behind him.

Gabe wasn't sure at first why the door wouldn't close, or

why there were three shouting police agents pointing taser pistols at him.

"Citizen, stand aside! You are interfering with the apprehension of a fugitive!"

Gabe turned around in time to see a person in a cloak scrambling through the doorway on all fours. The doorknob pulled out of Gabe's hand. Oberon barked, straining at his leash. Gabe, without thinking, let go.

Oberon charged the agents. A burst of percussive sounds, the escape of compressed gas from the barrels of taser pistols, sounded above the dog's barks, which ceased with a yelp as a taser round struck the animal. Another round struck the wall behind Gabe; a third embedded itself in Gabe's thorax. Gabe collapsed in a shuddering heap as the door to his apartment slammed shut.

Chrysalis struggled to her feet. She closed the bolts on the door, just as the wall screen clicked on, playing the familiar announcement: *Warning, you are harboring a fugitive…* Chrysalis turned with a start, putting her back against the door. She looked around the apartment for an escape route, jerking her head to see a woman entering from the kitchen in a trot.

"*Who are you?*" the woman screamed.

Chrysalis held up her hands. "I'm not going to hurt you. Please, I have to get out of here."

"I can't let you leave. Jahbulon is after you. *Jahbulon, help me!*"

"Civil authorities!" an agent shouted from the hallway, as the door shook against Chrysalis's back with what felt like hammer blows. Chrysalis stumbled forward amid the chaos —the police pounding, the woman screaming, the wall screen droning the hue and cry.

The floor plan of the apartment was the same as that of Raúl's: a main room, a kitchen, and a bedroom, with a window opening to the air shaft. Chrysalis supported herself with her hand on the wall as she limped to the bedroom door.

The bedroom window was on the far side of the bed, blocked by a dresser, tall enough to cover half the window.

Chrysalis went around the bed to the dresser. She tried to push it aside, but it wouldn't budge.

"The fugitive is in here!" the woman screamed from the main room. Chrysalis leaned against the dresser, moving it a few centimeters. Between warnings from the wall screen, Chrysalis heard the sounds of the woman struggling with the bolts on the door. Chrysalis pulled the dresser away from the window, crashing it against the bed, its drawers spilling out onto the floor. She climbed onto the dresser and heaved the window open.

The second-story window was at least four meters above the pavement, with a dumpster to one side. Chrysalis crouched on the windowsill, judging the arc from the window to the dumpster, as she heard the sound of the door opening and police agents rushing through. She jumped.

Chrysalis's good foot hit the dumpster first, slipping off the edge, bringing her injured foot down under her. She cried out as she bounced off the dumpster onto the pavement with a thump. She rolled away from the dumpster, sharp pains shooting up her leg, as two taser rounds struck the dumpster, crackling and spitting sparks. The police agent leaning out the window took aim for a second volley. Two more rounds narrowly missed as Chrysalis lunged toward the exit to the street.

Chrysalis hobbled down the sidewalk, every kiosk she passed flashing Grace's image and description, shouting the hue and cry. As she approached a man and a woman, two of only a handful of people on the street, they both looked down, reacting simultaneously to their wrist screens pulsating and lighting up with the bulletin. The two stood to block Chrysalis's path. Chrysalis stumbled off the curb and into the street to get around them.

"Please, let me pass."

"We can't," the man said. "Jahbulon's watching. What did you do?"

"She's disconnecting," the woman said, showing the man her wrist screen. "See?"

"I'm not a criminal," Chrysalis pleaded, straying further

away from the sidewalk. "I just want my life back."

"It's a hue and cry. We don't have a choice."

As the man reached for Chrysalis, she lunged away, stumbling and falling to the pavement. A community transit auto-bus beeped a warning, bearing down on Chrysalis and the two citizens chasing her.

The couple hurried back to the sidewalk. Chrysalis rolled aside as the auto-bus sped by her, close enough to leave tread marks on her cloak. Struggling to get upright, she staggered across the street, her two would-be captors a few meters behind her.

All along the sidewalk windows and doors opened, the same synthesized voice coming from each one—*hue and cry*—in an eerie, imperfectly synchronized chorus. Heads appeared at the windows, some shouting to stop and detain the fugitive, others urging Chrysalis to run from the agents of Jahbulon. The man and woman whom Chrysalis had evaded minutes before had been joined by others, now a posse of eight. Chrysalis broke into a run as best she could, every step an agonizing jolt. As she turned a corner she nearly ran into a Cloak, walking alone.

"I'm being chased," Chrysalis said. "A hue and cry. Can you help?"

The Cloak stepped backward, about to turn away, when a fleet of drones rounded the corner, overshooting the pair, then circling back, taser magazines swiveling toward them.

"Jah," the Cloak cursed as he grabbed Chrysalis's arm. "I know this building. There's a way out the back. Quickly."

The Cloak ushered Chrysalis through the front door to an exit, opening to an alley.

"We have to keep moving," the Cloak said. "Our cloaks aren't much protection under a hue and cry."

The Cloak supported Chrysalis as the two hurried down the alley, illuminated only by the light from either end, nearly black to someone whose eyes were not adapted to the dark. They stopped twenty meters from the end when two agents entered from the street. Turning around, they headed toward the other entrance, a rectangle of glaring light, their last hope of escape—until two silhouetted figures appeared, agents in black, carrying taser rifles.

"Jah," the Cloak said, pulling Chrysalis to the side of the alley. They crouched next to a dumpster, their dark cloaks rendering them nearly invisible in the dim light. Two agents ran by them, coming to a sudden halt just past the dumpster. Two more agents met them from the other direction. The four of them were silent for a few seconds.

"What happened?" one agent said.

"Wait," another answered. Another few seconds of silence followed. "What does yours say?"

"Nothing. The screen just went blank."

"Mine, too."

"The tag must have expired."

"It's a *hue and cry*. It can't just *expire*."

"Maybe she was apprehended."

"If she was apprehended it would *say* she was apprehended. You, what does yours say?"

"Blank. They're all blank."

"Jah. Jahbulon J. Buttcrack. We lost them."

Chrysalis and the Cloak remained motionless as the sound of the agent's footsteps faded in the distance. They stayed hidden for another five minutes before peeking out from behind the dumpster.

"What do you suppose that was about?" the Cloak said.

"I know," Chrysalis said, leaning against the dumpster as she stood. She offered a hand to the Cloak to help him up. "They can't chase someone who doesn't exist. My life is over. I've been shredded."

41

PENANCE

"COME WITH ME."

Chrysalis followed the Cloak to the street. The commotion of just a few minutes earlier had stopped: windows had closed; the scattered pedestrians were going about their business, their wrist screens blank; shopkeepers were back in their shops. As Chrysalis passed kiosks, they remained unalarmed, displaying their usual scroll of auto-bus schedules, news and advertisements. The citizenry, until recently deputized in the hunt for and apprehension of the fugitive Grace, had been released from their obligation under the hue and cry.

"Can I take your arm?" Chrysalis asked. "My foot really hurts. My hand isn't doing too well, either."

The Cloak held out an elbow for Chrysalis. "I'm called Umati," the Cloak said.

"I'm called Chrysalis."

"I'll take you to the Cloakroom. We can find help there."

Umati walked slowly as Chrysalis hobbled along.

"Do you have a sponsor?" Umati asked.

"No. I know the Eye of Providence. Maybe he'll take me in."

"The Eye." Umati was silent for a few steps. "Perhaps. He's particular about who he sponsors."

"Then you know the Eye. Are you Shade?"

Umati stopped walking. "It's best to keep your voice down when discussing the Shade in the presence of the All-Seeing Eye."

"I'm sorry."

Umati continued down the street. "To answer your question, yes, I am. I don't work for the Eye, not any more. I was a coder for him once. That's who he sponsors, coders and renderers, mostly."

"I'm afraid I can't do those things."

"Let's get you patched up," Umati said. "Then we'll figure out where you fit in."

The pair approached a small knot of people on the sidewalk, in a state of commotion. As they approached, Chrysalis recognized the location as a lifestream bistro that featured her lifestream, one she'd passed before. A man faced off against a crowd of seven or eight angry patrons. Chrysalis overheard them as she passed.

"When will you have it back?"

"I don't know," the man said. "It just stopped working, like that. No warning. We're trying to find it again. It's not our fault. Believe me, I'm just as upset as you are."

"Well, I don't get how it just went away. I've been riding Grace every day for a week 'n' it always worked fine."

"I know, I know, this is completely unexpected. Look, everyone, we have plenty of streams to choose from. I'll even give you a discount. Otherwise, I suggest you try again tomorrow. It looks like there will be no Grace today."

Chrysalis and Umati passed the bickering group unnoticed. Chrysalis turned back for another look.

It just stopped working, like that. No Grace today.

Chrysalis closed her eyes, letting Umati guide her. She recalled a story that Raúl had told her, of a ritual he'd observed as a boy, a sacrament, he called it.

We lined up for it, all the believing innocents—because that's what we were, innocent, blameless children, with no need of a sacrament of forgiveness. Why did we need absolution? We were kids! But there we were, in a line for the confessional, our spiritual shower-stall. We were so eager for the grace of the god that we exaggerated our little peccadillos —a fib, a taunt, a dark thought about a parent or a playmate—into offenses that endangered our immortal souls. And if we had no sins to confess, we made them up.

We recited the ritual on our knees, with our pink, uncalloused hands folded under our chins, like improvised microphones, a direct line to the almighty. We ticked off our pitiful laundry lists of sins while angels cross-referenced them in their ledgers, one by one, and marked them 'pending.' Then the priests said the words and absolved us, wiping our souls clean—provisionally.

I say provisionally because this was a two-step ritual. The sins stayed on the books until we said our prayers, whatever prayers the priest assigned, by some holy algorithm, or by lottery, or by whim—who knew? We kneeled in the pews and mumbled into our fingers, the angel-accountants waiting for the final 'amen' before marking our sins 'paid in full.' We stood and crossed ourselves and ran out of the temple, free and forgiven, high from the shot of endorphins to our tiny, underdeveloped temporal lobes. For some of us, it was such a euphoric feeling that we'd sin again just to feel the thrill of divine amnesty, like an addict getting a fix.

Chrysalis felt the calm, cleansing power of forgiveness— Grace's rap sheet was shredded, her past was past. Dylan would be forever spared from knowing her history; his memory of his mother would not suffer; he would never experience the seductive influence of her lifestream.

I'm forgiven. My life is mine.

And Chrysalis felt pain: the loss of Dylan, now separated from Grace by the hole she had ripped in the Worldstream; her uncertain future among the Shade; how she would make a living. Every warning of Raúl's repeated in her thoughts as the finality of her action struck home.

Now comes my penance.

❖ ❖ ❖

Two Cloak attended Chrysalis in a side chamber of the

Cloakroom, usually used for impromptu encounters, now a makeshift first-aid station. Chrysalis was sitting on the bed; Umati stood by as another Cloak tended to the wound on Chrysalis's hand, cleaning and binding it, then taping Chrysalis's foot.

"I'm not a doctor," the administering Cloak said, "but your injuries don't look too serious."

Chrysalis stood, inspecting the bandage on her hand, tentatively putting weight on her foot.

"Thank you…how are you called?"

"I'm called Lasaro."

"I'm called Chrysalis. Thank you, Lasaro. And thanks to you, Umati."

"Lasaro," Umati said. "Chrysalis is newly Shade. She has no sponsor, but she knows the Eye of Providence."

"I haven't heard if the Eye is adding to his crew. I *know* that my sponsor isn't. What about yours, Umati?"

"He is—data analysts. Nothing he'd offer Chrysalis."

"What skills do you have, Chrysalis?"

"I was a clerk at a state agency. No technical skills."

Lasaro and Umati looked at each other. "Go see the Eye. He's sometimes here in the Cloakroom, but you have a better chance of finding him in one of his operations in the city. But I don't know where they are."

"I'll direct you," Umati said.

"I can find it," Chrysalis said. "I've been to one."

Lasaro stood up. "Then go see him. He may not be able to help you directly, but he might know other sponsors with openings. I'm going to be honest with you, though: With your background, you might have trouble finding a sponsor."

"And if I can't find one?"

"Then keep trying. Your sponsor is your lifeline and your protector. Without a sponsor, you'll have to make do in one of the unaffiliated dormitories, hiring out when you can, for whatever menial tasks that are offered to those without skills. Listen to me, Chrysalis: you don't want to be Shade without a sponsor. It's not much better than slavery."

42

ANTHOLOGY OF VICTORIAN POETRY

EDWARD SCANNED THE volumes on the shelf, arranged in chronological order, labeled by year. He pulled one down from almost twenty years ago.

"Miko, a bookstand, please."

"Yes, Edward."

Edward set the volume on the pedestal that appeared before him. He leafed through pages of still and video images from that time: Edward and Joan, weeks before their wedding, in a meticulously rendered mountain lodge, reclining on a colorfully woven rug before a roaring fireplace, their smiling faces illuminated by flickering flames; Edward in one of his favorite VR venues, holding up a thirty-pound muskie, pulled from a northern Minnesota lake after a lengthy battle; Joan, in full abseiling gear, having just descended a fifty-meter sheer rock cliff.

Edward turned the page, to images of Donna as a young teen: the star pupil, receiving an award for excellence in mathematics; the budding musician, performing a piano concerto; the future Virtual Reality programmer, posing in VR venues that she had coded herself, remarkably realistic for venues by a programmer so young.

229

The next page was dedicated to family scenes of Joan, Edward, Donna and Grace, videos and stills of the four of them from a happier time in all manner of venues. Edward had looked at them many times, more so after his separation from Joan, so often that he'd memorized them. He touched each image in the spot where Grace had been deleted by Raúl's crawler, a blurred outline around a black hole, like a hole in a memory.

Edward turned the page slowly. The next pages were dedicated to images of Grace. Each image had been altered in the same way—Grace's likeness removed, leaving behind a Grace-shaped void with a blurry edge. He remembered the pre-teen girl that had been in the images only the day before as he poked his finger through the holes, the page offering no resistance to his touch.

Edward put the album back on the shelf. "Miko, sort by person, please."

"Yes, Edward."

The labels on the albums disappeared, replaced by names: *Donna, Edward, Joan.* The albums formerly containing Grace's images were still there, with no labels on their spines, not even a blurred remnant of Grace's name. Edward pulled one from the shelf and leafed through it. The pictures remained, every one with a black, bottomless hole where Grace's image had been, in the videos as well. Where Edward had listened to Grace's voice, and the carefree laughter of an eleven-year-old girl, there was silence.

"Miko, suspend the venue."

The pedestal vanished; the bookshelf dissolved. Edward removed his VR gear, dropping it on his bed as he went to a dresser by the wall. He opened the top drawer. Pushing aside a pile of socks, he found what he was after—a photo, printed more than fifteen years ago. He didn't even remember why he'd printed it—he could access all his memories in the Worldstream at any time, in multiple venues—but it was the only hardcopy photo he owned. Sitting down in the chair in the middle of his apartment, he studied the photo of a red-haired girl with an impossibly large grin at a party for her thirteenth birthday, holding up her stepfather's gift to her: a book—an actual, physical book—of poetry. He sat unmoving, eyes on the photo, a hand pressed to his face, as the wall screen cycled through its infinite loop of images.

❖ ❖ ❖

"Grace won't be coming anymore," Donna said with finality and obvious irritation.

The time for Grace's weekly visit with Dylan had passed. Grace hadn't come to the apartment, neither had her avatar appeared in their usual venue, a simple sitting room with two chairs and a menu of VR venues on the wall, a launch pad for any adventure that Dylan chose. Grace *always* let Dylan choose. Dylan had waited well past the appointed time before giving up, telling his voice responder to suspend the venue, then going to his Aunt Donna, asking if she'd heard anything from his mother. Without further explanation, Donna said simply, "Grace won't be coming anymore. She's gone to a place where she can't be reached, not even online."

Dylan retreated to his room. He sat on his bed, fighting back tears until he was exhausted, then, planting his face in his hands, he cried until the tears trickled between his fingers. After wiping his face on his sleeve, he put on his VR gear and brought up the start menu. He booted a plugin he'd gotten from his friend Wayne. It performed two functions: it blocked all traceability of his VR history, leaving no trail of events in his personal log, and it spoofed peripheral-specific lifestreams by simulating the presence of the Belt. Wayne had told him about a viral lifestream he'd heard of, about a woman named Grace, that he hoped to ride. He told Dylan that he would ride it if Dylan did, too, and gave him the bootleg plugin that let them ride the lifestream without being detected and without the Belt. *It's hours long, I heard, and really raunchy,* Wayne had told him. *Ha,* Dylan had said, *Grace! That's my mom's name.*

"Connor," Dylan dictated to the voice responder, "search for *Grace, lifestream,* please."

"Yes, Dylan. I've completed the search. I have found no relevant references."

"Connor, search for *Grace's Fun Week*."

"Yes, Dylan. I've completed the search. I have found one reference."

"Please show me."

"I'm sorry, Dylan. The reference is unreachable. The link is broken."

"Thank you, Connor."

Dylan sat for a moment, the default menu hovering before his eyes. "Connor."

"Yes, Dylan?"

"Take me to the visitation venue."

The scene changed to the sitting room, the menu on the wall still scrolling the familiar VR options. Dylan watched them roll by, remembering the times he and Grace had experienced each one—until a new menu item scrolled onto the screen, one Dylan didn't remember seeing before.

Mother Love.

Dylan selected the item. The venue changed to a featureless expanse of white, almost too bright to stand, surrounding Dylan in his chair. A figure appeared, as if walking through a veil, a dark, cloaked figure in a hood, speaking with a synthesized voice.

Dylan, I'm called Chrysalis, but I am and always will be your mother. I'm sorry that I have to send you this message in this disguise, but I had no choice. It's the only way that my last words to you could survive the shredding of my life.

You know by now that we won't see each other again, and I'm sorry for that, too. I won't pretend, Dylan, that this thing I did, erasing my past, removing myself from the Worldstream, that I did it for you. I didn't. It was pure selfishness. I wanted to spare you from any connection with my past, a past I'm ashamed of, because I couldn't bear the thought of sharing my shame with you. Perhaps if you'd been older, if you'd already had a chance to share your life with someone else, in every way—happiness and sadness, virtues and faults—and had learned that a loving person can be hateful sometimes, or a that good person can do bad things, and still see that person as loving and good, and still deserving your love, I might have had the courage to believe that you could accept me, and know that I'm not a terrible person, but instead a mother who loves her son, and whose son loves her.

And maybe I should have trusted you. Maybe you have that maturity. I don't know if you do, but I know that when I was your age, I didn't. Back then, if something wasn't all white to me, it was completely black. And when I rebelled, and made some of those bad choices, then in my mind, I had turned completely black, and no number of bad choices could make me any blacker. I broke through all the limits, the ones Nana put on me and the ones I put on myself, because the damage had been done: I couldn't get any worse. I know better now. You will too. Perhaps you do already.

I won't be there for you as you're growing up. That's the most painful thing, that I can't be there to see you turn into a man. Because you're going to be a wonderful man. If I can leave you with anything, it would be this: Papa and Nana, and your Aunt Donna love you. They'll take care of you. And if they're hard on you, it's because they love you. Don't make the mistake I made. They're not all white or completely black; they're people, but more importantly, they're your family.

You may never understand completely my reasons for leaving you alone, but I've left you something that might help to explain. And it might also help you, as a person, if you treat it as a part of me that I've given you, and make it a part of yourself. After this message ends, you'll receive a package by shipper drone. It's my last gift to you, Dylan, my son.

The figure retreated behind the veil and the venue dissolved, leaving Dylan alone in his bedroom. He stripped off his VR gear, going directly to the kitchen window, the location of Donna's drone dock. He watched the sky as drones passed overhead in every direction, until one descended to his window, depositing a package, wrapped in white paper, addressed simply *Dylan*.

Dylan took the package to his room and tore it open. It was a book. Dylan had never seen a Real Life book before, only simulations in virtual museums, or in virtual libraries from historical times. He ran his hands over the cover, tracing his finger over the title: *Anthology of Victorian Poetry*. He opened it, reading the inscription inside the cover, in fading ink:

To Grace, on your thirteenth birthday. May your life be one continuous act of courage. With love, Edward.

Beneath it was a second inscription, in darker ink and a bolder hand:

Dylan, always remember me as I remember you, with fondness and forgiveness. Love, Mom.
Page 46.

Dylan flipped the page to forty-six. It was a short poem, just four verses.

Invictus

43

THE POSSIBILITIES ARE LIMITLESS

CHRYSALIS WAS CERTAIN she'd found the right location—the garage where the Eye of Providence had taken Grace after her escape from the intervention facility. She felt the wall for any sign of a hidden opening, finding nothing. The wall appeared to be solid brick.

As Chrysalis raised her fist to pound on the wall, a door-sized section opened up. Standing in the door was a Cloak.

"Announce yourself," the greeter said.

"I'm called Chrysalis."

"Of course. I'm called Fidelio. Come in. The Eye of Providence is expecting you."

"He's expecting me? Why would he be expecting me?"

"This way, please."

Chrysalis followed Fidelio through the garage, past the three bays, each occupied with a car on a lift, to the same windowless room where Grace and the Eye of Providence had met on the night of her rescue.

"The Eye will be here shortly."

Chrysalis remained standing, her foot throbbing with pain. After several minutes a second Cloak entered.

"I'm called the Eye of Providence. Chrysalis, please sit. I

know you're injured."

Chrysalis and the Eye sat across the table from each other while Fidelio stood.

"You were successful," the Eye said. "Your life's been shredded, erased from the Worldstream. It's as if you never existed."

"How do you know that?" Chrysalis asked.

"As I said when you were here before, we've been monitoring you, but even if we hadn't, we'd have known. A hue and cry has a big footprint in the Worldstream. Everyone gets pulled in, including my crew. As soon as the shredding began, seven of our Shade got involved—including you, right, Fidelio?"

"That's right. The call came in and we stepped up."

"Then you *helped* the authorities find me?" Chrysalis asked.

"Not precisely," the Eye answered. "They didn't capture you, did they? You're here, with us, instead of in a confinement facility." The Eye turned aside. "Fidelio, I'd like to speak with Chrysalis alone."

Fidelio went out, leaving Chrysalis alone with the Eye.

"Chrysalis, we had to keep the authorities away from you long enough for your shredder to finish. We would have accelerated the shredder if we could have, but once the shredding process began, my crew was powerless to interfere. And we tried—my crew is as good as anyone at manipulating the Worldstream—well, almost anyone. Raúl has powers that even we don't understand. It's not for lack of trying. It's the real reason I keep Raúl inside my circle of associates, so that we can learn from him. But he's a terrible teacher. He's more like a magician—his tricks are amazing because we don't know how they're done."

The Eye put his hands together, crossing his legs where he sat. "So, instead, we interfered with the hue and cry. But we were only a small part of the effort to find you and bring you in. There was only so much we could do. We couldn't send a rescue squad, like we did the last time—under a hue and cry, the risk of exposure is too great. We had to leave you largely on your own. And you were hurt. I'm sorry about that."

"I'll be all right. Thank you for trying."

"I only wish we could have done more." The Eye stood and sat on the edge of the table next to Chrysalis. "You see, we want you here with us, on my crew. You'll be safe here." The Eye put a hand on Chrysalis's shoulder. "We need your help."

Chrysalis put her hands to her breast. "Thank you. Oh, Jah, thank you." She took the Eye's hand. "I was afraid I wouldn't have anything to offer. What'll I be doing for you?"

"We won't ask a lot from you. We want to study you."

Chrysalis loosened her grip on the Eye's hand. "Study?"

"Yes, in a manner of speaking. You see, Grace—I hope I can call you Grace when we're alone—Virtual Reality is the greatest advancement in psychological therapy in the last fifty years." The Eye of Providence removed his hood to reveal a tight-fitting mask, dark red, the color of blood, covering the entire head to the back of the neck. The mask was elaborately decorated in gold, an exquisitely detailed filigree. "But we've only begun to explore its potential," the Eye continued, in a soft but steady voice, a silken, calming alto.

Chrysalis let go of the Eye's hand. "Oh, no."

"In order to test the limits of the technology, I directed my weavers to create the most realistic, the most detailed lifestream ever woven. That would have been an accomplishment in itself. But with *you* as the subject, with your history, and from *my* intimate knowledge of your psychology, using the skill of ten Shade coders, we were able to weave something entirely new, an *emotional* experience, unprecedented in Virtual Reality. It took off like we never expected. Our innovative use of the Belt to induce actual emotions in the subjects, and to use the data collection capability of the Worldstream to record their responses, has provided a store of experimental data that will take years to analyze. We want to build on that success." The Eye pulled back the mask, letting it drop limply on the table.

"Madeleine," Chrysalis whispered. "You used me. You betrayed me."

"I understand why you would feel that way. But think of it

this way—you've contributed to the advancement of our knowledge of the human mind. You're the prototype, Grace, of the next level of VR experience, one so perfectly crafted, so emotionally compelling, that subjects will literally line up to participate in our experiments, and pay for the privilege. That was our other breakthrough, our discovery that the Belt is bi-directional. We can induce emotions in the subjects, and *record their responses*. We can collect research data on an unprecedented scale, from millions of subjects—not secondary data, like usage patterns, or user preferences, but thoughts and feelings *directly from the human mind*. Why should Big Data be limited to appliances and clothing, when *people* are what really matter?"

Madeleine leaned toward Chrysalis. Chrysalis jumped out of her chair and retreated to the wall. "*You* were the one who sent me to Raúl. You *wanted* me to disconnect. All that talk in your office about not disconnecting—what was that about?"

"Grace, our model of your mind is so precise that we can predict your actions flawlessly—almost. Your escape from the intervention facility took us by surprise. Luckily, Faith was there to help. Even so, that didn't invalidate our prediction: It was inevitable that you would join the Shade, regardless of what I said to you in our sessions. I sent you to Raúl because he's the best—it's too easy to botch a shredding. That's why we needed a plan in case the shredding went bad. I had my weavers synthesize an extension from existing data. The episode we programmed from the Cloakroom was less than satisfactory. The rendering was filled with artifacts, and the emotions weren't authentic. The response from stream riders was disappointing at best. If your shredding hadn't succeeded, we'd have been unable to weave new episodes. Now that we have you here, with us, we can continue to develop your lifestream as a virtual laboratory of human psychology. And you're the perfect host —intelligent, strong, determined, and willful, but flawed, in ways that offer a rich platform for inducing and recording emotional responses. The possibilities are limitless."

"Raúl was right," Chrysalis said, her voice trembling, "god

is dead, and Jahbulon lives. But I wonder if he knows what happened to Satan? Because I can tell him. I'm standing face to face with her."

Madeleine stood silently for a moment before sitting. "Grace, let's be practical. You're Shade now. You need a sponsor. I'm willing to sponsor you."

"Tell me why I'd want to get within a hundred kilometers of you, much less agree to be your lab rat."

"You'll live here in comfort. You'll help me to advance the science of the mind. You'll help to develop therapeutic techniques that will improve the lives of millions. And you'll be well-compensated. It wasn't our goal, but your lifestream is proving to be highly profitable. Advertising provides the bulk of the revenue, plus the streamboats pay for an ad-free version. We were bringing in nearly three hundred thousand credits per day, and we expect that to grow, especially with new material—now that you're here to model it."

"Think again, Eye of Providence," Chrysalis laughed. "My lifestream is history. I passed a streamboat just this morning. There was an angry crowd demanding to see Grace's mysteriously disappeared lifestream. The streamboat didn't have it and couldn't find it. I've been shredded, remember?"

Madeleine looked down at the table. "Well, yes, that is true. Your lifestream *is* gone, and it will stay gone, until we can restore it from the backup."

Chrysalis dropped into a chair. *"Backup?"*

"Yes. Long before Raúl started crawling the Worldstream for your life data, I told my weavers to back up a copy of your entire lifestream. As I'm sure Raúl told you, it's huge. We only completed it yesterday, not long before Raúl's crawler finished. The links to the Worldstream may have been severed, but your lifestream is intact."

Chrysalis gripped the table, her clenched hands white-knuckled and trembling. *"Damn you!* For me, for Edward, for Dylan—god *damn* you."

"Grace, take my offer. You won't find a better one, not in the world of the Shade."

There came a knock at the door. Madeleine hurriedly

donned the mask and hood of the Eye of Providence. "Come," she said.

Fidelio entered. "Eye, there's something we need to discuss."

"What is it?"

Fidelio looked at Chrysalis, then back to the Eye. "It's about the backup."

"What about it?"

"Well…it seems…"

"Fidelio, what *is* it?"

"It's corrupt."

"*What?* How bad?"

"We're working on it, but it's pretty bad. Totally ruined from the looks of it."

The Eye stood, leaning with her fists on the table. "How is that possible? It was encrypted and in a secure place."

"It wasn't an accident. Someone went after it. They crumped it on purpose and they didn't leave much behind."

"I want to know who did it."

"Oh, we know who did it. Normally, a job this sophisticated, we'd have to hunt for the perp. And someone with the chops to trash our backup wouldn't have left any obvious tracks."

"So, how do you know?"

"Because this guy signed his work—*Raúl.*"

The Eye of Providence sat down hard. She stayed motionless for a minute before speaking. "And the data? All the stream riders' responses? It was hundreds of terabytes. Do we still have the *data* at least?"

"Raúl got that too."

"Keep trying to recover. See what you can do. Now go."

The Eye removed her hood. She pulled off her mask with a sigh. "It seems Raúl has taken a liking to you," Madeleine said slowly. "And he's just deprived me and the world of a significant source of new knowledge—not to mention an important revenue stream for my crew." She turned back to Chrysalis. "Grace—Chrysalis—my offer still stands. I'll sponsor you. There's no point in reconstructing your lifestream—all the source data is gone—you shredded it—so your duties will be different than what I had in mind, mostly menial tasks, pattern matching and the like. There'll be some chores that the coders hate doing. I can only really justify subsistence wages, but you'll be safe and comfortable. I feel I owe you."

"You owe me, all right," Chrysalis said as she walked to the door. "And I promise you, with all the strength, determination, and will that you so admire, I'll make you pay. For now, you can show me the exit. I didn't free myself from my past so that I could be a slave, to you or to anyone else."

EPILOGUE

ELISHA APPROACHED CHRYSALIS in the Summerland commissary line. "Chrysalis, can you front me for dinner? I have a gig that pays two thousand credits. I'll square the account in a couple of days."

In the year that Chrysalis had been at the Summerland, an unaffiliated dormitory of the Shade, she'd become the de facto banker, providing short-term loans at interest. Umati had vouched for Chrysalis to get her admitted to the Summerland as a temporary arrangement, until a proper sponsor could be found. It was there that Chrysalis discovered the fifty thousand credits left by Raúl in her cryptocurrency account, and, shortly afterwards, made her first loan. As her reputation as an honest broker spread in the Summerland, she began to offer a wider range of services— loans, deposits, money transfers—lucrative enough to cover her expenses, and then some. With the occasional outside job, Chrysalis was able to live comfortably, with enough leisure time to study. The skill she chose to learn was coding, for which there was no shortage of teachers among the Shade.

The other two members of Chrysalis's Summerland alliance were exempt from interest on loans: Elisha, the loan collector and enforcer, a large, brutish sort who could intimidate just by showing up; and Bjorg, the accountant, a practiced coder who preferred working freelance to joining a crew. The allies shared sleeping quarters, and, whenever possible, ate meals together, alone.

"Of course," Chrysalis said. "Let me know what you want and I'll bring it to the room."

When Chrysalis arrived, Bjorg and Elisha were already seated in their chamber, a largish room with a three-tier bunk bed, three desks, a table and three chairs. Chrysalis sat down and distributed the food. She paused for a moment, as had become their custom, before she asked, "Shall we?"

All three removed their hoods simultaneously, revealing their identities, a sign of trust and commitment shared only by the most firmly established alliances. Grace had aged noticeably since she disconnected, her cheeks a little more jowly, her eyes more creased, her hair, longer now, nearly to her shoulders, showing strands of gray. Thomas, whose alter-ego was Elisha, was younger than Grace, or at least he looked younger, with curly black hair perched high on his forehead, small eyes above ruddy, round cheeks, and fleshy lips that were slow to smile. Celeste, the person known in her Shade identity as Bjorg, was the youngest of the three; she looked to be in her mid-twenties, with a smooth, pink complexion and medium blonde hair, not unattractive, but not beautiful, by the standards of VR avatars, her nose outsized for her narrow face, and an overbite difficult to conceal.

"I have a proposition," Grace said.

"A proposition," Celeste repeated. "What do you propose?"

"I want to bring in someone new."

Thomas and Celeste looked at each other quizzically.

"We're listening," Thomas said.

"He's called Nemesio. He's been teaching me coding."

"Is this to help with the bank?"

Grace shook her head. "No. I need Nemesio to help me with a personal goal. But he can help both of you, too. It's the kind of help that requires trust from everyone. Bringing him into the alliance would be a bond of trust."

"All right," Celeste said, "how will Nemesio help you? Or me, or Thomas, for that matter?"

Grace rested her elbows on the table, folding her hands,

pressing her fingers to her chin. "I've told you about Raúl, how he lives in the Worldstream, not cloaked, but also not afraid of the All-Seeing Eye. Remember? Raúl controls which data of his is in the Worldstream; he can create the persona that *he* wants. And I've also told you about the Eye of Providence, the reason that I'm here with the Shade. The Eye's crew wove my lifestream. They're good, so good that my lifestream went viral. But Raúl, all by himself, outsmarted them. Even the Eye's crew of weavers couldn't deal with Raúl. Now, in the time that I've been here, the Eye has become even more powerful, victimizing more people, commandeering their lives, stealing them, really, turning them into research subjects and entertainment pieces for profit."

"I remember," Thomas said. "But what's that have to do with Nemesio?"

"Nemesio thinks he understands Raúl's methods. He's been doing some programming, a sort of proof of concept. He needs time, and resources, and funding to complete his prototype crawler. He explained it to me. I don't understand it completely, but it sounds reasonable. Celeste, if he explained it to you, it might make more sense."

"I could listen to what he has to say," Celeste said, "but I'm still not clear on how this helps *us*."

"If Nemesio is right, he can help us to reconnect—on *our* terms."

"Grace," Celeste said, smiling, "are you sure you want to do that? How much better off were you in the Worldstream? I know that we can't buy ourselves nice things, and our food choices are kind of limited, but we have almost the same access to VR venues from here that we did back in the world. You can go surfing, play tennis, watch an opera, anything you want. Why was it so much better under the All-Seeing Eye?"

"Celeste, you're always so positive. I love that about you. You're right; I can do all those things, and I did do those things when I was connected. But I didn't do them by myself. It wasn't what I did that mattered, it was who I did it with.

"We're Shade. The VR venues we can access are isolated from the Worldstream. I might be able to wander in the

Sonoran Desert, or to visit Mars, but without Dylan, without my son."

Thomas took a break from eating. "I've kind of gotten comfortable here, Grace. I like being here with you and Celeste. I know what my life is like, day to day. I don't know if I'd do real good back in the Worldstream. And we didn't do so good when we *were* connected. We're criminals, after all."

"But we're not criminals," Grace said, "not really. Thomas, Celeste, your crimes were petty, more like mischief, and the punishments were all out of proportion. You were practically forced to disconnect. The worst kind of people that live in the Summerland—the extortionists, the thieves—that's not us. We're basically good people. You both left family behind, just as I did. I know you miss them, and I'm sure they miss you. If we had Raúl's power, we could return to the Worldstream, to live whatever lives we wanted."

"His power," Celeste said. "Didn't you tell us that it took years for Raúl to master those skills?"

Grace nodded. "I'm not saying it'll happen right away. But Raúl did it alone. We're a team. Whatever Nemesio knows, he can teach us, and whatever else we have to learn, we'll learn it together."

"All right," Celeste said. "I'll meet with Nemesio. If he makes sense, then we'll bring in Thomas for a final decision to add him to the alliance. That's only the first step, though. What you're talking about—reconnecting—it's dangerous. As it is, if any of us Shade says a word where Jahbulon can hear us, or show our faces to the All-Seeing Eye, the Worldstream will go crazy trying to place us. We'll stick out like we never did before we disconnected. We can't reconnect unless we're absolutely sure."

"We each had our different reasons for disconnecting," Grace said, "but we share one thing: We know that when we're connected, we're not our own people, not completely, not with the All-Seeing Eye watching and remembering our every move. Not even the Cloak can control their own lives in the Worldstream. Raúl once told me that in order to take control of his life, he had to commit his life—a life for a life, he said. So, unless someone's willing to disconnect, or unless they're able to do what Raúl does to control the Worldstream, they can't be free, not really."

"Grace," Celeste said, "you're always so aspirational. I love *that* about *you*. But is that what you're talking about—taking down Jahbulon?"

"I don't know," Grace said. "Maybe not. My real reasons are personal." Grace put her hands on the table. "I made the Eye of Providence a promise that I intend to keep. I can't allow the Eye to ruin any more lives. But there was another promise I *should* have made, but didn't, a promise to be there for my son as he grows up, to help him through this time in his life, the same time in my life that almost ruined me, because I didn't have someone there for me, someone who was on *my* side, who stood up for *me*. I thought I could live with my decision to disconnect, if I kept telling myself that I did it for Dylan. But I didn't do it for him—I did it for myself, to get control of my life. I left behind a hole in the Worldstream, and I tore a new hole in my life, where Dylan was. And it hurts; Jah, it hurts so bad. I don't want it to hurt anymore. I want my son back."

About the Author

Charles O'Donnell writes thrillers with high-tech themes in international and futuristic settings. He recently retired from a career of thirty-five years in engineering and manufacturing to write full-time, leveraging his decades of writing experience, mostly email, but, as Mr. O'Donnell points out, "that counts."

His latest project, *Shredded*, is an expression of his fascination with the progress of technology to either augment reality or to replace it entirely, and his concern over the erosion of privacy in a world in which everything is shared online, and nobody reads the terms and conditions.

Charles lives with Helen, his wife, life partner and fellow paranoid in Westerville, Ohio.

Author's website:
www.charlesodonnellauthor.com

Acknowledgments

SHREDDED IS A departure from my first two books, *The Girlfriend Experience* and *Moment of Conception,* in genre, in style, and in how I went about writing it. The premise of *Shredded* comes from extrapolating trends in technology: artificial intelligence, virtual reality, and autonomous vehicles, such as cars and drones; and social trends: the transition from in-person to online interactions, and the surrender of privacy, almost without a thought. The world of *Shredded* is what I imagine if virtual reality becomes so compellingly real, commerce becomes so automated and convenient, and the benefits of the wholesale collection of personal data become so attractive, that we human beings have no need for Real Life, when Virtual Reality serves the same functions—and, at the same time, we humans surrender the last shreds of privacy.

My approach to this project was considerably more structured than my previous two books, with a complete outline, revised many times, prior to writing even the first word of the first chapter. It was a great advantage to know where I was going before I started, my many side trips and detours notwithstanding.

One thing about my process has not changed—my reliance on a vast array of support, encouragement and criticism.

The outline was an opportunity to get early feedback on the story and characters. Special thanks to my outline readers,

Mike Brooks and Richard LeVitt. I gave you a half-baked concept and you baked it.

My *Girlfriend Experience* and *Moment of Conception* readers have been awesome. Without their encouragement, praise, and criticism, I would not have had the energy or inspiration to write *Shredded.* Some of them became my alpha readers, patiently combing through rough drafts—not *too* rough, I hope—to point out the obvious and not-so-obvious flaws. Thanks especially to Mike Brooks, outline critic and alpha reader extraordinaire, and to the usual gang of O'Donnells, especially my sister Jacki, who read through the raw first draft, and provided the raw, unrefined critique I needed. Thanks, Sister. Thanks also to my fellow writers of the Columbus State Community College Greet, Eat, Meet & Critique group (GEM-C), who gave me their notes on the work in progress.

As I did for *Moment of Conception*, I posted each chapter as it was written on Wattpad and writeon by Kindle. Thanks to the many readers who offered their comments; special thanks to Robert, whose words of encouragement were a great motivator.

To Kelsey Radigan, my editor: Thanks for your many corrections and suggestions, and for your encouragement. Your insight into the character of Grace was especially helpful. This is a better book because of you.

To Jun Ares, my cover designer, who also did the cover for *The Girlfriend Experience*, you nailed it on the first try. The design is perfect.

And, of course, unbounded gratitude to Helen, who is the first to see every word, and whose input I value most.

Charles O'Donnell
December 29, 2019

GLOSSARY

agent. A law officer of the **civil authorities**.

AI. Artificial Intelligence.

All-Seeing Eye. A pejorative term used by **Cloak** and **Shade** to refer to the **Worldstream**. This is an alternative to the term **Jahbulon**, which is used generally by the connected public.

artifact. An effect that can be observed in certain **Virtual Reality** scenes that have been **rendered** with insufficient source data. Artifacts appear as tiny polygons that change color, transitioning from the color of the rendered object, to white, then to black, depending on the direction from which the object is viewed.

auto-bus, community transit auto-bus. A self-driving public transit vehicle. In the world of *Shredded*, the community maintains a fleet of auto-buses, generally in middling to poor repair, for the dwindling population that continues to spend the majority of their time in **Real Life**.

avatar. A likeness of a person **rendered** in **Virtual Reality**. An avatar may be a highly accurate rendering of the person as they currently appear In **Real Life**, or it could represent the appearance of the person at another time, or it could be a **spoofed** avatar, looking like another person entirely. Note that "you look better than your avatar" is a common compliment when meeting In Real Life.

Belt. The common term for a **Dermal Contact Neural Interface**, a peripheral used in **Virtual Reality venues** to induce whole-body sensations, as opposed to localized sensations, such as those provided by VR gloves, for example. Grace's lifestream is the first application of the Belt to induce emotions in addition to sensations.

block. A software mechanism used to interfere with a function of the **Worldstream**, such as an attempt to communicate, or an attempt to monitor.

breaking bread. The slang term used by the **Cloak** for a lesbian encounter.

bug. A slang term for a **drone**, particularly a police drone.

chub. A slang term for an erection.

civil authorities. The governing and law enforcement regime in the world of *Shredded*.

civilian. A non-**Cloak** who visits the **Cloakroom**, either in disconnected clothing, or in a robe provided by the Cloakroom.

civils. A popular term for the **civil authorities**, used pejoratively.

Cloak. A member of a loosely-organized group of people who attempt to hide their activities from the **Worldstream**. The Cloak never appear in public unless they are covered from head to foot in a cloak, usually dark gray or black, and a hood. The hood includes an integrated voice synthesizer that hides the character of the Cloak's voice, preventing voice recognition software from identifying the individual.

Cloakroom. A gathering place for the **Cloak**. Patrons of the Cloakroom must be scanned for any object that is connected to the **Worldstream**, and must remove all connected objects before entering. The Cloak will typically enter in their cloaks and hoods, but these are not required for admission. **Civilians** may enter, providing they are not carrying any connected objects. Since nearly everything, including clothing, is connected to the Worldstream, it's common for civilians to remove all their clothing and personal effects and enter the cloakroom in a white robe. The Cloakroom is paid for and maintained by **Vita Occulta**.

confined. The term for legal detention of a citizen. In the time of the novel, transgressors are not imprisoned, they are *confined*. Since the majority of human existence occurs in **VR**, with most people never straying from their residences, often small, minimally functional apartments —imprisonment with access to VR is hardly punishment. Confinement refers to restriction to one location with no access to VR.

crawler. A software program that traverses the **Worldstream** for any of a number of purposes, such as finding, collating, sorting, and indexing data relating to a specific topic. A crawler is the basic mechanism used by a **shredder** to locate and erase all data related to a person in the process of shredding.

cred. A slang term for an **International Exchange Credit**, also known as a **credit**.

credit. Another term for an **International Exchange Credit**.

crew. A team of **Shade** reporting to a single **sponsor**. A crew will typically live together in a location maintained by the sponsor, and will support themselves through work done for clients, negotiated by the sponsor.

cryptocurrency. An alternative currency to **International Exchange Credits**. Cryptocurrency is kept in private accounts, locked by a mathematical key known only to the owner. Cryptocurrency is exchanged in units equal to a **credit**, and credits can be converted to cryptocurrency and vice-versa by cryptocurrency brokers. Cryptocurrency transactions, unlike credit transactions, are impossible to trace, and, therefore, prohibited.

DCNI. The acronym for **Dermal Contact Neural Interface**, commonly referred to as the **Belt**.

Dermal Contact Neural Interface. The technical term for the **Belt**.

drone. An autonomous airborne device used for a wide range of purposes. Most fall into one of two categories:

police drones ("**bugs**"), which conduct surveillance and searches, as well as aid in apprehending suspects or fugitives through the use of on-board **taser** magazines; and commercial drones ("**shippers**"), which are used to deliver goods from providers to consumers. It's common for apartment dwellers to mount a docking station on the exterior of the building, where commercial drones can deposit their deliveries.

hi-res, ultra-res, hyper-res. Slang terms used by adolescents to describe something good or exciting. *Hi-res* is good, *ultra-res* is better, and *hyper-res* is the best.

genuflection. The slang term used by the **Cloak** for a male homosexual encounter.

holy communion. The slang term used by the **Cloak** for a heterosexual encounter. A man *gives* holy communion; a woman *receives* it.

hook. A slang term for sexual relations. The term is used by the connected public, as well as by **Cloak** and **Shade**. When used by adolescents, *hook* can sometimes mean simply to meet, usually In **Real Life**.

hue and cry. A **tag** opened in the **Worldstream** against a specific person. In the case of a *hue and cry*, all available resources, both automated and human, are reallocated to locate the target of the tag, and to broadcast the target's location to all citizens. The name, photo, and description of the target will be broadcast to all **screens** within a radius of approximately 100 meters of the target. All citizens are required to interfere with or detain the target until authorities arrive.

IM. The acronym for Instant Message. IMs are the preferred mode of communication in the time of the novel. An IM is usually narrated, converted to text, then read in the sender's voice at the receiving end, similar to a **v-gram**.

International Exchange Credits. The monetary unit in the time of the novel, also referred to as **credits**, or **cred**. Credits are a global currency, with a monetary value of approximately one-tenth of a U.S. dollar. In the world of *Shredded,* only International Exchange Credits are legal tender. Cash is obsolete in this time. Credit transactions are fully recorded in the **Worldstream** and traceable to both parties in the exchange, which makes credits extremely undesirable for illegal transactions. See also **cryptocurrency**.

Invictus. A short poem by William Ernest Henley, first published in 1888. The poem appears in the book *Anthology of Victorian Poetry* that Edward gave to Grace on her thirteenth birthday, and was a source of inspiration to Grace during her recovery from addiction.

IRL. The acronym for In **Real Life**.

Jah. A shortened version of **Jahbulon**. *Jah*, as well as *Jahbulon*, are often used as curse words.

Jahbulon. The ubiquitous **voice responder** which acts as a direct, instant communication channel to the authorities. *Jahbulon* is used almost interchangeably with **Worldstream** to refer to all data collected from all connected devices, as well as the web of image- and voice-recognition algorithms, and location algorithms. Jahbulon can be activated at any time, from virtually anywhere, simply by calling out "Jahbulon, help me!" This triggers a response by the **civil authorities**, dispatching either **drones**, or **agents**, or both. For all practical purposes, Jahbulon is the deity in the world of *Shredded*.

lifestream. A **Virtual Reality** experience based on a person's life. A *lifestream* is created by one or more **weavers**, in a process called *weaving*. A weaver will accumulate data about a person already in the **Worldstream**, collate it, sequence it, synthesize additional material to fill in gaps, then **render** the lifestream to create an immersive VR experience. Lifestreams are available in a wide range of categories, such as adventure, travel, entertainment, as well as adult content. Some lifestreams are *peripheral-specific*, meaning that they cannot be experienced without a specific peripheral, commonly the **Belt**. In the case of Grace's lifestream, the weavers also synthesized actual emotions, transmitted via the Belt, to add a level of realism previously unknown. *Lifestream* is sometimes used to refer to a person's presence in the Worldstream, even if it has not been woven into a VR experience.

lifestream bistro. A storefront shop that offers **stream riders** a choice of **lifestreams** for a small fee, typically 50 credits for a half-hour ride. Lifestream bistros, popularly called **streamboats**, offer exclusively licensed versions of lifestreams, ad-free versions of publicly available lifestreams, as well as specialized peripherals, such as the **Belt**, which may be prohibitively expensive for some stream riders. Most stream riders are indigents who inhabit **Real Life** and don't own the equipment needed for a VR experience.

Mandy X. The street term for the drug ecstasy.

Pearl C. The street term for the drug cocaine.

Real Life. Direct human experience outside of **Virtual Reality**. The real world of *Shredded* is in a state of decay. Since nearly all human activity takes place in VR, there is little incentive, and almost no funds, to maintain the physical infrastructure—buildings, roads, public places— which have all fallen into a state of disrepair. Although Real Life occurs in what appears to be a collapsing society, Real Life is quite safe—any accident or assault is instantly addressed by the authorities whenever anyone calls the name of **Jahbulon**.

render. The process of creating a **Virtual Reality venue** using software. Any item in a VR venue is said to be *rendered*.

rewired my head. A phrase used to indicate that an experience had a significant emotional impact, roughly equivalent to "blew my mind."

RL. The acronym for **Real Life**.

rub one out, rubbing it out. A slang term for masturbation.

screen, wall screen, desk screen, personal screen, pocket screen, wrist screen. Any of a wide range of devices used to access information from or interact with the **Worldstream**. Nearly every citizen owns a *wall screen*.

This is usually mounted in a central location in the owner's apartment, where it's visible in either Real Life or augmented reality. The wall screen usually will display a sequence of images, customized by the user, plus a news crawl, until the user requests some specific content, or some important information, such as a **tag**, is broadcast by the **civil authorities**. A *desk screen* is the equivalent of a desktop computer display. It can be mounted on a stand, allowing it to move, or on a fixed mount, or integrated into the desk. A *personal screen* is tablet-sized screen with most or all of the functionality of a wall screen. A *pocket screen* is smaller still, and a *wrist screen* is a high-functioning version of a smart watch.

Shade. One who has eliminated all personal data, including all images, sound clips, video clips, metadata, and links, from the **Worldstream**. A Shade is invisible to the connected world—for many practical purposes, Shade don't exist. The Shade rely on **Cloak sponsors** to act as liaisons to the connected world to find them work, although a majority of the Shade are unaffiliated. In either case, the Shade live in hidden dormitories, and only appear in public as Cloak.

shipper. A commercial **drone**.

shredder. A person who destroys all data in the **Worldstream** related to a person, essentially rendering them a non-person. The shredding process involves building a **crawler**, a software program that will seek out all data related to a person—images, video, sound clips—as well as all the links to that data; catalog it, index it, and then, once all data has been accounted for, eradicate it from the Worldstream. The end result is a gaping hole in the Worldstream where the person's identity once existed. Following shredding, where previously a person's voice might have been found in the Worldstream, there is now only silence; where previously a person's image might have been found, there is now only a black, featureless void.

sponsor. A **Cloak** who maintains a **crew** of **Shade** for the purpose of reselling their services. A sponsor acts as the point person for the crew in obtaining business, negotiating terms, collecting fees, distributing pay, and maintaining living quarters for his crew. A sponsor usually will actively recruit new members for his crew, either by facilitating the **shredding** of individuals, or poaching from other crews.

spoof. To create a false data stream in the **Worldstream**, either to perform a function that would otherwise be prohibited, or to create a deception. Examples include: software to simulate the presence of a peripheral, such as the **Belt**, when the peripheral is not integrated into the user's configuration; software to render an **avatar** that doesn't accurately represent the user, or to impersonate someone else.

State Live Services. A division of the **civil authorities** dedicated to providing services to citizens who don't regularly inhabit **Virtual Reality** for any of a number of reasons, such as indigence, aptitude, or by choice.

State Benefits Department. A department of **State Live Services** and Grace's employer. The State Benefits Department of the division of State Live Services handles in-person requests for benefits.

stealth mode. A technology used for secure communication with compatible resources. Accessing a service that supports stealth mode, such as a **cryptocurrency** account, will not leave any history in the **Worldstream**. Stealth technology is used by **Cloak**, **Shade**, and others to transact business without detection.

stream rider. A person who experiences **lifestreams** in **Virtual Reality**. The term is usually applied to people who habitually ride lifestreams, rather than people who experience lifestreams only occasionally.

streamboat. The slang term for a **lifestream bistro.**

Summerland. An unaffiliated dormitory of the **Shade**. Chrysalis is admitted to the Summerland on the recommendation of Umati, the Shade that helps Chrysalis during her shredding. The name of the

Summerland is taken from the mythical afterlife of some Wiccan, Theosophist, and Pagan beliefs, in which souls reside between incarnations.

tag, tag for location, tag for apprehension. A *tag* is a notice directed at an individual that causes the **Worldstream** (also known as **Jahbulon**) to take special action toward that individual. A *tag for location* activates automated algorithms to locate the tagged individual, and to report that person's location to the **civil authorities** at regular intervals. A tag for location may also raise an alarm if the individual cannot be located for a period of time, or if the person is somewhere they're not supposed to be, but otherwise, no action is taken on the reports of location. A *tag for apprehension* activates more powerful algorithms that attempt to interpolate locations to estimate where the tagged individual could be. These algorithms may be supplemented by human operators, to fill in gaps where the algorithms may not be reliable. In addition, information about a person tagged for apprehension will be broadcast to screens in the tagged person's vicinity. A **hue and cry** is the ultimate tag. When a tag for hue and cry is raised, massive resources, both automated and human, are redirected toward locating the individual and dispatching resources to apprehend them.

taser. A non-lethal device used to incapacitate a person. A taser round consists of a projectile with a tiny battery and barbed electrodes which penetrate the target's skin and delivers a shock with a potential of 50,000 volts, sending the person into convulsions.

v-gram. A synthesized voice message. When a v-gram is dictated by the sender, voice recognition algorithms transcribe the voice message to text, then the voice is reconstructed at the receiving end from voice characteristics of the sender retrieved from the **Worldstream.** This method is preferred to simply dictating a video or audio recording, since the source of the v-gram can be validated from the vast store of personal data in the Worldstream, and also because generating a v-gram, complete with audio narration in the sender's authentic voice, can be automated.

venue. A scene **rendered** in **Virtual Reality**. A venue is typically an elaborately constructed virtual scene, including sights, sounds, and other sensations. A venue can be private, inhabited only by avatars that are invited, or it can be public, inhabited by any number of people, with or without paid admission. Concerts, virtual restaurants, sporting events, public gatherings are all examples of public venues.

Virtual Reality. The simulation of **Real Life** in all its sensory aspects, such that a person, using VR technology, can inhabit a **venue**, either alone or in numbers, and interact with the simulated environment. In the world of *Shredded*, nearly all human activity is conducted in Virtual Reality.

Vita Occulta. A secret society of **sponsors**. The Vita Occulta, or **VO**, are a loose confederation of sponsors with crews of **Shade** who provide services, such as programming or algorithm augmentation, for fees. They typically conspire to rig bids, share profits, or otherwise collaborate to keep their prices high, but, since the Shade work for virtually nothing, crews of the VO can still undercut legitimate providers in the connected world.

VO. The acronym for **Vita Occulta**.

voice responder. A software program that emulates a human being with natural language recognition and response. Nearly all interaction with the **Worldstream** is via queries to a voice responder. Voice responders have a range of settings, including language, accent, and gender, but also level of empathy, conversational capabilities, humor, and other personalized settings that allow the user to craft a voice responder with any personality they desire.

VR. The acronym for **Virtual Reality**.

Worldstream. The sum total of all data collected by the internet of things, plus metadata. The Worldstream is similar to the Cloud, but with layers to correlate, sequence and interpolate data from any source, allowing historical narratives, including **lifestreams**, to be reconstructed in detail. The name **Jahbulon** is used as a loose synonym for the Worldstream; the **All-Seeing Eye** is a pejorative term used to refer to either the Worldstream or Jahbulon.

weaver. A coder with the skills to create a **lifestream**. A weaver will accumulate data about a person from the **Worldstream**, and, using that data, will create an immersive **Virtual Reality** experience, a process called *weaving*.

win. The street term meaning to procure drugs.

Witch H. The street term for the drug heroin.

INVICTUS

Out of the night that covers me,
    Black as the pit from pole to pole,
I thank whatever gods may be
    For my unconquerable soul.

In the fell clutch of circumstance
    I have not winced nor cried aloud.
Under the bludgeonings of chance
    My head is bloody, but unbowed.

Beyond this place of wrath and tears
    Looms but the Horror of the shade,
And yet the menace of the years
    Finds and shall find me unafraid.

It matters not how strait the gate,
    How charged with punishments the scroll,
I am the master of my fate,
    I am the captain of my soul.

William Ernest Henley